LITTLE ODESSA

ALSO BY JOSEPH KOENIG

Floater

JOSEPH KOENIG

LITTLE ODESSA

VIKING

VIKING
Viking Penguin Inc., 40 West 23rd Street,
New York, New York 10010, U.S.A.
Penguin Books Ltd, 27 Wrights Lane, London W8 5TZ
(Publishing & Editorial) and Harmondsworth, Middlesex,
England (Distribution & Warehouse)
Penguin Books Australia Ltd, Ringwood,
Victoria, Australia
Penguin Books Canada Limited, 2801 John Street,
Markham, Ontario, Canada L3R 1B4
Penguin Books (N.Z.) Ltd, 182–190 Wairau Road
Auckland 10 New Zealand

First published in 1988 by Viking Penguin Inc.
Published simultaneously in Canada

LIBRARY OF CONGRESS CATALOGING IN PUBLICATION DATA
Koenig, Joseph.
Little Odessa.
I. Title.
PS3561.03345L58   1988   813'.54   87-40314
ISBN 0-670-81954-9

Printed in the United States of America by
Arcata Graphics, Fairfield, Pennsylvania
Set in Gael

For Barry Mennen

LITTLE ODESSA

ON A night her feet ached so bad that it was an effort to grind her hips, a sailor at a ringside table began hooting at Kate Piro. "Knockers like those you don't trip over, doll," he hollered. "Pick up your dogs."

Three expense-account types guzzling watered margaritas traded catcalls with a party of bulldykes in a private booth. Kate edged close to the bank of speakers, taking shelter behind a wall of sound.

"What do they expect, these jerks?" she asked the organ player in the three-piece house band. "A donkey show?"

The organist was an aging hippie with shoulder-length salt-and-pepper hair, a saddle nose from a bad coke habit. "Hee-haw," he said.

Kate danced away from the speakers and the booing grew louder. Going blindly through the motions she felt her body bathed in warmth, sensed a rosy current wash down her bare breasts almost to the gold chain around her hips that was the bulk of her costume. Some frat rats applauded the show of color like it was part of the act. Kate's feet quit hurting and she tossed her shaggy, jet black fall. Her rouged nipples became erect and the frat rats cheered some more. The sailor pounded his hands together, tipping over an eight-dollar bottle of Bud.

Kate spun across the stage showing off her tight little ass. The perfect ass—she wanted that in quotes on the marquee. This week, for five shows a night, she was M. Anita Supreme. Matinees, under the curly platinum wig, she was Hellen Bedd. Of all the ways of trading off your looks, this had to be the worst—if you didn't object to hooking, which she did.

Giving herself to the follow spot's clinical glare, she high-stepped onto a narrow runway extending the length of the room. She broke a light sweat and her taut body glistened blue, then amber, then cherry red under the revolving gels. The heavy musk of masculine perspiration wafted back from the crowd, propelled by ceiling fans. The runway was her home turf, the end zone. Soon she'd have them eating out of her hand.

Kate gave them her high kick and gave it again, keeping half a beat ahead of the music. Ray Charles now, the organist switching to electric piano. With her eyes shut it wasn't half so bad, almost like a smoky hotel disco, a disco with a serious draft. She kicked high once more and came down off-balance. A stiletto heel snapped and the cold floor drove splinters into her hip. The music crashed, too, and the boos started again. Someone in a Burberry topcoat came careening up the aisle, elbowing the hostesses in outfits as elaborate as hers.

Kate squinted into the darkness, kneading her bruised side. Weaving drunkenly beyond the footlights was a short black man whose cheeks were a labyrinth of thick scars. Horrible, like banded snakes slithering beneath his leathery skin. He leaned against the runway showing tobacco-stained teeth and yelled something she didn't catch, made his meaning clear by thumbing his nose. Kate rubbed her hip and pretended not to notice. The drunk had his say and lurched back into the tables flicking a cigarette at the runway.

The glowing butt arced over the boards and landed between Kate's breasts. Before the pain registered, she swept it away with the back of her hand. A cinder burned the blushing flesh and she wet her fingertips with saliva and pressed them to the hurt. Then a curtain of red dropped before her eyes and she scrambled to her feet,

hobbled down the long runway through a gauntlet of ex-
pectant cheers and clutching palms.

The drunk crashed toward the exit, tangling himself in
a velvet rope hung from brass stanchions and a bouncer in
a powder blue tuxedo. The bouncer, a journeyman light
heavyweight known as Young Washington, applied a left-
handed grip to his throat wondering where to hit him first.
He was leaning toward a rabbit punch when Kate jumped
off the runway and kneed the drunk in the small of the
back.

The drunk didn't seem to mind. Kate balled her hands
into delicate fists and hammered the thick cords in his
neck. The drunk butted Young Washington and broke
free, turned around to exhale a beery laugh in Kate's face.
Then Young Washington jumped on his back and Kate
stepped out of her good shoe and bashed the short man
over the ear with the pointed heel. She hammered him
three times more before his head opened and blood ran
down the sleeve of the bouncer's blue tux.

Young Washington, also a bleeder, had an aversion to
gore. He kicked open the door and threw the drunk into
yellow snow, and the wind-whipped chill chased Kate
back onstage. She kicked off the other shoe and finished
her number barefoot to a standing ovation.

The drunk, as it turned out, was a thirty-seven-year-old
Nigerian by the name of Princephilip M'Lule, a second
secretary with Lagos's United Nations mission. In a year in
New York he had collected $565 in unpaid parking tickets
and a record for shoplifting at four East Side department
stores—forgiven in the best tradition of diplomatic immu-
nity. A cabbie pulled him out of the snow and brought him
to Lenox Hill Hospital for a sewing session with an intern.
When he was feeling more himself, he asked for the secretary general. Told that it was two A.M., he demanded to
see the mayor. He settled for the desk officer at the Sixteenth Precinct house on West Forty-eighth Street, where

he came to press assault charges against M. Anita Supreme.

The deskman, who had had his fill of UN delegates, was something of a diplomat himself and did not mention the price tag dangling from the sleeve of the new topcoat. He said knowledgeably, "You want her name and number, call the club and ask. Probably quote y'a price, too."

Princephilip M'Lule, addled by too much drink and a slight concussion, responded in Yoruban. "The young woman with the firm breasts must be punished under our laws. At our convenience we will seek extradition."

The deskman made no sense of it. "Like I say," he tried again, "you want in her pants, call." He paused to sip coffee from a chipped earthenware mug. "You're serious about bringing charges, I'd advise strongly against it. Be a long time before this comes to court. You'll be dictator back home and the publicity'll become a heavy embarrassment for you. Whyn't we just leave it where it lays?"

Princephilip M'Lule pounded his fist on the side of the desk and asked to see the commissioner.

"Okay, okay," the deskman said, steadying his coffee with the flat of his hand. "Have it your way." To a bearded man in a Hasid's caftan waiting for an elevator he said, "Infante, tell your buddy Bucyk to haul his ass down here. When he says he's too busy, tell him he gotta go to the Starlight Lounge to pull in one of the bottomless girls. Then stand back, Infante, you don't enjoy being trampled to death."

Detective Stanley Bucyk came down the stairs two and three at a time, massaging a compact holster into place beneath his left arm. He braked at the high desk and muscled the short black man out of the way. "You're kidding," he said to the desk officer. "About the Starlight, I mean."

The deskman shrugged. "Ask him," he said, nodding in the direction of Princephilip M'Lule. "And enunciate,

Stanley. The gent's from Nigeria. I don't know that he understands a lot of English."

Stan Bucyk, standing five feet, eight and three-quarters inches tall in his low-heeled Foot Savers, was forced to bend his head when addressing Princephilip M'Lule. The Nigerian, in his $250 alligators, was five-two, two and a half, and about as wide around. Definitely not NBA material like that other Nigerian, what's-his-name down in Houston. "What happened to you, bro?" Bucyk asked.

Princephilip M'Lule put a hand to his bandaged head. In passable English he said, "I was assaulted by a crazy woman."

"Not your noggin," Bucyk said. "Your face. It looks like you were branded or something."

Princephilip M'Lule's narrow eyes came together over his blunt nose.

"He's with the UN," the deskman explained.

"Why didn't you say so in the first place?" Bucyk asked sourly. He went toward the elevator. "Handle this one yourself."

The deskman said, "Naked ladies give me a tummy ache when I can't have 'em. It's your case, Starlight peeler and all."

"What peeler?" Bucyk asked. "Those girls come on-stage, they're already peeled like bananas."

"Then all you gotta do," the deskman said, "is cream."

Bucyk retreated to a corner where the glare from the overhead fixture was weakest and leaned against a Pepsi machine. He motioned for the Nigerian to follow and draped an arm around his shoulder. "What's your name?" he asked.

"Princephilip M'Lule," the short man answered.

"I'm Bucyk," he said. "Listen, Phil . . . can I call you Phil? . . . you're making what we call a tempest out of a teapot here. I see where your feelings are hurt, maybe worse than your head. But you wanna be accepted by the movers and shakers in this town, you can't go around doing a federal case out of every little thing. What do we say we go home and get a good night's sleep and forget all about it? Few days, the bandages'll come off and it'll be like nothing ever happened, right?"

Princephilip M'Lule smiled at Bucyk showing a mouthful of yellow teeth. "If you don't run her in inside of thirty minutes, asshole," he said, quoting from the Clint Eastwood doubleheader he'd caught at a Chelsea second-run house, "I'll have your ass in a sling by morning."

"You bet," Bucyk said, and asked nicely to see some ID.

Bucyk went upstairs for the Taiwanese London Fog knockoff with the zip-in lining that he'd picked up for a song on Orchard Street. Outside, a six-year-old Reliant from the first batch of compacts the department had put on the road was waiting where he'd left it on the sidewalk. Some asshole, some *real* asshole, had parked in the gutter, pinning him there. He steered cautiously along the curb, honking the occasional pedestrian out of the way. Where the line of unmarked cars broke for a hydrant he squeezed into traffic.

He went across Forty-eighth Street to Broadway and down to Times Square, parked beside another hydrant and climbed a gap in the mound of garbage bags barricading the sidewalk. The Starlight Lounge shared a former legit theater with a fag strip show—BOYLESQUE, the sign offered—and a rap center–whorehouse. Bucyk craned his neck at an athletic Miss California with blond hair down past her hips, about forty-eight teeth. Underneath the marquee, behind smudged glass, were hand-colored photos of an Oriental girl, Misty Chin, coming next week. A plexiglass sign with movable type and no pictures promised M. Anita Supreme every two hours.

A well-built black man nursing a split lip let him inside, did not look happy to see him. "You doin' here?" he asked. "Ain't even the tenth of the month yet."

Bucyk ignored the question. He was eyeing the stains on the sleeves of the bouncer's blue tux. "Main event?" he asked, taking the gummy cloth in his fingers.

"TKO in the second," Young Washington bragged.

"Which side of the decision were *you* on?"

"Undefeated and still champeen."

"Yeah." Bucyk let the sleeve drop. He bulled his way toward the stage where a malnourished redhead with needle tracks on both arms was doing a carpet act for empty seats. "That Anita Supreme?"

"M. Anita," Young Washington corrected him. "Man-eater, get it?"

"Now I do."

"Now too late. She done for the night."

"Where's home?"

"Don't know. You want to talk to her, you don't have to either. Find her backstage."

"In her dressing room?" Bucyk asked, brightening.

"Call it that."

The bouncer marched Bucyk around the perimeter of the room, prodding a GI nodding in his beer. They went onstage sidestepping the supine redhead to a PRIVATE sign stenciled over a filigree of felt-tip graffiti. Young Washington opened the door with his shoulder. "This way," he said, ducking inside a low corridor lit by red exit lights at both ends. "You grinnin' for?" he asked without turning around.

"Am I?" Bucyk asked, trying on what he hoped was a more serious expression.

"You know better'n me," Young Washington said and tossed a folding chair out of the way.

Bucyk unbuttoned his coat against the wet heat spitting from steam pipes sagging along the ceiling. "Warm in here."

"That the way the girls like it."

They squeezed past a bed done up in tigerskin chintz

leaning on its side against the wall. They came to a door guarded by a faded gold star. Greasy handprints made a brass bull's-eye of the knob. Bucyk put a hand on it and Young Washington brushed it out of the way, pointing to the star. The bouncer knocked twice and then twice more.

"Who is it?" came a voice from inside.

"A fella to see you," Young Washington said.

"Tell him to get lost. With my love."

"Not this one," Young Washington said.

"Why not?"

"He a police fella."

"Don't these guys read a paper? Don't they know the Supreme Court says T and A's family fun?"

"Have to ask him yourself," Young Washington said. "He look mean."

"Didn't like the show, huh? Tell him half a sec."

They heard water gurgling from a basin, the clatter of hangers sliding along a pipe. Young Washington edged around Bucyk, careful not to bump shoulders. "You on your own now," he said.

"Thanks."

"You grinnin' again, man."

Bucyk made no attempt to hide it. "I know."

With little enthusiasm Kate called out, "You can come in now."

Bucyk took hold of the knob and twisted it, spun it 360 degrees before he pushed open the door. The room was hot, hotter even than the corridor, and small; he'd seen caskets that looked larger. The woman slouched before a cluttered makeup table was also small, and young—about twenty, he guessed—and better-looking than anyone in a rattrap like this had a right to be. In the sympathetic glow of the cosmetics mirror he saw a peaches-and-cream cameo with taffy hair in a stylish chop, dangling silver earrings. She wore a lapis lazuli choker, half a dozen bracelets on each arm, two rings minimum to a finger, more jewelry than he thought was decent. More clothing, too.

Much more. The perfect ass was covered in designer jeans, and an NYU sweatshirt showed the buoyant outline of a rarer perfection. She opened a large leather bag and swept the tabletop clean. She located Bucyk in the mirror and asked, "What can I do you for?"

An honest response Bucyk couldn't give without jeopardizing his rank and the pension it would bring in eight years, five months and fourteen days. "I'd like a word with you," he said.

"Just the one? If it's clean, that'll be a first."

Bucyk heeled the door shut. He stood awkwardly behind her and then tested his weight on a sprung easy chair, jumped up quickly holding a paperback book.

"I was looking for that," she said, reaching over her shoulder.

Bucyk, grown nearsighted in his middle thirties, held the book at arm's length. "*Winesburg, Ohio,* by Sherwood Anderson," he read. "Heavy going."

"The cover's just for show. It's a Harold Robbins, *The Betsy.*"

"Yeah?"

She snatched the book away and dropped it in the bag with the rest of her things. "Not really," she said.

"I'm Bucyk."

"And I'm sick and tired of waking my lawyer in the middle of the night every time the NYPD makes like Pearl Harbor on Times Square."

"I look like a Jap?" Bucyk asked.

"My mistake. You're the dance critic from the *Times.*"

"Wrong again."

"An admirer? I don't see any flowers."

"Strike three," Bucyk said. "I'm a fight fan . . . and I hear you've been duking some of yours."

Kate swiveled around in the rickety, straight-backed chair. "A fat guy tell you that? Little black guy with, like, these awful tattoos all over his face?"

"Could've been his brother."

"Did he tell you the rest of it? How he tried to barbecue me?"

"All he gave out was you'd assaulted him. He wants to press charges. I'm here to take you in."

"On that tight little squirt's word?"

"The squirt's an accredited member of the Nigerian mission to the UN. We checked."

"Oh shit," Kate said.

"My sentiments," Bucyk told her. "But if you can prove he tried to hurt you, I'll have you home in bed . . . back home before morning. So what do we say you grab your hat and go?"

"I never wear a hat."

She found tinted lenses with large Fiorucci frames in the bag. She was, Bucyk decided, the first woman he'd seen who looked just as good in glasses. Better actually, more private, which made her sexuality less calculated, a lot more devastating. What *was* a girl like her doing in a dive like this?

Kate pushed back from the table and Bucyk helped her into a heavy shearling coat hanging from a pipe. She tugged at a thin chain and darkness flooded the room. In the ruddy aura of the corridor she met Bucyk's stare. "Trying to make an honest living," she said.

She led him out a side door into an alley in sight of the car. He scampered between the garbage bags and started the engine while she went along the street for easier footing in the snow. Bucyk met her at the corner and she came off the curb on her toes as if she were expecting him to run out and hold the door. He managed not to. He leaned across the seat and lifted the button and she slid beside him and dropped the bag between her feet, dug out *Winesburg, Ohio.*

Bucyk hung a right at Eighth and went back uptown. He switched on the dome and a high-intensity light came on over her end of the dashboard. "Thank you," she said.

"You don't see many girls, I mean women in your racket reading books like that," Bucyk said. "Reading."

Kate closed the slender volume over her index finger. "Do you have dealings with many of them?"

"Not enough."

She turned back to Winesburg and didn't look up again until they were on West Forty-eighth.

Bucyk paraded her past the deskman and then they went upstairs. In a large room leaking clutter from a Bearcat police scanner overweight men were eating to stay awake. He sat her at a plain table scorched around the edges. He dumped an ashtray in a wastebasket and lit a True menthol, offered her one that she refused.

Behind a glass partition a light-skinned Puerto Rican with a cast on his leg was talking to a uniformed officer. "The fuck you mean I fell off a fire escape?" he asked. "They found me, I was on the roof."

Bucyk crooked a finger at Infante, who was looking more himself in a blue quilted vest. He brushed long blond hair out of his eyes and came over with a thin sheaf of papers.

"Say hello to Paul Infante," Bucyk said. "He's gonna help us with the paperwork."

Infante put a knee up on the chair beside her. "First we have to show you a UF61 form with the details of the complaint against you."

"Don't I get to see my accuser?" she asked. "I thought that's the way the law worked here."

"You do," Bucyk told her, "but only if you go to trial. Till then, he's calling the shots."

"Detective Bucyk, this is not going to be as quick and painless as you said it was, is it?"

"Not really. Not for you."

"I'm going to have to spend the night in jail, aren't I?"

"A part."

"You mean what's left of it."

"That's right."

"Can I make a call?"

"You don't need a lawyer yet."

"My family," Kate said. "They'll worry."

"Soon," Bucyk promised.

Infante came up with the UF61 and read out the complaint. "That the way it happened?" Bucyk asked her.

"You forgot the part where he burned me, where he mashed Washington's face."

"We didn't forget. He did. It'll all come out eventually."

"Okay, now," Infante said, "we need some personal info before we send you down to Central Booking. Can I have your name please?"

"Kate Piro."

Infante put down his pen. "Just Kate? Kate's not short for anything?"

"It's short for Ekaterina. My full name is Ekaterina Malutina Shapiro."

"DOB?"

"I'm not familiar with that term."

"Don't be cute on me."

"I never heard it before."

"Date of birth," Bucyk explained.

"January 12, 1965."

"Place?"

"Odessa."

"Where's that?"

"Texas," Bucyk answered for her. "In the oilfields, right? I passed through once on my way to Fort Bliss."

"Ukrainian Soviet Socialist Republic," she said without looking at either of them.

"How's that again?" Infante asked.

"Russia."

"You're a Russian?"

"*No.*"

"We won't send you back," he snickered.

"I'm Jewish."

"*Mazel tov.* Can I see your green card?"

"I don't have one any more. We got out in 1974, with one of the first batches of Jews Brezhnev let go. I'm a naturalized citizen."

"Lucky break," Infante said.

"Luck had nothing to do with it. My father was a stevedore, not like those chess players, those Moscow intellectuals. The government saw a good deal and let us go for wheat."

"You sound sorry."

"You've stopped writing, Detective."

"Address?"

"Forty-two thirty-seven Neptune Avenue. Apartment 4D."

"Where's that?"

"Little Odessa."

"Huh?"

"In Brighton Beach. Brooklyn."

"The rest you give when you're booked," Infante said. "Sign here and you're on your way."

"Can I call now?" she asked.

"Why don't you wait a while?" Infante said. "See where you stand when you get downtown."

Bucyk fished in his pocket for a quarter. "There's a pay phone out in the hall," he told her. "You're on your honor."

When she stepped from the booth he was waiting for her, looking like a schoolboy with her bag over his shoulder. "Let me tell you what's gonna happen now," he said, walking her downstairs. "First you're going to Manhattan Central Booking. They'll take your prints and send them on to Albany by computer and they'll mug you front and side. That's color mugshots I'm talking about. They'll put you in a cell while a DA draws up a formal complaint and then you'll go up to the Criminal Courthouse at 100 Centre Street. You'll be interviewed there by someone from the Vera Institute of Justice, a background check to help determine what kind of bail they'll ask. If I wasn't working for the other side, I'd advise you not to tell them how you dress for work. You'll pose for more pictures there, black-and-white Polaroids they'll clip to your bench warrant.

"Are you still with me? All this is gonna take a good ten, twelve hours, and that's if there's no glitches. This is New York, so count on glitches. Tomorrow you'll go before a judge and he'll set bail, probably let you out on your own recognizance, you don't have a record . . . and then they'll drop the charges," he said. "Piddlyshit thing like this, you don't do time. The process, that's the punishment right there. You see how it works?"

She shook her head. "Where will you be, Detective Bucyk," she asked bitterly, "home in bed, watching TV, out for drinks with your friends? Why didn't you just say you couldn't find me?"

Bucyk avoided her face. "Tell me about Russia," he said.

She came out of jail shielding her eyes against the sunset, put on her glasses and headed across Foley Square to the IRT. A blue Ford station wagon with a mismatched fender skirt cut her off crossing Pearl Street. She started to say something but changed her mind, swung the bag over the other shoulder and went around behind it. The driver backed up, blocking the way, and she turned to look for a cop. Bucyk cranked down the window on the passenger's side. "Need a lift?" he asked.

"No, I—" A cab bleated past, nearly clipping her heels. Bucyk opened the door and she jumped in.

"How bad was it?" he asked.

Her nose reddened, but there were no tears. She hid her face in a crumpled tissue and when she took it away her color was as even as when he saw her at the Starlight.

"What are you doing here?" she asked.

"I moonlight for one of these, you know, car services," he said. "Business wasn't so hot, so I thought I'd see if I'd catch you, case you needed a ride home or anything."

"How long were you waiting?"

"Not long," he told her. "A couple hours, could've been."

"Thanks."

"Was it terrible?" he tried again.

She didn't answer right away. "Worse than that," she finally said. "Much worse."

"Did they try to . . . do anything, those characters—?"

"The other women? Four or five of them, maybe four or five *didn't*. We found each other in that big cell and stayed together and after a while the others sort of gave up. I didn't sleep."

"Anyone you wanna press charges against? I'm good at that."

"No," she said. "I just want to go home and take a hot bath."

They went around City Hall Park onto the Brooklyn Bridge. He looked down through the cabled grid at the sliver of a not very large island that marked the boundaries of his world. Two years in Texas after high school and a week each November getting loaded at a deer lodge in the Poconos, spring and summer visits with his brother in Atlantic City, that was his experience with the rest of it—the mainland, he liked to call it. Brooklyn, shrouded in its stolid nineteenth-century waterfront, was almost as great a mystery as the woman beside him.

Kate couldn't keep her eyes open. Her jaw sagged and her lips parted and he heard her heavy breathing. He pulled into the right lane and slowed to forty to study her face at rest. Without makeup her skin was still flawless, unlined even around the eyes, not a hint of the smacked-out hardness that went with Times Square. She showed little of what she had been through other than arms holding herself tight. Inside the heavy coat cloaking her voluptuousness she looked about sixteen, which Bucyk was surprised to discover did not excite him all that much.

He followed the BQE around the corroding Brooklyn shore. Poking through the haze was the Erector-set skeleton of the parachute jump, a relic of the 1939 World's Fair, of the ritualized silliness of Steeplechase Park, "the funny place," and of Coney Island in its heyday, of the boardwalk, of Brooklyn. A grave marker two hundred fifty feet high.

He put a hand on her shoulder and after a while he shook it. "Where do we get off?" he asked. "I've never driven this way before."

"Huh . . . ? I don't know," she said. "I always take the train."

"The D? Not exactly your Moscow subway. I've seen pictures. It's a regular museum."

She yawned. "I've never been to Moscow. Wait . . . we're on the Belt. You'd better turn here."

He exited at Ocean Parkway and took it toward the beach. Almost immediately she said, "You just went past it."

"What?"

"Neptune Avenue. My block."

At Brighton Beach Avenue she pointed him in the shadow of the el. The dark streets were crowded with middle-aged men and women, uniformly thickset, in shabby clothes or flashy. Discount store closeouts—the women in cloth coats and peasant scarves, burgundy pants and patterned jackets for the men, lots of patent leather. And everyone dragging a net shopping bag as if the shelves might be bare tomorrow, forgetting where they were.

They wore put-upon expressions that made him wonder how they had looked before. *More* put-upon, he decided.

An express train gathering speed overhead showered the street with sparks, but no one ducked for cover, no one took an extra step. Whatever they once had been put through, they would spend the rest of their lives taking it easy now that it was over. Nothing would ever get them moving again.

"There's no young people here," he said.

"The Russians are desperate for workers and soldiers so they keep everyone but the sick and old. The few young ones who got out, most went to Israel. But things are bad there now with the economy and military service till you're fifty-five, so they're starting to show up here . . . I see you don't take cabs."

"Why do you say that?"

"The drivers, they're all greenhorns."

Though he prided himself on a beat cop's eye, he could see nothing especially Jewish about these people. Nor did they seem Russian, lacking the sloping cheekbones and oriental cast, the furious eyebrows that he associated with comatose old men in greatcoats at Red Square funerals. There was some resemblance to the Czechs around York-ville, but not enough so you'd confuse them. What they looked like most were the generic poor.

"I bet there aren't many like you at NYU," he said.

She turned to him with a puzzled frown. "I don't know what you mean." The frown met his and followed it to the school insignia on her chest. "Oh this," she laughed. "I don't go to NYU. . . . It costs three hundred dollars a credit and what would I take up besides space? But it's a nice color, don't you think? And sometimes, when I'm in the Village, it gets me in their library."

"You don't go to college?"

"Starlight U."

"You can't be president, you weren't born here," he said. "So what are you going to do with your life? You don't want to be M. Anita Supreme all the time."

"I'm not," she told him. "In the afternoon I'm Hellen Bedd. And Sundays," rattling her bracelets, "I'm a belly dancer at an Egyptian restaurant on Seventy-second Street."

"Kind of skinny for that, aren't you?" He'd wanted to make a joke of it, but it came out wrong. "What do you call yourself there? . . . C. Anita Camel? Harem Scarem?"

"Little Odessa."

"You like to dance? You're good? I missed you at the Starlight."

"Thank God," she said. "No, I'm not making a career of it, if that's what you want to know. I've got real plans."

"Like what?" he asked.

"I'm going to start modeling school, when I scrape up a few extra dollars."

"Those places are a rip," he said. "They tell fat girls they look like what's-her-name, Twiggy."

"I have to work on my diction," she said. "I want to lose this accent."

"You don't sound like a Russkie."

"Not Russian. Brooklyn. I want to do TV. Every once in a while I find a modeling job on my own, showroom stuff. If things work out, pretty soon I'll have to give up dancing before my face . . . before I get too well known. At least I hope so."

He went up Brighton Fifth Street, banked with the decaying brick and stucco bungalows of recently arrived Jamaicans, the old summer colony of the Brooklyn elite now in the throes of third-world liberation. He turned again on Neptune and she pointed out a five-story elevator building indistinguishable from hundreds of others, save for *LEVANTINE HALL* in script over the entrance. He put the wagon in park, killed the engine. "Well—"

"Straight ahead will put you on the Belt," she said. "Maybe you can find a fare going back."

"Hack commission catches me, I'm dead," he told her. "I don't have a license to cruise."

"Anyway, I appreciate the ride."

"Don't mention it," he said, and laughed uneasily. "It was the least I could do after running you in."

She grabbed her bag and opened the door. He stopped her with a hand on her wrist. "You don't really live with your folks?"

"Why?"

"I thought I could come upstairs, we could have a cup of coffee together."

"That would be nice," she said, "but I'm asleep on my feet. How would you feel if I dozed off while we were talking?"

"I wouldn't mind."

"Yes you would." She smiled too sweetly. "Besides, my mother would hit the roof if I brought home a *shaygets.*"

"A what?"

"Good night," she said. "And thanks again."

Fuck you, too, lady. "Well then, s'long."

2

NATHAN Metrevelli, jiggling a sifter full of seeds and broken twigs over a Formica tabletop, said he hated sleeping alone. "If I wanted to be by myself all the time, I wouldn't have moved in with you. There are plenty of rich women I could be just as lonely with."

Kate dropped her bag at the door and went inside the tiny kitchen. "You know, there's more to life than sex and money," she said, "but they're acquired tastes."

"Well, yes," Nathan admitted without turning his head. "That's why every day I try to set aside a few hours to eat, go to the *schvitz*, watch TV, work—"

"Hah," Kate said, "what do you know about that one?"

"About eating? Just wait and see. When are you starting supper?"

She threw her arms around his neck, nuzzled him. "Nathan, Nathan, why do I put up with you?"

"Because," he said, "I'm not like other men, who never get past your obvious charms. What I love you for . . ."

"Yes, Nathan?"

"Is your body."

She slapped his face.

"Ow," he said, spilling some of the grass from a yellow square of gummed paper. "Those rings feel like brass knuckles."

"They're supposed to."

He crooked an arm around her neck and bulldogged her cheek to his, quickly let her go. She stood over him and cupped his chin in her hand, guided his mouth to her lips. "Your body," he said again.

She studied the upside-down face. The cleft jaw made a fine, worried pinhead above the red-rimmed cyclops' eye of his mouth. The curly dark brown hair, a beard from a Chagall painting of a shtetl rabbi. She wondered if she seemed as ridiculous to him, and then realized he wasn't looking. Inside out was the only perspective that interested him.

"Do you know why?" she asked.

He waggled his chin, shaking the stubbly pinhead. "Why what?"

"Why I put up with you?"

The arm snaked around her waist and pulled her onto his lap. His eyes widened in mock apprehension. "No, Kate, I don't. Wh-y?"

"Because you're so damn useful," she said. "When all the other girls at Lincoln were rebelling against their parents, when they were doing reds and drinking that awful peppermint schnapps, sniffing glue and getting knocked up, the real dumb ones, I didn't have to. I had Nathan Metrevelli, the Bad News Boor. Just being with you was worse for my reputation than anything the others tried."

No, that wasn't smart. Never be too candid with Nathan, especially when you're going heart to heart with him. Nathan could dish it out with the best of them, but he caught everything coming back with a glass ego.

"So you had time for homework and made good marks," he said. "What did that ever get you?"

"Nathan Metrevelli all over again."

He moistened his lips and put the joint in his mouth and drew it out again. He leaned over the stove and Kate caught a whiff of singed hair before the sweet mustiness of the Maui Wowie. He filled his lungs and puffed out his cheeks, croaked, "Wanna hit?"

"Nathan," she said, "I'm twenty-two years old and I dance bottomless on Times Square. I don't need you to be bad for me any more."

"My pleasure," he said and waved the joint under her nose. "You sure?"

She brushed his hand away. "I'm trying to be serious."

He took another hit. "What's more serious than grass? Grass is my livelihood."

"No, Nathan." She slid off his lap. "Though you won't admit it, I'm your livelihood. Dope is your hobby."

"Six of one, half a dozen of the other," he told her. "My parents didn't drag me all the way from Tbilisi to push a hack."

"So you push grass instead?"

"How many years in this country and still you don't understand the language?" Nathan said. "I don't push grass, I *deal* it. It's a seller's market. My customers are lucky to be getting it. I don't have to push it on anyone."

"You push it at me. All the time. Breathing around you makes me goofy."

"Here," he said. "It'll give you an appetite."

He put the joint to her lips and she inhaled lightly. "Damn it, Nathan, at least you found grass. What have I got?"

"Artistic freedom," he said.

She went back for her bag and carried it into the bathroom. She ran water in the tub and tested it with her hand, tempered the numbing flow with a surge hot enough to take off skin. She added some more of the cold, so that she could almost stand it, and went into the bedroom.

An unmade mattress covered most of the scuffed parquet floor. Kate stood beside a mahogany dresser that was the only piece of furniture she had ever purchased new and brushed her hair at a wall mirror. She lowered the venetian blinds and kicked off her shoes, wriggled out of her jeans, pulled the sweatshirt over her head.

Redness had spilled over the burn on her chest. She felt a twinge beneath her breasts and found two small blisters she hadn't known were there. Her hip was black and blue to the middle of her thigh. She heard a chair scrape against the kitchen linoleum and then Nathan came into the room with the joint glued to his lip.

"Dressed for work? You just got home."

"Sometimes, Nathan, it stops being funny."

"Who's being— Hey, what happened to you?"

"I was shot," she told him.

"Perfect aim," he said. "Who'd you make jealous, a gal with a shotgun?"

"Nathan, you're incorrigible." She laughed in spite of herself. "No, it wasn't a shotgun. You only see pistols at the Starlight, pistols and long knives."

"Whoever did it, it looks nasty." He pressed his lips to her chest and kissed it several times. "Feel better?"

"Uh-huh," she sighed.

"I don't know about you, Kate," he said, and went from the room. "Sometimes you act just like a little girl." The medicine cabinet squeaked open and Nathan returned with a tube of Noxzema. "A kiss can't make the pain go away. You need something stronger."

He tossed the Noxzema on the dresser and nudged her onto the mattress, knotted his fingers in the taffy hair. She wrapped her arms around his back. Nathan ran his lips to her breasts, raising away to study the burn in the weak light slicing through the blinds. Kate undid the buttons on his shirt.

"What *did* happen?" he asked

"It's nothing," she breathed, and pulled him back down.

Nathan touched his fingers to the redness, resting his palm on her breast. "It doesn't feel like nothing." He put his hand on the other breast. "No way is this nothing."

She backhanded his elbow out from under him and he fell heavily on her. She circled her arms around him again and held him close. Feeling for his body melting against hers, she kissed him. His shoulders stiffened and he arced his neck.

"What is it?" she asked.

"You never did tell me," he said.

"About last night? Later, Nathan. Why don't you get out of your clothes?"

She unlocked her arms and he rolled off. He picked up the roach from the ashtray beside the mattress and took a deep hit, then another. "What's for supper?" he asked.

She pulled the curtains inside the tub and raised her face to the scalding needle spray, scourged the corruption of her night in jail. Another milestone on the merry-go-round, and Nathan along for the ride. What was with him anyhow? He was more impossible now than ever. Ask him and you'd hear a lot of crap about a man caught between conflicting cultures and values, with only his dope and his woman to keep him going. Jesus, Kate thought, he came over when he was eight. New York was all he'd ever known. Most likely he was moving blow again, and most of it up his own nose.

It was snowing when they went downstairs, stinging pellets that eddied about their eyes and collected in the folds of their clothing. In the early darkness Brighton Beach Avenue was dug in behind steel gates. Nathan took her hand and they darted across the stairstep shadows of the el, homing in on the dull beacon of an all-night fruit stand. Next door was the Café Kharkov and a booth beneath a watercolor of the frozen Dnieper shore.

Their waitress was a pale dumpling of a woman with mottled, bleached hair. She unburdened herself of a couple of soiled menus and looked exasperated when Nathan didn't open his. "How's the salyanka?" he asked.

"*Srednya*," she answered expressionlessly.

"Not so good, huh? Well, I'm not crazy for lamb anyway. I'll have the chicken chahombili. . . . What about you, Kate?"

"Dalma."

The waitress removed the extra settings unhappily, reproving them for not being a four. As she backed through the swinging doors Nathan placed his wool astrakhan hat on the seat beside him like an invited guest. "I talked to your sister last night," he said.

"I didn't know you could."

"About you, Hannah'll always talk. I wanted to know where you were."

"What time was this?" Kate asked.

"Around three. I didn't know what was keeping you."

"You called my mother's house at three A.M? What did . . . after the screaming stopped, what did Hannah say?"

"She said you'd told her you were staying with Irina in the city."

"I wasn't."

"I know," Nathan said. "I called there, too."

"At three o'clock?"

"More like three-thirty," he told her. "I thought the train might be stuck, so I waited up. Care to tell me where you were?"

"In jail."

Nathan tore a piece from a loaf of dark bread and began buttering it on both sides. "Gave everything you had at the Starlight? I'm sorry I missed it."

Kate's face reddened. "Damn you, Nathan, can't you be on my side . . . just this once?"

"Who was he, Kate? One of the sleazebags who runs the club, or some jerk-off from the street?"

Kate gathered her coat around her shoulders and slid out of the booth. "Good-bye, Nathan," she said. "Enjoy the chicken."

He clamped a hand around her arm. "Who?" he asked again.

"If you must know, it was a *schvartzer* in a fur coat and a felt hat with a wide brim. He had a diamond in his front tooth and I think he was diseased. You know how I'm drawn to men who drive avocado Lincolns."

"Just so long as it wasn't some lowlife," he said.

He let go of her arm and she slumped down in the booth. "Nathan, why do you do this to me all the time?"

"Do what?" He bit off a corner of the bread. "You said jail, so I said pimp. Or you did. Where's the harm? I'm sorry I called your sister so late, but I was worried about you. Do you blame me? . . . Now, what happened?"

"There *was* a black man involved," Kate said. "A fat little guy, Prince somebody from somewhere. He scorched me with a cigarette."

"Is that what happened to your chest?"

"Uh-huh. Have you ever burned your lip on a roach? Multiply the pain by ten and you'll have an idea how it felt. And then I—" She began to laugh.

"What's funny?"

"It wasn't funny at the time," she said. "I saw red, Nathan, flaming red, and the next thing I remember I was leaping off the runway and chasing the fat guy through the crowd."

"*You* were chasing *him?*"

"And then Washington tackled him and I didn't have anything else handy, so I opened his head with my shoe."

"That's funny?"

"I guess you had to be there," Kate said. "Anyway, this prince guy turned out to be a UN ambassador, or like that, and he called the cops. And I ended up in a cell with all these awful women I'll bet started out dancing at the Starlight."

"I suppose you had a lot in common . . ."

Kate's face got redder and some of the color spilled over

her eyes. Nathan didn't notice. "A lot to talk about," he went on. "Why didn't you call me?"

"Because," Kate said evenly, "I didn't want to wake Phyllis Stern."

"Huh?"

She opened her palms and pushed them at him. "Please, Nathan, don't start. Your 'Who me?' routine hasn't worked in years."

"I don't know what you're talking about. I haven't seen Phyllis."

"Maybe the lights were out."

"You're spending too much time on Times Square," Nathan said. "You're starting to fantasize, like everyone else there."

"Her earrings, Nathan, the nice silver ones I always admired. She left them under the pillow last weekend."

Nathan fielded that one slowly and then he bobbled it. "Very good, Kate," he said. "You almost had me going there, you sounded so serious."

"It's not good and I am serious. Nathan, open your eyes. I'm wearing them."

The kitchen door swung out and the waitress placed a steaming casserole dish in front of Nathan. When she went away he said, "They look very nice on you, Kate."

Kate asked, "Remember what I said would happen if you two were so much as seen together again?"

Nathan wrinkled his brow. "Something bad, wasn't it?"

"Bad for you, Nathan."

He brushed the moisture from his hat and put it on his head. "You want me to pack my stuff?"

"What stuff? All you brought with you were your scales."

"I'm not going to make a scene, Kate, if that's what you want."

"I won't hurt you, Nathan. I'm not wearing heels."

"That's not what I meant. I just don't want to fight."

"No," she said. "I didn't think you would."

He got up to leave. "Bye, Kate."

"Good-bye, Nathan. Give my best to Phyllis."

The waitress came back with the second order and Kate pushed it out of the way without tasting it. "Nathan, you shit," she called after him loud enough for everyone to hear. "I love you."

3

PLAYING *The Price Is Right* in Abu Safwat Khader's office over the Arabian Knights on Seventy-second Street, Kate guessed that the furnishings had set him back a cool $200 to $250. The estimate took in two olive-green file cabinets, a Mr. Coffee coffeemaker, a yard-sale desk, a pen-and-ink drawing of a soccer goalie—or was it a framed Rorschach inkblot?—not a single chair. She held her bid on a separate lot of factory-new Barcaloungers that cluttered the small room. She counted six of them upholstered in tangy simulated leather, two gray, two black, two in chocolate—one the dark bittersweet kind, the other lighter, milkier.

In the year she had been dancing for Abu Safwat Khader she could not remember him in another kind of seat and only rarely in the upright position—about as often as he had seen her in anything besides sheer veils and the slippers with the curled toes that already were crushing her feet. Khader's real name was Howard Ormont and he had papers from a court in Washington, D.C., to prove it. At another time he had been called Fatti Ben-Zvi and made his home on Kibbutz Altalena in the Negev. His first sixteen years, three spent hiding from the Nazis in Samarkand in the central Soviet Union, he was Isaac Grynzpun. He had paper to prove this, too, a certificate from a yeshiva in Glukhov, the Ukrainian town where his family was buried.

He dated his love affair with Barcaloungers to his nineteenth birthday, which he had celebrated sowing land mines along the Hulda Road with the Haganah's Givati Brigade. A sniper opening fire from a shallow wadi tore a small hole in his back, a painless wound he shrugged off until a sudden shortness of breath forced him to sit down and gulp uselessly for air. As he was blacking out, he toppled backward and was able to fill his lungs again. He lay beside the Hulda Road for forty minutes waiting to be evacuated, holding each new breath in his chest as though it might have to last forever.

The medics explained that he had suffered a sucking wound; the bullet had opened up the pulmonary cavity, allowing the outside air to push against his lungs. That he had fallen on his back and plugged the hole rather than slumped forward and died he interpreted as meaning he should spend what future he had reclining. Four years later, he came to New York.

With skills as a farmer and a sapper he went bankrupt in his first business venture, a kosher restaurant on the gray steppe of the Grand Concourse, newly *Judenfrei* in the wake of the postwar migration of Jews to the Long Island suburbs. Like many Israelis he spoke fluent, unaccented Arabic, and with embarrassed Egyptians backing him he opened an Arab restaurant on upper Broadway. Though his political loyalties were a poorly kept secret in Manhattan's tangled Mideastern community, the partners prospered on the strength of his easy manner and weathered good looks. The Arabian Knights was his third and most successful enterprise.

"Half of which, along with the most vulgarly large diamond of your choice," he told Kate between shows on a torpid summer night, "is yours anytime you say the word." He flailed a cigar about his head with thick hands, skywriting the offer in gray ash.

"That's very generous of you, Howard."

"Abu, remember? Or we'll both be out on the street. And don't look so morose when it's my heart you're trampling on."

"Abu."

"Do I frighten you? To look at me now would you suspect I killed seventeen men with these hands?"

"Is that so, Abu?" Knowing what was coming next, preparing a smile.

"Sad to say, it is. It happened years ago, when I was young and didn't know better. Just before I lost my first restaurant I let go the cook and took over the kitchen myself. The carnage . . ." He hung his head.

Kate forced the smile, but not hard enough.

"Not funny? Let me try again."

"It's not you," she said. "It's . . . really, it's nothing."

"Yes," he said. "I see that." He squeezed her arm, kept his hand there a little too long. "Then there's still hope for me?"

Again the watered smile. Kate turned toward the window and probed between the gritty blinds, staring out at the abandoned benches of what had been Needle Park. "Howard, we've been through this so many times. You're very sweet and extremely attractive and you know how fond I am of you, but it wouldn't—"

"*Sha,*" he said with a finger to his lips. "Let me make a proposal of another sort, one I think may ease this existential trauma afflicting you."

She bent the blind back. "I won't be part of your harem," she warned.

"Maybe some other sheikh's? How would you like to be in the movies?"

"Which one, the Baronet or the Quad?"

"Please, I'm talking from the bottom of my heart."

She laughed out loud and immediately regretted it. "Howard, that line won't work on anyone over fifteen. It was worn out before movies were invented."

"Listen," he said, stretching out his legs and leaning back so that all she saw above his chin was the ruby tip of his cigar. "Two landsmen, friends of mine . . . well, maybe not friends but fellows we can do business with, are shooting a film and shopping around for a belly dancer and naturally they told Abu. And I'm telling Little Odessa."

"Why come here when they could just pluck a girl off the street back home?"

"For one, the street is Hollywood Boulevard. They, too, have expatriated themselves. For another, not many Palestinian girls would be caught dead in an Israeli movie, since that is likely what would happen if they were. And also because these fellows accepted incentives from the mayor's office to use the Astoria sound stages. . . . They're anxious to meet you, Kate. I've gone out on a limb touting you."

"Hang on tight," she said, brushing aside the tassles from her spangled halter to play her fingers over her ribs, "or did you tell them about these bones you say scare off your customers? Why not turn them on to one of the other women?"

"Feh. Belly dancers they can find anywhere. A presence like yours—"

"They'll hide behind a veil."

"Don't worry about details. Worry instead about getting the part. It's a small one, but it pays handsomely for a few days' work, and who knows where it can lead?"

"I still don't see why they'd want to use—" She pulled up short. "Oh no," she said, hovering over the Bar-calounger, snatching the cigar from his teeth. "Get yourself another girl. I didn't give up flashing my *tuchas* on Times Square to do porno flicks."

"Would I ask that of the future Mrs. Abu Safwat Khader? This is going to be an R-rated production, could be a PG. Very soft at the core, very classy. You wouldn't even have to go nude much."

"But I do have to audition for these friends of yours?"

"Call it a screen test."

"I think we both know what that means."

"No, no . . . trust me. These guys are for real, their

money is. What if I invite them to the show, let them have a look at you?"

"It's your restaurant," she said with a quick hunch of her shoulders. "I just dance here."

"Kate, you're doing yourself a terrific favor." He took back the cigar and patted down his jacket for matches. "Now do us both another one."

"Yes, Howard?"

"And put a little meat on those bones."

The rumble of Indian tablas ionized the stuffy room. Kate went to a tortoiseshell compact to plump her lips with Carmine Karma, darken her cheeks with powder. A raven fall swallowed the taffy hair. She hooked her fingers in cymbals the size of half-dollars and clattered them like tinny castanets, tugged at the rhinestone halter so that the pale fullness of her breasts spilled over the top. She said, "Your friends, the *machers*, they're downstairs? Maybe I should lose my top."

"Just put the left in front of the right, the left foot in front of the right, and they'll have enough to see."

She hiked her veils around her hips and tiptoed two flights down. Howard ran interference as she dashed into the alley past a disbelieving old man scavenging returnables from a dumpster. They came back inside through the kitchen, where he fed her snips of toasted pita smeared with tabouleh while a skirling clarinet set her swaying like a cobra in an air-conditioned basket.

The sound thickened under the weight of a Moroccan oud and Kate stepped out between the tables. The musicians, in burgundy fezes and embroidered vests, lowered their instruments as she acknowledged the casual applause. She circled the floor slowly as they started up again, tried her feet in the familiar places. Feeling her body come alive, she rewarded the crowd with a rare smile. Though she wouldn't admit it, she loved what she was doing, considered the eight weeks with a fat women's dance class in the basement of the Bensonhurst Y the best investment of her time she'd ever made.

The volume picked up and the tempo grew frenzied, faster than the psychedelic storm which climaxed her routine at the Starlight. Acidophilus rock for the yogurt set, Howard called it. She shut her eyes, undulating in place, the sweat running freely between her breasts. What she lacked in technique she masked with enthusiasm and the youthful suppleness of her body.

Beyond the colored lights the house was half full, couples mostly, patriarchal Turks sipping sweet Arab coffee at tables barely large enough to balance a demitasse. The pillows in the window seats were empty. She searched the room, but saw no one with the casual arrogance that would give away Howard's movie friends.

The music stopped on a dime and she came to a halt two cents later, arching her arms shakily above her head. The backbone of a round of polite applause was a violent pounding from the kitchen door. The crowd tried again and she held her pose, then exited through the clamor.

"You saw," she said, steadying her voice with a hand against her chest. "So what was that crack about not eating enough?"

Howard tossed his jacket around her shoulders and nudged her out of the draft. "An invitation to join me for dinner. I have another favor to discuss with you," he explained. "I want you to spend a few nights at my place."

Kate accepted a glass of mint tea, trying not to look too annoyed. "I thought we'd covered that."

"Did I say I would be there with you?" He dug under her shoulders for a blue-and-white El Al ticket envelope. "I go on vacation next Sunday night," he said. "Four exciting weeks in *eretz Yisroel*. I want you to stay with Isaac Grynzpun."

"Who's that?" The annoyance starting to show.

He replaced the ticket in the jacket, brought the lapels

together under her chin. "Don't worry, you'll have him eating out of your hand."

"Who is he?"

"My best friend and trusted adviser," Howard said. Kate pulled a sour face, but before she could say anything he added, "My wolfhound, the great grandson of my companion in the years when the Germans were chasing me all over Russia. Like myself, a survivor. It's a fine name, don't you think?"

"A Russian wolfhound? I didn't know you like dogs."

"Don't call him that, not if you want to stay *his* friend."

"Why, being a dog's not good enough for him?"

"He thinks he's American," Howard said and ushered her into the dining room.

They took seats at the window booth closest to the kitchen. One of the musicians followed carrying menus. "What's good," Howard told him. An order, not a question. The man in the fez nodded and went smartly away.

"You never danced better," Howard told her.

"That's a hell of a compliment."

"No, by any standard tonight you were excellent."

"The *macher*s, what did they say? I looked everywhere trying to pick them out."

"You didn't look far enough," he told her. "They're still in California."

She studied the smoked tumbler as if it were a crystal ball. "I thought you told me—"

"Did I? You must excuse me if I did. Tonight's audition was for my benefit only. The way you danced, I'll tell them to come for a look soon as they arrive in town."

"When will that be?"

"Some time after I'm gone. They'll show up without introducing themselves, and there will be your big opportunity without your even knowing it. You had better be this good every night."

"What if they're here when I'm not dancing?"

"We can't let that happen. That's why I'm leaving you in charge of the Knights as well as of my house. You book the dancers."

"What do I know about running a restaurant?" she frowned. "What do I know about dogs?"

"Who else can I ask, my former partners, those crooks? They stole my profits and sent them to the PLO. You have to do these things for me."

"Howard, I can't."

He dropped his voice, quieting her. "The restaurant practically runs itself, so you'll be taking twice the pay just to dance. Did you hear? The cook will help with the ordering. As for staying in my place, you're entitled to a little luxury for once in your life. I know the way you live in Brooklyn. Ask me how and I tell you frankly I don't pay you enough to live better. Am I wrong so far?" Without waiting for an answer he said, "So if you won't live with me, live with Isaac Grynzpun. And maybe if you get along with him as well as I do, you'll be there when I come back."

"No, Howard, there's no chance."

"It's up to you. I'll be gone a month, so indulge yourself, play the big shot. What have you got to lose?"

"I know what you think will happen. . . . You're going to be disappointed."

"Don't be so sure of yourself, Ekaterina. You wouldn't be the first girl seduced by luxury. I live extremely well, you know."

"There are more important things than money."

"True, but most of them grow old fast, as old as this," he said, tugging at the loose flesh under his chin, "and sick, while having the bad taste to remain as poor as they ever were."

"If that's what you want to believe—"

"Tell me about it, tell me about it after." He shredded the wrapper from a fresh cigar. "Let me offer a deal. Stay at my place a few weeks and if you still feel the same way, don't be there when I come back. I'll call from Israel before I leave to give fair warning."

"What if I want out?" she asked. "What happens to Isaac?"

"Don't be silly, Kate. He'd never let you go."

He caught her wrist and slipped the foil band on a finger. She peeled it off and rolled it into a silver ball, flicked it away. If he was disappointed, he didn't show it. When she sniffed at the thick panatela like she'd never seen one before, he offered a light. She bit off the end on the second try and puffed three times without coughing, exhaled coolly and examined it again, then knocked off the ash and slapped him on the shoulder. "You're on," she blurted.

And was more surprised than he was to hear it.

The centerpiece of Howard's West Seventy-sixth Street brownstone was a burnished gingerbread staircase with potted ficus trees and bench seats on each balustraded landing.

"Real chestnut," he bragged, rapping his knuckles on the banister as though the heavy thud would erase any doubt. "When I moved in, it was hidden under fourteen separate coats of paint. It took two months to strip down to the original wood, everything hand-carved. The house was built in 1883 for Miss L. Hamilton Wynne."

"Who's that?" Kate asked.

Howard shrugged. "I'm new here," he explained.

What Kate liked best about the place was the ailanthus forest in the backyard which shut out the sounds of traffic, and Isaac Grynzpun, who lay across his master's bed with one bloodshot eye trained on the TV. She plopped down beside him to scratch his ear and was rebuffed with a discreet growl.

"He's not very sociable," she said. "Or did you forget to feed him?"

"Shhhh," Howard said, leading her away. "He's watching the news. I'll introduce you when it's over."

They climbed to the third floor where a grand piano was stuffed inside a dark salon like a ship in a cheerless bottle.

Another shrug from Howard. "Don't ask me," he said. "It was here when I moved in."

Kate ran her fingers over the keyboard and whisked the greasy dust against the palm of her other hand. A louvered screen intercepted the light entering through a window with a pine sash, and she raised the slats to peer out at a street mirrored in brownstone from Amsterdam to Columbus. Ginkgo trees grown sturdy beneath a sodium-vapor sun came together in a yellow canopy. A green sedan idling at the curb caught her eye, and she glared at a man looking back through field glasses.

"Howard, do you know you have a spy?"

"Once I saw a mouse, but this is the first I hear . . ." He went to the window as the sedan pulled into traffic and rounded the corner. "I don't see anything."

"That car," she said. "There was a man in front watching through binoculars."

"The lady next door is dying. The apartment hunters have been circling like buzzards for weeks."

"He was looking here," Kate said. "I'm sure of it."

"Could be he thinks I'm sick, too."

The door inched back and Isaac Grynzpun padded inside. He was the biggest dog Kate had seen, with a small head as high as her chest. "Isaac," Howard said, "this is your new mistress, Kate Piro."

The dog looked up intelligently and Kate expected some rare trick. Instead, he sat on her foot and allowed her to stroke his long neck.

"He weighs a ton," she said, struggling to free herself. "Does he bite?"

"Yes. And he chews. . . . Say hello, Isaac."

Kate stroked the animal cautiously. After a while she told Howard, "He didn't say anything. Does he like me?"

"He likes all women."

"What does a Russ—a wolfhound eat?" she asked. "Caviar?"

"Strangers, if you tell him," Howard said. "Isaac is the world's greatest watchdog, more efficient than the burglar alarm that is connected to the Forty-eighth Street station house, by the way. He'll also eat roast beef—yours, if you're not careful. I feed him dry dog food and table scraps."

"Where do you keep it?"

"In the kitchen cabinet. Isaac will show you when he's hungry. There's plenty of food more to your liking in the freezer, and towels and sheets and so forth in the linen closet outside my bedroom. And . . . I almost forgot." From a leather case he removed a key with metal filings clinging to the sharp edges. "I had this made up for you," he said. "Yesterday."

"What about the mailbox?"

"What mailbox? The postman drops the letters through a slot in the door."

"I never thought of that," she said. "I've always lived in apartments."

"You'll get used to this, so quickly the other will seem strange," Howard said. "I did. . . . Any more questions, you'd better ask now."

"Just one. How do I thank you for everything?"

"That," he said, "I'm leaving up to you."

4

THE TOWELHEAD was a closet fruit; Harry Lema could tell. In the six weeks they had shared a room at the Duffy-Lawes House on West Ninety-sixth Street, Harry had never seen him near the showers, or even change out of his clothes. The towelhead had vile habits, and the room—with its soft pastels and indirect lighting and the furniture that looked like it had been ripped off from a suburban kindergarten—stank to the high heavens. He smoked clove cigarettes. He farted in his sleep. He brushed his teeth once a week and cooked all his own meals on the two-burner hot plate on Harry's side of the room. Arab stuff. Lamb three times a day, stewed in garlic and paprika and onions, the greasy smoke hanging in the air till Harry's clothes and hair reeked. The window, like all the windows at Duffy-Lawes, was bolted shut. If Harry smashed it one more time, they would put him back in Great Meadows.

Harry had been calling the halfway house home for nearly four months now, finishing off concurrent two-year beefs for a string of houseboat burglaries at the Seventy-ninth Street boat basin that had brought him to the city. Had he accepted the terms of early release, he would have been out on the street by May. But he couldn't be bothered with supervision, the endless tug-of-war with a parole officer, the job interviews and urine testing and all the rest of the crap that was as comforting as mother's milk to the Institutional Man, which was something Harry Lema was sure he wasn't, as sure as he was that the towelhead was a fruit.

Harry pressed the pillowcase against his face, breathing

through the thin cotton. Then he pounded the mattress and sat up as the dark little man shoveled more condiments into the bubbling pot. Harry held his breath, trying not to deck the towelhead, not with less than two weeks until his time was up. He reached over the edge of the bunk for *The American Turfman* and used it to stir the heavy air.

He had finished an article about a son of Secretariat who was an odds-on favorite to break his famous sire's speed records when he put down the magazine. The towelhead, whose name was Ali, was standing with his back to the wall, not moving, staring up at him with parted lips.

"Yeah?" Harry said.

Ali opened his mouth, showing Harry spotty rows of teeth and primitive dentistry. He raised his arms over his head and brought them down quickly in a flapping motion, like he was trying to lift off for a short flight. Harry turned the page. Crazy fucking towelhead, he was thinking as the little man reached over his own shoulder as though he wanted to pat himself on the back and then resumed waving his arms.

"Never get off the ground," Harry said, and read another half-column. When he looked down again the towelhead had stopped flapping, like he was coming in for a landing, and his skin was the same light blue as the walls.

"The hell's the matter with you?" Harry glanced into the pot, noticed that the food scarcely had been touched. "You chokin'? That what you're trying to tell me?"

Ali pumped his head up and down.

"That's what I figured," Harry said, and went back to his magazine.

He was reading about a great-great-granddaughter of Nasrullah when the towelhead knocked over the pot and the grease oozed into the rust-colored carpet that made Harry sick to be around it. Ali had turned a darker blue and was sagging against the wall. Harry watched him for a while. He said, "Quit carryin' on, huh?"

Harry folded a corner of the page and placed the magazine beside the pillow. He switched off his reading lamp. He slid down from the bunk, avoiding the greasy spot in the carpeting as he got into his slippers and went across the room. The towelhead was flailing wildly again, and the back of his hand caught Harry under the chin.

"Butt out?" Harry asked. "That what you want?"

The towelhead flapped faster.

"Then try and be a little cool about this."

Harry stepped behind the shorter man and put a half nelson on him, then slid his hands around the thick waist, picturing the Heimlich maneuver poster on the wall of the Duffy-Lawes kitchen. He tightened his right hand into a fist and used the left to sweep it upward into the towelhead's gut. "Better?" he asked.

Ali's head shook violently.

Harry dug the fist higher and deeper. "That do the trick?"

The little man twisted in his grasp. Harry surrounded him with his body and raised him off the floor. "Got it that time, right?"

Ali made no sound. His arms hung loosely at his sides and his head had stopped moving. Harry shrugged. He spun him around and drove a short punch into his stomach, dropping him to his knees. A pulpy mass struck Harry beneath the eye. As he flicked it away, he saw that it was an undercooked piece of lamb.

Ali was down on all fours taking deep, mournful breaths. His color was coming back. Harry climbed into the bunk and found his place in *The American Turfman*.

"I owe you my life," Ali blubbered.

"Keep it under your hat," Harry said. His wrist had begun to throb, as though he'd sprained it, and he probed the tender joint with his fingers. "In this town, anyway."

Ali dragged himself to his feet and looked at Harry with tears running freely down his cheeks. "Anything you want

that I have in my power to give to you . . ." He came close
to the bunk and embraced Harry's ankles.

Harry squirmed away and pulled his legs after him.
"Knock it off," he said. "I was bein' neighborly is all."

"This is not something I forget. I am in your debt."

"Don't bother. It's on the house."

"No," Ali insisted. "It is a debt that must be repaid."

As the Arab retreated to his side of the room and sat in
one of the kindergarten chairs, Harry inched back to the
edge of the mattress. "Why?" he asked. "What're you
givin' away?"

"One million thanks to you, my friend."

"Shove it," Harry told him.

"One million and one."

Harry put down the magazine. "What's the one?"

Ali's eyes lit up as though Harry had done him a greater
favor than before. "It is something you may wish to know
about when you are back in circulation." He swiveled
around in his chair. To Harry he looked good as new,
better even. "There is a vault, in a house not very far from
here. I understand that you are a safecracker . . ."

"Something like that." Harry sat straighter.

"Inside this vault is never less than fifty thousand dollars,
and often more."

"Belongs to a dealer, huh?" Harry rubbed his wrist
again. "Thanks," he said. "But no thanks."

Ali got out of the chair. He went down on his knees
again and began picking scraps of meat off the rug.

"I said it's a dealer's stash, right?" When the Arab didn't
respond, Harry dropped down from the bunk and
grabbed him by the collar, backed him against the wall.
"You were sayin' . . ."

Ali smiled ecstatically. "It belongs to my former partner."

"Partner in what?"

"The restaurant business."

Harry glanced at the overturned pot near the hotplate and laughed. "You gotta be jivin'."

The Arab put his hand on Harry's shoulder, but didn't try to push away. "Not so long ago, I was part owner of a restaurant with an . . ." He stopped, the word caught in his throat as if he was choking again. "With an Israeli," he finally managed to say, placing the accent on the second of four syllables, "and it was his habit always to keep large amounts of money in his vault."

"How come?" Harry asked. "He doesn't believe in banks?"

"His whole life he is a refugee, and so he sleeps better having cash within reach, even in New York."

"Where'd he get it all?"

"From me," Ali said unhappily. "He was skimming the profits from our business, cheating me and my brother and the IRS all at the same time. And now he is leading the good life on my money while I rot away on false charges that *I* stole from *him*."

"Where'd you say this was?"

"On Seventy-sixth Street, inside the largest brownstone on the north side of the block between Amsterdam and Columbus." He began scribbling on the back of an envelope. "His name is Ormont, and if you should find him at home you have my permission to kill him. To kill his dog, too, which is his favorite thing in the world and, I must warn you, the most ferocious son of a bitch I have seen. Here," he said. "One million and one thanks."

Harry glanced at the address. "Why you givin' me this? You'll be outta here pretty soon yourself, you could find somebody be glad to go in with you for a percentage."

The towelhead put his hand back on Harry's arm, winked at him.

For the first time since he'd been clean Harry Lema was back on the Lower East Side. On a wet, dreary afternoon he was wearing glacier glasses with brown leather blinkers, tapping his umbrella against the sidewalk as though he'd suddenly gone blind. Which, in a way, he had, courtesy of all the faces on the street he could live very nicely without seeing again.

What had brought him downtown were the secondhand clothing stores. He steered clear of trendy Saint Mark's Place, prowling the tired side streets off the Bowery that the new money hadn't discovered and the old wanted no part of. At a Volunteers of America thrift shop he found what he was looking for—a gray cotton jacket with *Speedy* in torn script over the breast pocket and frayed sleeves creased like a mummy's lips. He extricated a near match from a tangle of threadbare trousers in a wet wash cart and brought everything to the register.

The cashier was dressed entirely in black, showing off a tight body Harry rated a strong seven or weak eight and spiked hair between high, white sidewalls. "You want to try these on," she said, "there's a mirror behind the shoe department."

Harry took off the dark glasses. No, he said, the only pants he wanted to get into were hers.

The girl was in no mood for wise guys. She said, "You'd have nice eyes if they weren't so close together, like maybe your mom was screwing around with her brother. You ever ask her about that?"

A guard came over tapping a leather sap against his thigh, and Harry gave the girl her money and let the matter drop. His eyes *were* too narrow. They were also too blue and the gentlest thing about him, something many women—although not nearly enough—had noticed. In Cranston, Rhode Island, where he had passed long stretches of a troubled adolescence that ended when he was about thirty, passed them working a metal press while I-95 traffic hummed past the barred windows, some of the decreppos in the ACI medium-security weight room had noticed the same thing. And so he had raised an unencouraging full beard that came in scraggly and seemed to be losing territory ever since.

He walked back along Second Avenue, to a green Olds Cutlass they were still looking for in Riverdale. He tossed the package on the seat and plucked a ticket from the windshield, returned it to a Chevy parked beside a meter hooded in a paper bag. He drove downtown and turned east toward Tompkins Square. Take away the college kids pushing out of the Village, crammed five and six into eight-hundred-dollar cockroach flats, and the park looked about the same, a few raggedy green patches in a ground-glass desert, the benches lined with junkies in the clouded euphoria of their afternoon fixes.

He caught the FDR at Houston Street. He turned on the radio and switched off his mind and headed uptown on automatic pilot. The Harlem River Drive funneled him into Inwood and he followed the accusing finger of the island to a mock Tudor apartment house in the shadow of Baker Field.

He entered through the laundry room and emptied his package into a washer, watched it spin a while before running upstairs for something to read. Back issues of *The American Turfman* were spilled over the convertible sofa in his cubbyhole studio. He glanced at a sleek bay gelding in a blanket of Texas bluebonnets and did his best double-take, slapped his forehead with the heel of his hand.

"The flowers," he said out loud. "The fuckin' flowers. How can anybody be so dumb?"

Through a hole in the shade he looked out at the stadium clock. Nearly six-thirty—too late to take care of everything else and still hunt down a florist. He slapped his head again, but not so hard.

He filled a glass with chocolate milk and drank it standing at the sink. What now . . . call the whole thing off? No, that would be the sensible thing to do, a blot on a perfect record. There had to be something else.

Racking his brain, he remembered the winter he was so strung out that he ate sugar right out of the bowl, waking in the middle of the night with a craving for real candy worse than anything he'd ever felt for nose candy. Too wasted to move, he would phone Western Union and send himself a candygram—the big Whitman samplers, the gold Godiva *ballotin*, the heart-shaped boxes in February with the lace cards wishing, "Love, Harry."

He'd let his fingers start hiking again.

He found four pages of FTD florists in the yellow pages, dialed one on upper Broadway. "What I'm interested in," he explained, "is a bouquet with some bulk to it."

"I'm not sure I understand what you mean," the florist told him.

"Something substantial," Harry said. "No daisies or daffodils, something you could get lost in it."

The florist didn't answer right away. "Have you any particular flowers in mind?"

"I'll leave that up to you, so long as they're big ones, meaty, and lots of 'em."

The florist laughed uneasily. "This is some sort of joke, am I right?"

"No joke," Harry said.

"Then let me suggest mums. They're very fresh, very bright. A bouquet of chrysanthemums will run you—"

"I don't care what they cost," Harry said. "Are they big?"

"Oh, they're beautiful," the florist said.

"I didn't ask—"

"Nice and big."

"Good," Harry said. "Let me have a couple of bouquets' worth, make 'em up into one big one."

"That's hardly necessary. One will be quite sufficient by itself."

"Two's what I want," Harry insisted. "I can never seem to get my fill of . . . uh, mums."

"I feel *exactly* the same way," the florist said. "Where would you like these delivered?"

"The address is 330 West 218th Street, the apartment is 4F and the name's Lema. Harry Lema. Bill it the same way." He pulled out a drawer beneath the kitchen counter and began toying with the drawstring on a small flannel bag. "And hey, can I have 'em by ten? It's real important. Tonight's something special."

"Shall I include a card? We have them for all occasions."

"I don't need . . ." Harry wrapped his hand around the wooden grip of a small pistol and slipped it out of the bag. "You have anything in the way of, 'Sorry about your loss?' "

He held the gun to the light, admiring the sheen on the dark, stubby barrel. Then he put it to his temple and pulled the trigger twice. Though he had no reason to doubt it was the same empty starter's pistol he'd been hiding in the drawer, he blinked each time he heard the hammer click. He squeezed off a third shot at the hole in the shade squirting watery light into the room, then dropped it on the counter and went down for the wash.

It was ten past ten when someone buzzed up from the lobby. Half-hidden behind a paper cone dripping orange and yellow was a man in a rumpled uniform not very different from the freshly ironed one Harry was wearing. Harry saluted nattily, as though there were stripes on the other man's sleeve, and relieved him of the parcel, chased him away with a couple of dollars pressed into his palm.

He opened the paper and sniffed inside. Sweet—but not nearly so sexy as the Whitman sampler. Heavier, though, and lots bigger. The florist hadn't been shitting him about that. Jesus, it was all he could do to keep his arm steady. He stuck a few stems in a jar and let them stand under the faucet, hefted what was left and discarded a few more. They wouldn't be missed. The medicine chest mirror told him that whichever hand held out the bouquet it was impossible to see the other one behind it, or the small gun in his fist. He noticed a black-edged card on the floor and put it with the flowers.

Time to go and still he hadn't gotten his stuff together, hadn't even made up his mind what he was bringing along for the job. The thing he needed was a checklist; only it was kind of late to be thinking about that now. *The second-story checklist.* He liked the sound of it. Maybe he'd print up a bunch and sell them through the back pages of skin mags, like hair restorer. He could move a lot of them in Cranston, Rhode Island . . . that's for sure. Then a scolding voice, his own voice, told him: Harry, stop being so fucking cute. You better not be forgetting anything.

He got down on his knees and swept under the sofa for a blue nylon fanny pack. Empty, it didn't show beneath the uniform jacket, and with the pistol inside it hardly bulged. He put in two apples and a carton of chocolate milk and an egg salad sandwich from the refrigerator. On the tray below the freezer was a small steak wrapped in tin foil. Still thawing—but you like your meat raw, he figured, you don't mind it a little stiff, too. He stuck it in the pack, grabbed the flowers and headed for the door. Then he remembered the radio. Damn it, the checklist wasn't a bad idea. Inside a factory carton with the bill of lading still attached was a Motorola HT220 police scanner. He installed batteries and thumbed the tuner, his forehead accordioning as the Dyckman Street station house broadcast a report of a burglary in progress on West 215th Street. There goes the neighborhood, he thought. He clipped the scanner to his belt. He turned on the TV, switched on all the lights and sealed the apartment with a Medeco D-10 series high-security drop-bolt and a Fox police lock.

There was a ticket on the Cutlass, which he added to a dog-eared collection in the glove compartment. He caught the Henry Hudson at Dyckman Street and went downtown ten miles below the limit, taking no chances now. With the flowers on the seat it was just like prom night, the same tingle of nervous anticipation he never had his fill of. He took a sip of milk and tossed the carton out the window. Already he had to take a truly wicked piss.

The chef at the Arabian Knights was Homer Duff of Beckley, West Virginia, and Rhein-Main, West Germany, where he formerly was in charge of a U.S. Air Force mess hall. This was before he was given a less than honorable discharge without right of appeal for chronic alcoholism. When Howard found him, Homer Duff was living at the Salvation Army men's shelter on East Third Street, serving up great quantities of his specialty, which was anything groups of two hundred or more could get down without too many falling ill or becoming threatening. Luring him away with a free room above the restaurant and all the cheap wine he could drink, Howard gave him over to his Egyptians, who whipped him into a remarkably fast Mideastern cook whose one quirk was the southern tang he imparted to most dishes.

"What I think it is," Howard had confided to Kate, "is Homer likes to fry everything in bacon grease. Me, I keep kosher, so I try not to eat here. My customers, the regulars, never tasted anything like it and they love it. If they ever find out . . ." He finished the thought drawing an imaginary blade across his throat.

Howard's last night in New York, Homer Duff hosted a party at the Knights that began winding down about the time El Al Flight 016 landed in Tel Aviv. The following day, a Monday, he showed up for work ninety minutes late. On Tuesday he was missing for three hours before he lurched into the kitchen unshaven and reeking of Manischewitz dry white concord. Midway through a lecture from Kate he broke down and swore on the graves of his children that it would never happen again. That was the last she saw of him. Next morning, she was back at the Knights on four hours of sleep to supervise the kitchen that had become her biggest headache.

When Homer was gone three days, Kate brought in her own chef, until recently the proprietor of the Café Tolstoy on Neptune Avenue. Because he was unfamiliar with Arab cooking, a new menu had to be prepared. It featured karcho, a lamb and rice soup Kate decided was very Mid-eastern, and balyk, smoked sturgeon fillets she couldn't get her fill of and made no excuses for. Changes also were made in the floor show when she found she couldn't dance every night and keep the restaurant running. The new girls, booked through the same talent agency that had handled her on Times Square, knew nothing about belly dancing, "couldn't tell an oud from an Uzi," as Howard would say. But each one looked great in harem pants, and in the halter tops Kate would bribe them to dance right out of, and there were few complaints—none from the younger, freer-spending crowd that began flocking to the Knights on weekdays, when tables usually went begging.

On the first of the month the accountant came by to do the books. Kate watched anxiously over his shoulder till he told her to sit down and stop biting her nails, that the only discrepancy he could find was for $6.73, in their favor.

"What's the bottom line?" she asked, dropping into the dark brown Barcalounger. "Is it total disaster, or just a small one?"

"When is Ormont due back?" the accountant asked.

"Why?"

"Tell him to stay away. Tell him never to come near the club again."

Kate's stomach did the funny thing it did whenever Nathan dragged her onto the Typhoon and made her sit in the first car. "Oh my God," she said. "That bad?"

The accountant polished rimless glasses on his vest and pressed two fingers to the pinched bridge of his nose. "On the contrary," he said deliberately, as if choosing his words from a limited supply. "What I find here is the most profit the Arabian Knights has shown. The only problem is where we're going to hide this much money from the government. Suggest that Ormont continue on to China. For his own good have him keep his hands off the business."

Kate was waiting up in bed when Howard phoned the house. The overseas line crackled and thundered like a news remote at the edge of a great battle. Or was it his somber hello and perfunctory inquiry about the weather that came across as stiffly as the prologue to a casualty report?

"I have some bad news," he finally said.

"And I have some good. Which should we hear first?"

"Let me start. That way we'll end on a pleasant note."

"Tell me," she interrupted, "is everything all right with you?"

"Yes, fine," he said. "It's nothing like that . . . I spoke to the movie guys and, I'm sorry, Kate. They said no good."

"What . . . ? I can hardly hear you."

"No good," he repeated. "They said you danced like you needed trainer wheels. I told them they were out of their heads, but they insisted you were all wrong for the part anyway, much too tall and fair. Now you tell me, who's nuts?"

"I guess I am," Kate said. "I brought in some new girls on short notice. They weren't very good."

"When you knew these guys were coming to see you? Why?"

"I couldn't help it. Dancing two shows a night, running things. It was too much."

"I don't understand," Howard said. "I made arrangements. Everything should be smooth as silk."

"There were snags."

"What about Homer? Isn't he helping you?"

Only if he doesn't show his face again, Kate was thinking. Howard didn't have to know. "It depends on what you call help."

"I think I'm beginning to see. Did you count the bottles?"

"It's no big deal," she said unconvincingly. "About the movie, I mean."

"I'm sorry to be the bearer of such tidings, especially from so far, but I felt you should know right away."

"Forget it, I said."

"If it's any consolation, they loved the balyk."

Kate's stomach did the funny thing again. When she didn't say anything, Howard said, "So I told them, 'Now I *know* which of us is nuts.' "

"Well," Kate said, "Homer let me have a free hand in the kitchen."

"If that's where you'd rather be."

"No, not really."

"Maybe it's not such a bad idea. My friends said they had a great time, they only wished their production company ran as efficiently as the Arabian Knights. . . . They want to steal you away from me, Kate."

"What did you tell them?"

"That you were perfectly happy doing what you were doing."

"Good."

"They know I didn't mean it."

"Howard, when are you coming back? I'm tired of being a boss."

"There's an old girlfriend," he said, "not so old, actually, still very much a girl, who suddenly finds herself at liberty and who is making my stay extremely pleasant. I may be gone an extra week or two. . . . Now tell me, since we've gotten all the bad news out of the way, what is the good?"

"Last month was the best you've ever done. Your accountant says stay away as long as you like, and then a little longer."

"So do the *macher*s," he told her. "So I will."

The door chimed and Kate pressed the receiver tightly to her ear. "Howard," she said quickly, "someone's downstairs. I have to go."

"At this hour? Enjoy yourself, Kate."

"Good-bye."

She slipped into one of Howard's robes, yellow velour cut short above the knee, his knee, and went out of the room a couple of steps behind Isaac Grynzpun. One look in the fine antique mirror on the staircase sent her back. "Just a minute," she called out, dabbing at cheeks glistening with a disappointment that had taken her by surprise. Balling a wad of tissues in her hand, she hurried downstairs. "Who is it?"

She heard someone clear his throat, say "Florist."

"But I'm not expecting any . . ."

When Harry Lema saw Kate's tears, he forgot the hophead speech he'd been polishing on the stoop. He stood with one foot on the runner looking at the flowers and the gun hidden behind them, trying to figure where he had tipped his hand. "Are you Mrs. Howard Ormont?" he asked, moving cautiously up the steps.

"No."

"What's that?"

"I said no."

"Are you the daughter?"

"No."

"No?" Suddenly he saw the whole thing clearly. "Hey, don't look so sad," he told her. "Nobody died. These are for you."

"Who are they from?"

"There's a card." Harry stepped onto the landing and pushed the flowers at her and, as he did, showed her the snubbed barrel of his pistol. "I don't know what's eatin' you," he said, "but this is definitely not your night. They're from me."

Isaac Grynzpun bounded down the steps and Harry dropped his sandwich on the floor as he flung the steak at him. The dog snuffled the silver package, then turned up his nose and gobbled the egg salad, went back upstairs as Kate's heart sunk in her chest. "Who are you?" she demanded.

Harry didn't hear her. Now that she'd stopped crying, she hardly seemed upset. Maybe she had more important things on her mind. He'd change that fast. "You alone?" he asked. "We'll see," he answered for her, marching her upstairs ahead of him. "You'll show me."

"Who are you?" Kate tried again.

"Who the hell you think I am? I'm the burglar."

"Oh," Kate said.

"Oh? All you gotta say is 'Oh'?"

Oh God, a maniac with a gun, she almost said out loud. Instead, she tightened the sash around her waist and asked, "What do you want?"

"Don't be wise. You know what I want."

Kate turned to look at him and he nudged her ahead. A burglar, he'd said. If that was all, this might not be too awful. A big if. "Oh," she said again.

He stuck his head inside the bedroom, saw no one there. "Okay, know where I gotta go now?"

"No."

"The goddamn toilet."

She showed him to the bathroom. He stood her at the door and ordered her to turn her back. "No peekin'," he said as he tugged at his zipper.

He thought he was going to fill the bowl. He flushed twice and washed his hands, patted them dry in the fluffiest towel he'd ever felt, touched it to his face. He tore off a few sheets of toilet paper and blew his nose.

"What the—" He balled up the paper and tossed it in the bowl. "Place like this, run you at least eight hundred

K, unfurnished, has lousy John Wayne toilet paper like some subway craphouse."

"Who? The cowboy?"

Harry rolled his eyes up into his head. Good eight and a half, nine, a little higher if he could see more of what was inside the robe—and thick as a brick. "John Wayne toilet paper," he explained. "It's rough, it's tough, it don't take shit off no one." He flushed again. "Well," he said, "it's been fun talkin' to you, but now it's time to play *You Bet Your Life*. The topic I selected is your jewelry."

"What about it?" Kate asked.

"I'd like to steal it, you don't mind."

Kate felt tears again. "I don't have any jewelry, just costume stuff."

"And I'm the lady in black, never go anywhere without a bunch of flowers."

He sat her on the bed, tore apart the bottom drawer from a blond dresser on the wall opposite the window. Doing three-a-day B&Es for chump change he'd learned always work your way up to the top drawer, don't waste seconds shutting the lower ones. But this was a home invasion, his first, and the pace was all wrong, herky jerky, like a Charlie Chaplin short but without the laughs. Then the girl squirmed to the end of the mattress flashing sweet, milky thighs and he had all the time in the world. He pulled out the second drawer and poked inside, the third. "Gettin' warm?" he asked.

Kate bit her lip.

He turned the gun on her till he got some reaction, glistening pearls of sweat above her mouth. "You might want to point me in the right direction," he said, "give me a clue. . . . I won't tell."

"I don't live here," Kate told him. "I'm house-sitting. I don't know where anything is."

He dumped the top drawer on the floor and stirred a mound of white broadcloth shirts with his toe. "You expect me to buy that?"

"Please, it's the truth."

"How long you been here."

"Not long. A few weeks."

"Long enough," he said. "You should've figured it out by now."

"Howard . . . Mr. Ormont doesn't wear jewelry, not even cufflinks. He says gold chains do for a man's chest what curlers do for a woman's head. . . . I have these earrings." She took them off and held them out to him. "They're real silver. Take them and go."

Harry swatted her hand away. "I got my own," he said and began pacing the room. "Guy owns a restaurant, lives in a house like a friggin' palace and you're telling me he don't have a pot to pee in. That don't go down easy."

"He puts everything back into the Arabian Knights."

"He's good at that, pleading poverty? Listen, in case you just been born, everybody owns a cash business is all the time skimming the cream off the crop. You pay the IRS like Goody fuckin' Twoshoes, you better have a stomach for peanut butter three times a day. There's a pile of cash money layin' around somewhere and whether you like it or don't, you're gonna help me find it."

He ripped a picture off the wall, a signed lithograph of Picasso's *Ambroise Vollard*. "Let me explain what I'm doin', you don't get the idea I'm like some vandal gets off spray-paintin' his name all over the IND. I'm lookin' for a safe."

"That's a very valuable piece," Kate said. "Why don't you take it and go . . . ? It's insured."

It occurred to Harry that he would be glad to, if he had the right guy to move it, a guy with nice round arches on both feet. "I already got a picture," he told her. "Miss January . . . What's *your* name?"

Kate said nothing.

"I asked you nice, what is it?"

"Kate Piro."

"Make a deal with you, Piro," he said. "You're his bimbo,

it's only fair you get your cut, say ten percent. Call it a finder's fee."

Kate shook her head.

"Fifteen, robber, but that's high as I go."

He pulled another frame off the wall, a poster from a Toulouse-Lautrec exhibit at the Brooklyn Museum. He held it at arm's length admiring the color reproduction of *At the Moulin Rouge,* and then put his foot through it. "You ain't gonna help, I don't see why I should be nice to you," he said, touching the gun to her ribs. "Get up, we're takin' this act on tour."

She led him through the house in a cold sweat, chewing the inside of her cheeks as he ransacked closets and toppled the furniture, unpotted the ficus trees and tore down paintings, cursed his rotten luck. Then he hustled her back to the bedroom where Isaac Grynzpun was asleep on the floor.

"You gotta be the dumbest broad I ever met," Harry said, waving the gun wildly, "or the most stand-up. Either way, it'll cost you."

"How many times do I have to say it, I don't know where Howard hides his money? I don't know if he has any."

"You're lyin'. What it is, you're on some weird suicide trip. The way you were bawlin', I should've recognized it, you *want* to see what this gun can do. Okay, have it your way." He leveled the barrel, then dipped it toward the sleeping dog's ear. "One last time . . ."

"I can't tell you what I don't know."

Harry's face softened. "You win," he said.

And then he squeezed the trigger. The hammer clicked twice, three times, four times, clicked longer than Kate could scream.

"I'm what you call a sore loser," he told her later. "A thief, too, but that's where I draw the line." He offered his handkerchief and tried to look insulted when she shied away. "You don't believe me, let me show you the piece. What we have here is called a starter's pistol, can't do nothing to you 'cause it can't fire real bullets. And I don't mess with blanks. Sensitive ears. Looks scary if you don't know about guns, but, hey, I don't have to tell you."

He shook the apples out of the pack and zipped the gun inside. "One for you," he said, polishing the smaller, greener one, a Granny Smith, on his sleeve.

"The way I see it," he told her, "is round one goes cleanly to you. But it's no KO, so you've got to come out of your corner when you're feelin' better. Just 'cause you know I won't hurt you, don't think you're off the hook."

"If you meant that, you'd leave me alone," Kate said. "Don't you see I couldn't help you if I wanted to?"

Harry bit into his apple and chewed thoughtfully. "It pains me to have to admit this, but you're startin' to convince me."

"It's the truth. Why can't you just go away?"

"Because," he said, "I put a lot of time and sweat into this and I'm not gonna see it go down the tubes 'cause you're not pullin' your end."

"You make it sound like we're partners."

"You might not like the split, but that's the way it is."

Kate inched away. No sense in trying to reason with him, he really believes it.

"What I'm gonna do," Harry went on, "is give you more time to find where Ormont keeps his dough. A few days, that's what it takes. I'll be in touch and, when you have everything ready, I'll stop by and pick it up."

"You won't be offended," Kate asked warily, "if I tell you you're crazy?"

"Feel free to speak your mind," Harry said. "We're friends. Fact is," he told her, stretching out on the bed, "I'd like to get to know you better."

Kate's heart began pounding and her arm snaked out

toward a glass ashtray on the nightstand. Harry got there first and moved it out of reach. "Why don't we do dinner one night, catch a movie?"

"That's a swell idea. Just leave your name and number and I'll call you."

"No, I mean it. Guy in my line of work doesn't meet too many women like you."

"That's your problem," Kate said. "Do you think I'm enjoying this? Do you think I'm going to write Dear Abby and tell her some screwball with a gun broke into my place and I'm worried he won't call?"

"You should understand, I can't take no for an answer."

"It's the only one I have."

"That," Harry said, "is 'cause you haven't heard the rest of it. Till you come up with the goods, I'll be holdin' a deposit, something you'll want back."

"I don't know what you're talking about."

"Him," Harry told her, prodding the sleeping wolfhound with his foot.

"Isaac?"

"That his name?"

Kate nodded.

"Isaac's gonna be bunkin' with me for a while. You don't see him again till I get what I want."

"You'll be sorry," Kate said. "He's vicious."

"Yes," Harry said, reaching down to scratch the dog's ears, "I see that." He sat bolt upright. He turned up the volume on the police scanner till the bedroom reverberated with a call for detectives to respond to a liquor store holdup on Seventh-sixth and Broadway. "Had me goin' there," he said sheepishly.

"What's that?"

"It's . . . like *Dragnet.*"

"*Dragnet*'s been off the air for years."

"For you," Harry said. "Me, nothing I like better than keepin' an ear on the cops, specially when I'm havin' a lousy day at the office."

He unhooked the radio from his belt and put it beside Isaac Grynzpun's ear. "Come on, boy," he said. "Wake up. Time to go."

"You can't possibly believe this is going to work."

Am I gonna see one red cent from the job? Not likely. Am I gonna see you again? Seventy to thirty says I don't. Long odds, but I'll take them, even if I end up out a few bucks for the Kal Kan.

"I know it don't sound real bright," he said aloud. "But you have to realize when Ormont comes home and finds his dog gone, there'll be hell to pay. What are you gonna tell him, the burglar's holdin' the mutt for ransom?"

"Do you think he'd be happier if you cleaned him out?"

"No," Harry said, "not from what I hear about the guy. Thing is, you tell him the dog's gone, he'll figure you screwed up and lost it and it'll be your ass. The dog's here and you say you got taken off at gunpoint, he'll kiss it, this is your ass I'm talkin' about, he'll feel so guilty leavin' you all alone."

"Not Howard."

"Then you're gonna have a lot of explaining to do, about the dog."

He slapped the animal on the rump. "Hey, c'mon big fella. Let's go."

Isaac didn't budge.

"What's wrong with him?"

"Ask him," Kate said.

"I'm askin' you."

"I've never seen him like this."

"He off his feed?"

"You saw. Maybe your sandwich didn't agree with him. All I give him to eat is red meat."

"Egg salad on whole wheat's good for you," Harry said. Then, "Oh no, the steak."

He ran to the staircase, came back shaping a small silver ball and fired it into the wall. "I put enough downs in that chuck to stun a buffalo. I didn't know the fleabag was comin' home with me."

"Poor Isaac," she said. "It serves you right."

"Off the bed."

He sent her to the kitchen for some ice, and held it to the sleeping dog's neck. Isaac Grynzpun cocked open one large eye and let it close again. Harry wrapped his arms around the wolfhound's middle and wrestled him to his feet. Isaac went rubbery at the hind legs and sat down.

"Get me his leash," Harry said. When Kate stayed where she was he turned down the scanner and made himself comfortable on the bed. "Or, we can kill the night waitin' for him to sober up."

Kate unsnarled a silver chain and clipped it to Isaac's collar. Harry jerked the dog erect and steered him out of the room.

"Soon's he gets a whiff of fresh air, he'll be all right," Harry said. "I know, 'cause that's how I am when I get a little blotto. Now go down and hold the door."

Leaning all his weight against the leash, he let the wolfhound slowly downstairs. Then he gave some slack, and Isaac bellyflopped onto the stoop.

"Be talkin' to you," Harry said.

5

THE 911 operator couldn't be bothered—not unless someone had been shot, stabbed, strangled, raped, poisoned,
burned, drowned, beaten or bludgeoned, had suffered a
heart attack, overdose, stroke or crippling fall, had choked
in a restaurant or been hit by a car or bitten by pit bulls
within a two-mile run of an EMS ambulance. As Kate tried
again to explain what had happened, she was cut off and
a recording came on with the phone number of the
ASPCA.

"If this is an emergency, or you need further assistance,
please stay on the line and an operator will help you."

Kate kept her ear to the phone for four minutes before
someone said, "Yeah?" She recognized the voice as that of
the woman she'd just spoken to and slammed down the
receiver.

Information gave her the number of the Sixteenth Precinct. The desk officer sounded young and understanding,
and heard her out, interrupting only to dig for detail.

"Now let me get it straight, you're saying this Isaac
Grynzpun was sick and the intruder forced him to leave
the house against his will?"

"He's a dog," Kate said.

"That's pretty mild."

"Isaac Grynzpun is the dog, my boss's dog."

"Is anything gone with a value greater than one hundred dollars?" he asked with less understanding.

"My peace of mind."

"We've had forty-nine homicides in the Sixteenth so far

this year," he told her. "There were three hundred rapes we know about, so you can multiply that by five, probably one thousand felonious assaults and God knows what else and you're asking us to go hunting for a pooch? We chase the killers. We're good at that and we have a way with sex fiends, too. And that's about it. Every hairbag on the West Side knows it's open season on the citizens. So tell me, how come the citizens don't know?"

Kate didn't know either. "I . . . I'm from Brooklyn. He said he'd call again. I think the only reason he took Isaac is to get to me. He's got me spooked."

"I don't blame you," the desk man said, "but we're not bodyguards."

"Assuming I don't want to wait for him to kill me, can't you try and catch him now?"

"The best I can do is give you some advice, the same advice I give my own mother, who also doesn't have the good sense to take it."

"What's that?" Kate asked.

"Move to the country."

She sat on the floor sorting underwear and shirts, mountains of them, and filing them away in the dresser. She went to work with the vacuum cleaner and then milked it of two bags of dusty soil that she spread over the naked ficus roots. The furniture fit neatly in the floor plan flattened into the shag. There were chrysanthemums in the sink, though she couldn't remember putting them there. They looked better in a cut-glass vase. She tried them in the living room, the salon, the bedroom before she found the place she liked best, in the trash. She hung the pictures back on the walls. The poster was a total loss, but was worth about fifty dollars and could be replaced. She wished she could say the same for Isaac Grynzpun. If anyone asked, she'd be just as happy with a new wolfhound pup, but she doubted Howard wouldn't notice the difference.

Around dawn she threw herself down on the mattress and shut her eyes. Wasted effort. She thrashed the bedding to the floor, then stalked into the kitchen to put up a pot of coffee. It came to a boil about the same time that she did, and she dialed the Sixteenth Precinct again. To a fit of smoker's cough she responded, "Detective Bucyk, please."

"Doesn't work here any more."

"Do you know where I can reach him, Officer?"

"If you have to ask, I can't give out the information."

"That's great. Is Detective . . . um, Detective Infante on duty?"

"Just came in the door."

She had to wait several minutes to talk to him. The good part was she didn't have to listen to Muzak while she did.

"Infante here."

"Detective Infante, this is Kate Shapiro."

No answer. Then she could have sworn she heard gears meshing. She tapped the earpiece. Then, "Still knocking them dead?"

"You remember me . . . ?" she said. "It's been more than six months."

"Bucyk didn't give me a choice. Two things he never gets tired talking about, the time he murdered an eight-point buck at Tobyhanna, the night he went backstage at the Starlight. Trouble there again?"

"No, not there. I gave that up."

"Better than the other way around," Infante said. "How'd you make out in court with that African?"

"Not too badly. They fined me two hundred dollars. And I had to promise not to hit him again."

"So what's your pleasure now?"

"It's no pleasure. A man with a gun broke into my place early this morning and took . . . and took something of great sentimental value. When I tried to report it stolen, the police weren't interested."

"Brooklyn cops are like that," Infante said. "That's why they're in Brooklyn."

"This was on the West Side."

"Coming up in the world, aren't you?"

"I was beginning to think so," she said, mainly to herself. "But this could be a real setback. Detective Bucyk told me if I ever had a problem, he could help."

Infante exhaled hard into the mouthpiece and Kate heard his lungs wheeze. Had he been nicer the last time, she'd suggest a dry climate. "If the precinct can't handle it, I don't see what Bucyk can do," he said.

"That's what I'm trying to find out. Can you transfer the call, or tell me where to find him?"

"No."

"That's it? No? Pretend I was calling to give him a million dollars."

"As long as we're pretending, why not give him a tumble. I'll pass on the message, do that for you. Let me have your number."

Her fingers wrapped themselves in the cord, reeled in the clock, nearly snapped off the alarm button before she realized it was in as far as it went. Forcing open her eyes, she saw the phone beside the pillow and swiped at it, quieted it on the second try. "Hello?" she called out of the fog.

"M. Anita?"

"Unh?"

"This is Stanley Bucyk."

"Oh, Detective." Suddenly wide awake. "Thanks so much."

"Yeah, I called soon as I heard from Infante."

Kate turned the clock around. Bucyk wasn't exaggerating; it was still a few minutes before nine. "Did he tell you what happened?"

"Some of it. He said no one'd give you the time of day. Where are you now?"

"I'm on West Seventy-sixth between Amsterdam and Columbus. The police said they wouldn't waste their time on a robbery."

"The Sixteenth," Bucyk said. "Neighborhood like that they figure, why bother. Anybody in the Sixteenth gets taken off, she just flashes the plastic and forgets all about it."

"I wouldn't know," Kate said. "I'm visiting."

"Nice to have rich friends."

"I wouldn't know that either. This is my boss's place, he left me in charge while he's out of the country."

"In Colombia?"

"No," Kate said. "Israel. Why?"

"The Sixteenth," Bucyk said again. "Just a hunch."

"I was hoping he wouldn't have to find out about the robbery."

"What'd they get? Infante didn't say."

Kate gritted her teeth. "A dog."

"You're kidding, right? I couldn't find Rin Tin Tin for you if he wore bell-bottoms and talked French. Some med student's probably got him, trying to save the world from mildew, something like that."

"He isn't a German shepherd, he's a wolfhound, a very big dog. You don't see many of them. He wouldn't be that hard to find."

"Be a waste of time trying," Bucyk told her, his voice flattening like a fast leak. "Yours and mine both."

Kate gulped cold coffee, trying to fill the hollowness, making it worse. "You won't help, is that what you're telling me?"

"I'd like to, but . . . Jesus, I don't know. A dog."

Kate heard a familiar voice say, "That's not all he took."

"What's this?" Bucyk asked.

"He took some jewelry." What *was* it? A lie? Not really, more like a white one—and so easy to tell she wondered why she hadn't thought of it herself, why it had to slip out on its own. "Some jewelry and some cash."

"That's a whole other story."

"He even cut a picture out of the frame, rolled it up and took it away." A lily-white lie, boiled, bleached, 99.44 percent pure.

"Why didn't you say so in the first place?"

"I was so worried about Isaac, I forgot the other stuff for the moment."

"Isaac?" Bucyk said. "Hold on, let me get a pen."

Kate got out of bed and carried the phone to a yellow Barcalounger opposite the TV. "Take your time," she said, and leaned all the way back.

"What I'm gonna need for starters," Bucyk said, "is a list of everything that was stolen and a description."

"That's easy. He's nearly all white, with a—"

"The jewels. We'll want to notify all the hock shops, Forty-seventh Street, the diamond bourse down on Canal. I'll pull some strings, get burglary working on it. Some detectives will want you to come down and talk to them."

"Oh no," Kate said. "I can't."

"This time they'll be on your side."

Sure, but for how long? "I don't have a list. He just scooped it out of a drawer and stuffed it in his pocket. I didn't even know it was there."

"Tell me about the money," Bucyk said.

"It was . . . money. What about it?"

"The amount taken, the denominations."

"I don't know. Can't you start looking for Isaac?"

"It'd be good if I had a picture to work with. There any around?"

"I'll have to look," Kate said.

"I'm only a few blocks away. How about I come over and help. We're gonna do this right, I'll have to see the place anyway."

"But I've already cleaned up. You wouldn't find any clues."

"We'll leave that to the techs," Bucyk told her.

"Techs?"

"The crime lab. You know, fingerprints, footprints, like Sherlock Holmes. The works."

The hollow feeling again, only stronger, strong enough to swallow her whole. "Detective Bucyk," she said stiffly. "I didn't think this was going to become so involved. Maybe we should forget about it."

"Infante said something about a gun."

"Not a real one," Kate said. "A beginner's pistol."

"A what . . . ? Doesn't make a difference. It's still armed robbery, and we can't forget it. That would be against the law. I'll be over in ten minutes."

Six to be exact.

"You're looking good."

"Thank you, Detective."

"Very good."

She stood on the landing searching for a compliment to toss down to him and saw a number of possibilities grinning back at her. Bucyk was tan. He'd lost weight, a good twenty pounds, and about a year from his face for every five of them. He wore a nice suit. The way he was looking at her, the suit seemed the safest way to go. "So are you," she said as if she had to. "And very prosperous, I might add."

He parked a dark gray fedora on the bannister and jogged upstairs. A cloud of sweet wintergreen got there first and Kate prepared to block his lips with her cheek. He went for her hands instead, taking one in both of his and not letting go till it was time for the grand tour.

"Nice place you have here," he said as she brought him to the third-floor salon and seated him on the piano bench.

"I'm only a guest, remember?"

Bucyk surveyed the room, squinting into the darkness as if his eyes were filled to capacity. "Why buy the cow when you get the milk for free?"

"Nothing's free," Kate said gravely, and some of the

elasticity went out of Bucyk's face. "It's my job to look after the house, the dog, the business. Only I've managed to make a mess of everything."

"What business is that?"

"My boss owns the Arabian Knights."

Bucyk seemed to be torturing his memory. Then he snapped his fingers. "You said you danced there."

"Not any more. It's all I can do to keep it running."

"You like it better backstage?"

"Oh, I'm still performing," she said, "juggling the accounts, balancing the books, walking a tightrope over a very deep drop."

"You're lucky to find a boss who'd give you a break like that."

"That's why I'd hate for him to find out what happened. He's been good to me. Very good."

You made your point, Bucyk wanted to say. "So I see. Well, let's hope he doesn't have to. How much time do we have?"

"Before Howard comes home? I'm not sure. A few more weeks."

"Howard?"

"Mr. Ormont," Kate said. "My boss."

"That's not a lot." He pulled a small pad from his jacket and scribbled a few words on the back without taking his eyes off her. "I'm on a pretty tight schedule myself."

"I haven't even asked about your new assignment," Kate said. "Have you transferred out of the West Side?"

"Out of the department," Bucyk told her. "Strictly speaking, I'm no longer a cop."

"Then this isn't an official investigation?"

"Far as you're concerned, I'm a private eye. I owe you one after what happened last time."

"Oh," Kate said, starting to relax. "Oh."

"You're welcome," Bucyk said.

"Who are you working for now?"

"For you."

"I mean—"

"Don't ask, 'cause I can't say. It's interesting work, important work, and it pays better than being a flatty. I'm happy I made the change. Are you?"

Kate was looking absentmindedly out the window. She didn't seem to hear.

"Well, are you?"

"Ask me when this is all over," she told him. "Where will you be looking?"

"For the dog, or the other stuff?"

"For the man who took them. I won't rest easy till I know he's not coming back."

"You'll tell me all about him, his MO and everything."

"His what?" Kate asked helplessly.

"Sorry, I forgot," Bucyk said. "His modus operandi, how he parts his hair, and I'll start making calls in the other room."

"Where will I be?"

"Right beside me, waiting for one from him."

He stayed till four, till she chased him out saying she had to get dolled up for the club. So did he, he told her, and tapped a fresh crease in his hat. Some Arab cooking was just what the doctor ordered and anyway he'd feel more relaxed keeping an eye on her all night. She cut him off with a polite, "Nothing doing." She'd had her fill of staring eyes and they didn't relax *her* one bit. The Knights was perfectly safe and she could always catch a ride home with the cook. He wouldn't take her no for an answer till she exchanged it for his home number and promised to call if there was trouble.

The pounding on the door came in short, demanding bursts in time with the pounding in her head. She deadened the pain with two aspirins and then sleepwalked downstairs to deal with the noise. Through the fish-eye lens in the peephole she saw Bucyk marking time on the stoop with rain running from his hat. She let him stand there a little longer while she went back for a robe.

Bucyk scrubbed his shoes on the mat and came upstairs behind a brown bag that he had been shielding under his jacket. There were thin spots in the paper where the water had gotten to it. "I brought breakfast," he said. He was waiting for some kind of reaction. Anything. He didn't give up until she put the bag on the floor without looking inside. "Croissants . . ."

"It was very thoughtful of you," she said, too tired to argue.

"This isn't a social call," he announced, starting to cut his losses. "I've got a buddy, defrocked cop, can hook an automatic trace on your line. It's illegal, and he's in dutch with the department as it is, so he isn't banging down the door to do it. But he will. In the meantime, I can't hang around every day so I'm going to install a wire, record all your calls. I'll show you how to work it so you erase the hot stuff before I pick up the tapes."

"There's something I—"

"You hear from the guy with your dog," he cut her off, "you try and set up a meeting, then you get back to me. He won't go for it, just keep him talking—about himself, if you can. He's as bright as he sounds, he'll probably drop his Social Security number. He doesn't, at least we'll have a good listen at his voice."

"There's something I have to tell you first."

"You don't like croissants? I can run around the corner for some danish."

"About the jewelry," she began uncomfortably. "You see, I never expected—"

"No need to get into that now," he said. "There's too many things we haven't covered yet."

"But this is important."

"Tell me later. The only thing's important now is I catch up on how you made it into the high-rent district."

Kate forced a smile, but had to give it up. Bucyk tried it on and bent it back into shape. "Think you've got problems? The guy who took your dog, he doesn't know it yet, but he's already got one foot in the slammer."

Kate sighed deeply and her chest heaved, spreading the robe at the lapels. Bucyk wanted to ask if she planned on doing it again. "Call me Stash," he told her. "For Stashu, my name in Polish. Think you're the only one with an old country?"

"Were you born in Poland?" she asked, grateful for the reprieve.

"Try Scranton," he said. "The family came to New York when I was two. If you have to have an old country, Pennsylvania's mine, but I'll answer to Poland." Eyeing her, he ran his fingers along the banister, taking in the atmosphere. "You know, there's a number of folks come to mind wouldn't raise a stink trading places with you."

"Do I seem like I'm feeling sorry for myself? I'm getting good at that." She brought him into the kitchen and tore apart the soggy paper, put out the croissants on a plate. A light came on under the percolator. ". . . It's the way my life is going. I can't get myself arrested, is that the expression?"

"You're talking to the right guy."

Kate smiled weakly. "I'm tired of dumb jobs, of living in other people's houses. My brain is shriveling from lack of use." When Bucyk let that go by she said, "I do have one."

"I don't believe I'm hearing this," he told her. "A kisser like yours, the world's got to be beating a path to your door."

"To nail it shut," she said.

"You were gonna be a model."

"And then I was going to manage a restaurant, act in a movie. I was going to do a lot of things."

"A movie? You didn't say anything."

"There's nothing to say. I was turned down for the part."

"X-rated?"

Kate glowered at him.

"A real one," he said. "Well, what do you know about acting?"

"The role called for a dancer. If that's out, what's left?"

"Plenty of things," Bucyk said.

"Name one I can tell my mother about."

"After breakfast," he promised. "I'm starved."

6

WITHOUT the contacts it was a little better, as if the fuzziness was something to take cover in. She tried focusing on the corners, projecting herself out of the spotlight's stark assessment. It was how many months since she'd put Times Square behind her and now she was mortified doing a shimmy they taught in a Bensonhurst Y. She told herself she finally must be growing up. But the idea didn't take. More likely it was just that she was out of practice—and ashamed to show it. Before the next performance she'd give a piece of her mind to the talent agent who touted the girl that canceled.

One of the waiters intercepted her as she hurried off to perfunctory applause. Squinting into the lights, she scarcely recognized him. His hairline was receding and he seemed to have aged suddenly. Then she realized why. "You're out of uniform, Malik," she said.

He opened his mouth, but no words came. Like the ventriloquist's dummy in that scary old English movie . . . what was it called? "A customer took my fez," he stammered, "and he won't give it back."

She straightened the settings at an empty table so he wouldn't see her trying not to laugh. *Dead of Night*, she remembered, and felt the flesh creep along her arms. "Where?" she demanded.

"Thirty-four."

She tucked herself inside her halter as she stormed across the floor. Alone at a booth for six was a man in a herringbone jacket with a burgundy fez cocked over an ear, like a straggler from a Shriner's convention. "Sir," she said, coming up behind him. "That's not a souvenir."

The fez dipped over a plate of pelmini, then bobbed up again.

"Sir?"

A voice she'd heard before told her, "Take a load off."

"Who—?"

"Join me, Kate?"

"Oh!"

"You still shake up a storm," Nathan Metrevelli said.

"Thank you, Nathan, that's kind."

"In a way," he agreed. "Looking good, too."

"So are you," Kate said.

"I've been working out."

"Working, Nathan? Will wonders never cease?"

Nathan chewed thoughtfully and then sipped from a cup of mint tea. He looked betrayed. "Working *out*, Kate. Going to the gym every day. Schlepping weights."

"Why don't you just try working. It's lots easier."

He unbuttoned his jacket and flexed a stringy bicep under her nose. "A body like this requires plenty of upkeep," he said as if he could mean it. "I'd have to move pianos, become a stevedore."

"So what? It's honest work."

"Now there's a contradiction in terms."

"For you, Nathan. Only for you." She picked at the pelmini with a spoon from a vacant setting. "What's new?" she asked. "Besides your body, I mean."

"I've given up dealing, Kate."

She put down her spoon. "What's the gag?"

"You were right all along," he said. "I don't see any potential for growth."

"What are you doing?"

"*Not* dealing. It's a case of addition by subtraction. A shady element's been moving into the industry, guys with sloping foreheads and big guns. I tried carrying one for a while, but my jacket didn't lay right and it made my ribs sore. And what chance does a greenhorn stand against those cowboys? So now I hang out in the gym."

"That's an improvement."

"Not really," he said and went back to the pelmini.

Kate snatched the fez by its tassel and swung it onto her lap. "Aren't you going to ask about me?"

"I heard," he told her. "That's why I dropped by. I had to see for myself. You don't dress like most big shots, but you run a great place. Any future in it?"

"Not that I can see."

"So where do you go from here?" he asked. "Forty-second Street again?"

"I'd sooner starve."

"That's no answer."

"Just trying to get used to the idea," she said.

"We could do it together. I'm taking an apartment over the boardwalk."

"What about Phyllis?"

"She wants to get married. Have kids, if they're girls. Since I quit dealing, she thinks I got religion. If I stay with her, I'm afraid I will."

"You could do worse," Kate said.

"You don't know Phyllis."

"I know you, Nathan."

"It would be different—" he said before something in his own voice stopped him.

"Would it?" Kate asked.

"This time," he began again more deliberately and, he hoped, more believably, "it will work."

"But will you?"

As if he couldn't bring himself to say it, Nathan nodded. Kate thought she saw him shiver, too. "Is it a big place?" she asked.

"Four rooms," he said breezily. "A sublet with a two-year lease."

"The problem," she said as though she'd thought it out a long time before, "is that whenever we try to live together I never have enough space. I think we'd be cramped."

"I won't be in your way."

"I love you, Nathan, and after all these years of trying not to I don't see much hope I'll stop, God help me. But you know me too well, you know how to bring out something that makes me want to kick the person I am when I'm with you. It's a neat trick. I can't tell if you do it on purpose and I doubt you can either. I promised myself I wouldn't take it any more."

"A simple no will do."

"That was a yes," Kate said. "A qualified one."

Nathan's fork clattered to the floor. "Say that again."

"You caught me at the worst possible moment. The only kind I seem to have any more. I need you, damn it."

"Could've fooled me."

"But I won't move back to Brooklyn," she insisted. "Will you come to my place, tonight?"

"I haven't moved out of Phyllis's yet. She'll kill me when she finds out where I was."

Kate's lips toyed with a cold smile. "Stay with me, then. I'll protect you—"

"That's cute, Kate. But so is Phyllis. She'll put my stuff out on the street."

"—if you'll protect me."

"Phyllis has no grudge against you. She says nice things about you sometimes."

"I'm not talking about Phyllis. The other night a burglar broke in where I'm living and scared me out of my wits. A wild man. It's a miracle he didn't attack me. He says he's coming back, Nathan." She reached across the table and pinched his bicep. "I'd feel better having you around."

Nathan took his arm off the table. "You said I depress you."

"We'll hardly ever see each other." She smiled. "I'm here all the time."

"I don't know," he said. "That's not exactly what I had

in mind." He gave the idea more thought. "Is it comfortable?"

"Elegant is more like it."

"What about noise? Is there any construction on the block?"

Kate shook her head. "You can sleep as late as you like."

"It might not be too bad." He pushed his chair back, reaching for his wallet. "Great meal," he said. "Do you take rubber?"

"You mean plastic."

"I brought checks," he explained.

"Leave a nice tip," she told him, motioning for a busboy. "You bruised Malik's feelings when you swiped his hat. Dinner's on me."

They walked uptown along dark streets alive with coffee shops and fruit stands that never shut, the roar of the IRT piped through broken sidewalks. Clinging to his elbow, Kate steered him onto Seventy-sixth. When they came to the brownstone she pressed the key in his hand and stood on the next to bottom step until he unlocked the door and went in. Then she hurried past him and put the light on in the anteroom. Without a word Nathan took in as much as there was to see.

"Say something," she told him.

"Say what? I can't even make a joke about what you're doing in a place like this. If I did, you'd slap my face."

Kate came near and reddened his cheek with the flat of her hand.

"Ouch," Nathan said. "What's that for?"

"For what you're thinking, whatever it is." She took back the key and dropped it in his pocket. "That's for you, too," she said and then led him on a quick tour of the house. "Well," she asked in the salon, "do the accommodations suit you?"

"I can't say till I've seen the bedroom."

Kate walked stiffly to the doorway. "Yours, Nathan? Or mine?"

He got up from the piano bench and followed her to the stairs. "You're putting me on," he said uneasily, "aren't you?"

They went down two flights before she said, "All these closets and I've only found one blanket. I guess we'll have to share it."

"That was good, Kate. You had me faked out."

She let him kiss her. It had been a long time since she'd slept with him, longer than they'd ever gone before. He felt almost like a stranger. Oddly, she thought, it was the familiarity of his touch that excited her most about him, knowing that he understood exactly how to please her because he'd trained her desires himself. Well, she decided quickly, a stranger could be exciting, too. "It's like you said," she whispered, backing him into the bedroom, "what goes around, comes around."

"I did?"

The first call came at five-thirty. A woman with an accent that sounded like she'd learned to talk from machines was saying that Tel Aviv would be phoning. Kate went to the mirror to brush her hair, to the kitchen to put up a pot of coffee, back to bed to wait. Nathan didn't stir. The second call woke her, too.

"Ekaterina . . . Did I get you up?"

"Me . . . ?" She stopped, waiting for her head to clear. "No."

"Good." He was laughing. "Let me tell you why I called and then you can go back to sleep. Those friends of mine . . ."

She rested an elbow on the nightstand, nearly tipping over a cup of stale coffee. She moved it out of the way and leaned back, careful not to disturb Nathan. "What friends?"

"The movie guys," Howard said. "You remember. They put an idea in my head. A good one, I think."

"I'm not too keen on show business right now."

"Forget about that. I want you to stay at the Knights, to help run it for as long as I have it. I'm offering a piece of the action. Do you hear?"

Kate dug her knuckles into her temples. "What?"

"I met with them here just an hour ago and they still haven't stopped raving about the time they had. These guys are tough cookies, real *momzers*, If you made them even smile, the rest of my customers must be in heaven. I can't afford to lose you."

Kate yawned.

"What do you say? I'm offering a fifteen percent interest with no equity from you. Giving it away."

"That's very kind of you, Howard," she said. "What's the weather like over there?"

"You're still disappointed, aren't you, that the part fell through? Don't be. It may not be as glamorous, but this is an excellent opportunity. A partnership in a Broadway restaurant, at your age? If you want my honest opinion, this is better for you, more realistic."

Kate reached around the recorder and pulled the phone into bed. Nathan opened his eyes, then shut them again. "I'm not sure," she said.

"If you aren't, who is?"

"What I mean is, it's a wonderful offer. Really, Howard, you're too generous. Only I'm not so certain I'm the reliable businesswoman you think I am. There's been all sorts of trouble lately. You wouldn't believe it."

"At the Knights?" he said slowly, afraid to ask. "Do I still have a restaurant to give pieces away?"

"Not there. We're still doing well."

"Then there is no trouble." He sounded relieved, about two tons lighter.

Kate didn't. "No . . . it's, you see, there was this . . . I don't know how to say it, but—"

"Have you any idea what this call is costing?" he interrupted. "It can wait until I get home. Now, are you telling me yes or no?"

Am I telling him about Isaac?

"Kate?"

Why spoil what was left of his vacation? "It sounds good to me."

As if it made a difference. As if he'd let her near the place once he found out.

"Then give yourself another raise immediately. Say to four hundred dollars a week?"

"If you think it's okay . . ."

"I do," he said.

"I'm tired, Howard. I want to go back to sleep."

"One other thing. I won't be back till after the fifteenth. You do know what the fifteenth means?"

Kate shook her head, then said, "Uh-uh."

"All over the West Side, everybody gets taken care of on the fifteenth. The police, the health inspectors . . ."

"It was like that at the Starlight, too."

"Of course it was. Now listen carefully, this is very important what I'm trusting you with. On the chance I got held over, I prepared everything before I left. The money is in a hiding place built into the stairs between the first and second floors."

"Jesus," Kate said, "now you tell—"

"Do you hear? Untack the runner and the three middle steps are actually one piece of wood you can pull out with two fingers. Inside you'll find some packages wrapped in paper. These are of value only to myself. So don't touch. On top are two sealed envelopes. The thicker one is for the police. Remember to have both of them at the Knights on the fifteenth."

"How will I know who to give them to?"

"These people are not shy. They will introduce themselves."

"This is a hell of a way to run our business, Howard."

"It's the only way. That's why it is essential you do it this one time. I'll be home by the twentieth. After that, I'll handle it."

"So soon?"

"Should I stay longer?" Amused rather than insulted. "You sound disappointed."

"I was getting to like it here," she said. "I guess I'll have to start looking for a place of my own."

"Will you?" Howard asked. "I'm disappointed also."

She hung up. As she put the phone back, she saw Nathan watching her out of one eye. "Who was that?" he asked.

"Howard . . . Mr. Ormont. The man whose place this is, my boss at the Arabian Knights."

Nathan squinted at the luminous face of an alarm clock. "What did he want at six A.M.?"

"He asked me if I'd like a piece of the restaurant," Kate said. "Can you believe it?"

Nathan opened the other eye. "How does he expect you to pay? Dance it off?"

"He's giving it to me, Nathan."

"No one gives anything away."

"But he is. No strings attached."

"Is it worth anything?"

"We're clearing about fifty-five hundred a week and he's letting me have fifteen percent. What does that come to?"

His eyes were closing again. "Dunno," he mumbled.

"It's a lot, though. More than I'll ever see doing anything else."

Nathan put an arm around her. "Marry me, Kate?" he said, and began snoring.

The blue car was double-parked with the engine running when she came out of the club. It moved slowly into traffic, sidling up to her at the corner. The driver whistled softly and she pretended not to hear. Bucyk liked that. He tapped the horn and her eyes stayed at the red light. He liked that, too. "Need a lift?" he finally said.

She stepped quickly into the crosswalk without looking either way.

"Kate?"

"Oh," she said and backed onto the curb. "It's you. Are you driving tonight?"

"I gave that up when I got the new job. Didn't need to any more."

She went to the passenger's side and tossed a leather bag onto the seat, pulled the door shut after her. A taxi swung around them as the light turned red again.

"We've each of us put one lousy job behind us," he said. "That's progress, isn't it?"

Kate looked like she was debating it.

"I thought you said you had a guy riding shotgun," he scolded.

She made an empty gesture. "You didn't have to do this. I shouldn't be taking up so much of your time."

He headed uptown along Broadway with the needle glued to thirty, making all the lights just as they turned amber. "You're not taking any I can use. I worked nights so many years, I don't know how to sleep till the game shows come on the air. Before you called, I was mostly studying the various test patterns."

"Thanks anyway."

He followed Seventy-sixth to her block and parked at the fire hydrant. Then he opened his wallet for a laminated card which he placed on the dash over the steering wheel.

"What's that?" Kate asked.

"Shows you're a member of the Patrolmen's Benevolent Association. You keep it in plain sight wherever you're parked in the city, you never get a ticket. Want one? You might say I stocked up."

"I don't have a car."

"That's right," he said awkwardly.

"Well, thanks again," she said. "And good night. Maybe he'll call tomorrow."

Bucyk touched her elbow, slid his hand along the fine arm to her shoulder. "I'd like to come upstairs," he said.

"But it's nearly four o'clock."

"And Mom's up, that right . . . ? Like last time?"

"She might as well be," Kate said. "She knows everything I do."

"Then we won't do anything she hasn't heard about before."

"We won't do anything at all." Kate's nostrils flared. He didn't like that. "What are you getting at anyway?"

"I'm trying to get at you," Bucyk said. "What gives?"

"Not me, Detective. I'm sorry."

"Don't be sorry. Be agreeable."

"I'm sorry if you misunderstood my intentions," she told him. "I didn't mean to lead you on."

"You didn't."

Backing out of the car she said, "I'll be home all afternoon if you want to stop by for your recorder." She paused, then shut the door. "After five, my boyfriend can let you in."

"You never said . . . I didn't know you had one."

"It was news to me, too." She smiled.

Some of the slack went out of his eyes. "One thing has nothing to do with the other. I'm still gonna help you find the guy who has your dog."

"You're sure you want to?"

Bucyk nodded. "Like I told you, I owe you one."

7

AT CODDLED Canines on Madison Avenue a salesclerk was trying to interest Harry Lema in a Gestalt dewoofer for his dog.

"Which means what?" Harry asked.

"Let me show you," the clerk said, removing a heavy choker from a display case and attempting to cinch it around Harry's arm. Harry jerked away, his hands balled reflexively into fists. "Nothing personal," he said, quickly showing the startled clerk open palms, "but I have a thing about being restrained."

The clerk smiled knowingly. "Some of our best customers are people," he said. "Actually, the dewoofer is a very safe device. It's a top-of-the-line cowhide collar like any other, but with a computerized sensor built inside. The computer responds to any unnecessary barking by firmly instructing your pet to cut it out."

"Yeah?" Harry said, intrigued. He picked up the collar for a closer look, pinching a hard-edged bulge in the thick leather. "How's it do that?"

"By means of a lightweight, six-volt power pack also housed in the collar."

Harry tossed the dewoofer on the display top. "You mean it shocks the shit out of him whenever he opens his yap."

"Gently," the clerk said, "very gently."

"You call that coddling?" Because the salesman, who carried about 225 pounds on a thirty-inch waist, looked as though he might, Harry took a step back, then said, "I keep Isaac home with me, not in a concentration camp.

He's my good buddy, a man's best friend and all that. I wouldn't do that to a dog."

"But the dewoofer was invented by a dog handler from the Swedish army. It *can't* hurt."

"What else you got?" Harry asked.

"It depends on the animal's problem," the clerk said. "Could it be cage trauma?"

Harry shuddered. "Only if it's catching."

"Perhaps it's some form of anxiety hysteria? Our cananalyst offers therapy three times a week, individual and group, and Coddled Canines gives a money-back guarantee that when treatment is complete the animal will respond to your every command with an appreciative attitude and wagging tail."

"I don't know what the problem is," Harry said. "He just won't eat. I tried the canned foods and then the dry, but he turns up his nose at everything."

"Have you investigated our Gourmand Grub?"

"What's that?"

"A nutritious, flavorful, haute cuisine diet for the finicky eater prepared by our own trained chefs. Yesterday's menu, for example, featured an entrée of sirloin tips, and today there's roast beef au jus."

"Sounds yummy," Harry said. "I'll try 'em both." As the clerk reached under the counter for a couple of foil trays, he added, "Better make that two of each. Maybe the mutt'll go for it, too."

The clerk didn't laugh or stop stacking trays on the glass. "Some of our best customers," he said again, "are people."

Isaac Grynzpun liked the sirloin tips but loved the roast beef, loved it with the sirloin tips for dessert, and two days later Harry was back at Coddled Canines to start a tab. On the weekend, down close to sixty dollars, he phoned Kate at the house.

"It's me," he said.

"Who's me?" she asked grumpily.

She sounded exhausted—nervous, too—probably worrying her head off over the dog. He was on his way. "Me," he tried again. "The burglar."

Kate's throat caught so hard she was sure he heard it. She watched with some relief as Bucyk's wire took it all in. "What do you want?" she asked.

"You know what I want," Harry told her. "You found it yet?"

"I'm still looking."

"Open your eyes. It'll go faster."

"I still don't think there's anything here." She glanced toward the stairs. "I mean, where didn't you look?"

"Do us both a favor and don't think. Okay?"

"Okay," Kate snapped. "How's Isaac?"

"Cryin' his eyes out," Harry said. "He misses his own bed."

"Is he eating?"

"Is he *what?* Lady, eat's all he knows how to do. I'd of guessed what it cost to keep him in biscuits, I'd of taken you and left him to hunt for the stuff."

"That's cruel," Kate said. "Isaac can't survive on dog biscuits."

"You want it from him he ain't suffering? I'll call him." He whistled and Kate heard him say, "Hey, Isaac." Then he told her, "He can't come to the phone now, he's too busy stuffin' his face."

"Are you sure?"

"You're so worried, you'd be better off doin' what I told you, not asking if he's gettin' three squares."

"I can't help it if I'm upset," Kate pouted. "Isaac is my responsibility."

"No," Harry said as if he hated having to admit it. "He's mine now. You sure this deal wasn't your idea, to stick me with him?"

"If he's too much trouble, why don't you give him back?"

"You wanna take his place? I got plenty of biscuits left over. A little roast beef, too. TV's got ghosts, but I'm gettin' cable. You'd like it here."

"Oh, would I?" Get him talking about himself, Bucyk had said. Find out all you can. "Where, exactly, is here?"

"I'm exactly in bed."

"Thanks a lot," Kate said. "That's the most exciting offer I've had since you threatened to shoot me."

"Hey, don't be sarcastic," Harry told her. "You asked where I am, I'm tellin' you. I didn't say we had to stay all the time."

"Where would we go? Don't you think people might stare if they saw you holding a gun to my back?"

"Listen," he said, "this isn't gettin' us anywhere."

"That's your fault. If you weren't so unreasonable, we could work things out. You suggested we get together, why don't we?"

"For a crybaby," Harry said, "you're all of a sudden awful brave."

"You don't scare me any more. In fact, you never did. I think face to face is the only way."

"I don't," Harry said. "I don't like your attitude."

"But you just said you wanted to—"

"Forget what I wanted. Your bein' so cooperative, it makes me wonder. Turns me off, too. You've been robbed, you know? Ain't you got any pride?"

"Would you be happier if I was difficult? Should I work at that?"

"I got a hunch," Harry said, "you don't have to work on anything."

She was dialing his number when she heard his ring downstairs, one long, three short—Morse code, he'd said, for the letter B. She went to the landing deliberately avoiding the mirror, preferring to look half undone. Right off she hit him with, "You didn't tell me you'd bugged the phone, too." While he was deciding what to make of that she said, "He called."

"Something else we have to discuss, something shouldn't go on tape. That's why I dropped over." He saw the excitement wither on her face. "It can wait," he said. "What'd he give out?"

"A lot of nothing, really."

"He must've had something on his mind."

"He told me I had a poor attitude," Kate said.

"He's smarter than you let on."

She showed him the cassette and he dropped it in a pocket, went upstairs ahead of her like he owned the place. He kicked off his shoes and leaned back in bed while Kate perched on the footrest of the Barcalounger.

"I was running back everything we talked about," he told her, "and I got to thinking there's something more I can do for you, solve a number of problems at the same time."

"A new way to get Isaac back?"

"Forget the dog for now."

"I don't want to."

"Give me a minute to explain, huh?" Kate shut up and Bucyk used most of the minute to fumble in his jacket for a pack of fancy cigarettes in light brown paper. Another expedition inside yielded a silver lighter. He lit up with a flourish and waved away the smoke with his hand and she saw a pinky ring with a blue stone. "You should've figured it out by now," he said, eyeing her intently.

"I'm FBI," he said at last, and Kate leaned back to hear more. "That's the new job, doing contract work for the Bureau." He let that sink in. "You see why I couldn't let on before, before I got to know you better, why I was trying to?"

Kate acknowledged it with a barely perceptible nod. "Is that why no one at the station house would tell me anything?"

"They'd be in deep shit they gave out my hat size."

Kate sat forward again. "I feel so foolish, wasting your time on a dog. You must have found it comical, an FBI man . . ." The thought trailed off.

"Tell you the truth, I've been enjoying it," Bucyk said. "It's like . . . like a conductor's holiday."

"Aren't there enough kidnapped children to chase after? It's all you see in the papers."

"Only when it's interstate," he told her, "and even then, unless the vic's spitting silver spoons, it's small potatoes. I'm counterespionage," he puffed.

"You mean like James Bond?"

"You noticed the resemblance," he said, and Kate didn't know whether it was okay to laugh until he beat her to it. "It's kind of like that, only without the perks—the blondes, the Aston Martin. There's some running down spies and hunting for terrorists, but usually it's making sure our industrial secrets don't end up backside of the rusty rug, you know, with the Russkies."

"Don't look at *me,*" she said uncomfortably. "I may have been born there, but I'm not a . . . what do you call them, a sleeper agent."

"It's a load off my mind," Bucyk said. "I'll inform the director."

Kate flushed. "Why are you telling me this now?"

"It occurred to me maybe I could find something for you, something you could hang your hat on, subcontract work for me."

"Because I'm from the Soviet Union? I hate to disillusion you," she said, "but I'm about as Russian as a Cabbage Patch doll." The idea made her laugh. "Do you think I'm from a red cabbage patch?"

Bucyk wasn't laughing. "You got it right the first time," he said. "A doll."

"I still don't see what I can do—"

"Keeping tabs on foreign diplomats is our A-number-

one priority," he said. "There's a striped pants we're interested in who's attached to the permanent trade delegation
of an East European country I can't give out, and I was
thinking you two'd make a cute couple. It could mean a
feather in your bonnet and dollars in your pocket. The
Bureau is not a cheapskate. . . . You do speak Russian?"

"*Da*. With a bad New York accent."

"So does he," Bucyk said. "His father was Soviet . . . well,
that puss just squirted out of the bag . . . undersecretary
in the Soviet UN mission in the late 1950s and he was
raised here in the city. Went to the best schools, the Lycée,
Columbia University. Now he's back."

"And you want me to snuggle up to him?"

"Don't make a face. He's not your average vodka-blotter
in a drip-dry suit. The guy's debonair, drives a Porsche,
lives in a mansion out on the Island and hardly ever wears
his blue socks with the brown shoes. Has an eye for the
ladies, too."

"That doesn't sound like any Soviet envoy I've heard
about."

"Same here," Bucyk said. "What it seems, he's working
both sides of the street, socking away the rubles while the
proletariat's taking the lumps. If we could find out more,
we'd be able to stick it to him, turn him around or give him
back to the Russkies to use downwind on a rifle range."

"I thought the CIA handled that kind of thing."

"Overseas only," Bucyk told her. "Their charter doesn't
let them jaywalk in the States without clearing it first with
The New York Times. Forget all that crap you hear what
a gang of thugs the Company is, they follow the charter
right out the window. A setup like this, it's the Bureau's."

"I don't know what to say."

Bucyk inhaled deeply, stubbing out the tan butt on his
heel, held it at arm's length while Kate went out of the
room for an ashtray. "Thank you," he said when she came
back. "Say that."

"But why me? Doesn't the Federal Bureau of Investigation have enough trained women of its own?"

He flicked a crumb of tobacco from his teeth, making a spitting sound and a sour face at the same time. "You answered your own question," he said. "Trained women."

"What you're saying is no one else will take your money to screw him," she spit back. He didn't argue the point. Out came the cigarettes and she helped herself to one, took a light from his. She said, "It's no different with me."

"Sleeping with him's your choice. All we care about is putting him in place."

Kate hid a puzzled look behind a wisp of smoke.

". . . You know, getting him working . . ."

"I already have a boyfriend like that," she said, pleased with herself when Bucyk didn't come back at her right away.

"Or maybe you don't think we can meet your price."

Kate's nostrils flared again, and this time Bucyk loved it. "You really know how to butter me up," she said.

"Whatever it takes." He waited. Then, "Nothing I can say to change your mind?"

"Not even if he was chief of the KGB."

"Sorry I brought it up." He got off the bed and stretched. "Let me buy you supper. You look like hell."

"I'm not hungry."

He gazed past her and a little above, and she turned around to catch herself staring gauntly from the mirror. Her hands went automatically to sweep the taffy hair out of her eyes.

"It's not the do," he said. "Don't you eat any more?"

"I'm fine."

"Getting back to cases . . . your case . . . you still haven't told me everything's on the tape. What do you say you do it at a restaurant? You don't want to eat, you can watch me."

Kate began brushing her hair in the glass. She was hum-

ming. If she started talking to herself, Bucyk was going to
call 911. "Give me ten minutes to get ready," she said
without missing a stroke. "Please?"

They came out of the park off Columbus Circle, locked in
traffic which released them on Fifty-seventh Street. At a
bus stop in front of Carnegie Hall Bucyk put his PBA card
on the dash and they walked toward the Russian Tea
Room.

"Don't you think you're carrying this too far?" she said,
not hiding her annoyance.

He went to the window and looked in through a collection of tarnished samovars. He seemed surprised. "I don't
see what we're so worried they're gonna invade," he told
her. "They're already taking over."

A few doors away a twenty-story office tower hovered
self-consciously over its neighbors like the tallest kid in
class. A uniformed starter brought down an elevator,
monitoring its descent on a tiny screen as if he were pre-
viewing Hollywood's next blockbuster.

"Funny place for a restaurant," Kate said.

"It would be," he agreed. "We're going to an opening."

On the fourteenth floor they stepped off into a steamy
loft of summer furs and linen suits, straw hats of both
sexes. Track lighting rebounded off pale walls Kate decided would provoke less anxiety without the jumbled
canvases trolling for acclaim. Blocking access to the windows and fresh air was a table draped in a spotted cloth
she suspected had been snatched from a frame. At one
end was wine punch in a glass bowl and in a starched
waiter's jacket a thin-hipped young man, also starched,
ladling it out.

"An art gallery," she said, turning up her nose. "I
thought you were buying me supper. You didn't say anything about mooching it."

"We'll only be a minute," he promised. "There's something I want you to help me with."

He bulled through the crowd into elbow room which moved with them toward an office behind a butcher-block counter. Bony blond girls of a style which never changes, dressed in styles which change day to day, were drinking white wine from plastic cups, sipping like it was private stock. In a quiet gallery on the other side, paintings in ornate frames glowed warmly under incandescent bulbs, and Kate made out golden halos and Eastern churches. The program heralded RUSSIAN ICONS 1825–1917.

She went quickly past Byzantine caricatures of Saints Florus and Lavrus and Nicholas the Miracle Worker, whose reproving stares followed her around the room. Bucyk caught up to her in a corner, asking, "What can you tell me about this stuff?"

"You're being ridiculous," she said. "Next you'll want me to brief you on what they're saying inside the Kremlin."

"How'd you know?"

She glowered back at Saints Basil and Gleb, Saint Catherine the Martyr, laying blame for the pogroms her grandmother had sobbed over for sixty years. She sneaked away for some cheese and when she came back Bucyk was in the office making time with the blond girls. From the way they fluttered their hands they knew as much about the icons as she did. Then one brought him to a tall, broad-shouldered man with polished black hair, a cream-colored suit set off by a perfect tan. Kate carried her Brie close enough to eavesdrop.

"These the genuine article?" Bucyk was asking.

Kate expected the stranger to beg off. Instead, he put down his cup—some of the private stock—and looked at Bucyk earnestly. "Are you a collector?" he asked.

"Not just yet," Bucyk said. "This kind of stuff, it's a little out of my price range. But it's so damn beautiful, I wish I could afford it."

"I do too," the man with the polished hair laughed. "They're all first-rate pieces."

Kate saw that Bucyk was looking at the blondes. "Not real old," he said.

"For the most part, these are late-nineteenth-century works. The large orders for the Petersburg cathedrals had dried up by then and most painting was being done in rural villages by artists lucky to scrape together enough to eat. The artists considered this hack work, but were glad to get it. And so are we. Wonderful, don't you think?"

"Took the words right out of my mouth," Bucyk said.

"Is there anything else you need to know?"

"I'm still trying to digest what you told me. It was an education."

"Don't mention it. And if ever you're ready to enter the market—"

"Yeah, I'll come to you first."

The man with the polished hair went back to the girls and Bucyk picked up a catalogue and moved on. Kate followed him into the large gallery, where the punch was running out ahead of the crowd. "I didn't know you were interested in art," she said.

"Couldn't care less."

"You fooled me. That good-looking guy, too. And *he* certainly knew his stuff."

"Did he? What makes you such an authority?"

"Maybe I'm a sucker for a guy who knows how to wear a white suit," Kate said.

"So that's the trick."

"Or maybe it's just a guy who knows what he's talking about."

They followed the stragglers into the elevator, Bucyk sucking up what was left of his paunch to allow the gate to shut. "That your type?"

Out of the corner of her eye she saw him looking worried that she might say yes. His tough luck. "If I had a type."

"Pretty boys," he snorted. "I'm surprised at you. I figured you for an intellectual, you always have your nose in a book." They went out into a sunshower and Kate headed for the car. "Let's walk," he said. "I know a place . . ."

"This is a very expensive neighborhood."

". . . a place gives half off to cops. . . . So I would've guessed you went for the brainy ones."

"He didn't exactly come off as a dummy," Kate said. "There wasn't a lot he didn't know about those icons."

They crossed Sixth Avenue and turned downtown toward Radio City. "Where is this restaurant? It's really starting to come down."

"Smart," Bucyk said as if he didn't hear her. "Good-looking, a sharp dresser. A real piece of work, huh? You could go for a guy like that?"

If he had to know. "Any woman would."

"Why don't you, then?" He steered her inside a Mexican restaurant, shoved her a little harder than was necessary, and a short brown woman in a lace shawl showed them to a table under a piñata choking on its own insides. "His name's Mike, Mike Nicholas."

"How do you—"

"Let me finish. . . . Least that's what he's calling himself. If you want him, he's yours, only you have to share him."

"You're not making sense. Share him with who?"

"The Bureau."

"Oh," Kate said, picking up her menu and putting it down without opening it. "I'm starting to see."

Bucyk had stopped looking jealous. "You're interested?"

"No."

"You do a good imitation."

"You know perfectly well what I'm talking about. If I

didn't have a boyfriend, I might be interested in getting to know him, not in setting him up for the FBI."

Bucyk wasn't so sure. "These general principles, or he rates special consideration for having a good tan?"

It didn't deserve an answer. She reached for the menu again.

"Make you a wager. Take up with him . . . I'll help with introductions. And you still think he's such hot stuff, keep him with our blessings, he's yours. You don't, we take him off your hands. All we care about is you get him to hold off on going back to Russia. Fair enough? Your boyfriend never knows unless you tell him."

"And what if I don't think it is fair?"

"Then I gotta eat the paper with his phone number on it."

Kate said, *"Bon appétit."*

"That a yes or a no?"

She searched the tables for their waiter. Bucyk waved him away. "You take this on, I'll have your dog back inside of a week. Guaranteed."

"Do I get that in writing?" She laughed without smiling.

Bucyk tore off a corner of the menu and scrawled a few words. Kate pushed the cardboard back at him without looking at it. He glanced again at what he had written and then put it in his pocket. "Okay, I'll hold it for us," he said.

"I didn't agree to anything."

"Didn't you . . . ?"

8

THE ZOO went up early in the Depression, a Hooverville for animals. Forget the busloads of children and the orang-utan she was convinced had come to know her and it was a joyless place, not enough sky and no grass, prison archi-tecture—socialist realist lions with the breeze in their pit-ted manes poised heroically over a kill at the entrance to the Palace of the Felines. And inside, if you could stand the stench, the big cats pacing, going nuts by the mile as they measured their punishment cells.

But Nicholas was "a sucker for bears," his brand of na-tionalism, Bucyk had said, and Kate found him at the crumbly dens where the polar bears lumbered down a concrete bluff for a vegetarian lunch slopped out of a keeper's bucket. She inched along the rail groping for something to say. Bucyk's suggestions were as leaden as the ones he'd tried out on her and so she'd insisted on a free hand. Now that it was time, she was fresh out of ideas and she wondered if dropping a hankie might do the trick. She had no hankie. What she said was, "I didn't know they eat lettuce. I mean, where do they get a taste for salad at the North Pole?"

Just terrible, and Nicholas didn't even seem to hear. Then he tossed a peanut through the bars and looking straight ahead said, "Seal meat is their favorite food. But that's not to say they're strict carnivores. They'll fill their bellies with seaweed, or grass when they're hunting on land."

Very romantic. Well, you can't judge a book by—

"Then it's not one bit fair."

He emptied the bag and dry-washed his hands. He turned to look at her and for an instant she thought he recognized her from the gallery. No problem, till she realized she'd forgotten what she planned to say if he did. "What isn't?" he asked.

"Keeping them penned up like that, like they've been bad."

"It could be worse," he said. The voice was silky, a light tenor with no more accent than hers, which was none at all. "I've been to zoos where they make them earn their keep—dancing, balancing on rubber balls, wrestling their keepers. They may seem bored, but take my word for it, doing nothing can be paradise."

"Oh, have you had much experience?"

"I was talking about the bears," he said sharply, and Kate tried not to hold her breath as she waited for him to walk off. He pushed his sunglasses back over the polished hair. His eyes were brown, heavily lidded and lashed, and held their own with the rest of his darkly appealing features. "But yes," he conceded, "I've had some, though not nearly enough as I'd have liked."

"I was sure I'd seen you here before." Beating him to the punch. Just in case.

He looked surprised. "I don't think so. This is not a place where I spend much free time." He backed away from the rail and crumpled the bag into a trash can. He lowered his shades and she was sure he was saying good-bye. Then she realized this was his way of signaling that act one was over. The shades came up again and they walked together to the monkey house.

They went in past a family of Arabian baboons done in white marble, and along one wall a cage full of the real thing. A large old male with broken teeth was rocking on his haunches, yawning, and Kate came near clucking her tongue. "Poor thing, he can hardly keep his eyes open."

"I hope you're not thinking of tucking him in bed," Nicholas said. "What he's doing is called 'rage yawning,' showing his fangs."

"You didn't learn that from the plaque on the cage. How do you know so much about animals?"

"I'm an expert," he said. "A free-lance expert, on any and all things."

"Does it pay?"

"Why do you want to know?"

"I'm not after your job," she laughed. "It seems like pleasant work, being an expert. There are things I'm expert on, too."

"Yes," he said. "I see that."

It was a clumsy line, she thought, too obvious—almost crude. In spite of herself, this spy business was getting to be fun. Every word sounded on so many levels that the most innocuous remark seemed to thunder between them. She wanted to blush, to trump him at his own game. She tried conjuring up the first time she'd gone bottomless at the Starlight, putting a hand to her chest to feel for warmth. She felt nothing. "What would you say was my field of expertise?" she asked.

With his head cocked to the side he reminded her of a Coney Island storefront gypsy trying to guess her weight and age. "Whatever, I'm sure it's something that's fun."

"It depends on how you look at it. I have a restaurant on Seventy-second Street, a Mideastern place." They left the monkey house, dragging across a plaza where two harbor seals slapped gritty breakers from the lip of a blackish pool. "I still don't know what *you* do," she said. "Why are you being so mysterious?"

"I am, aren't I?" Offering nothing. "Does it make you uncomfortable?"

As if it was the most natural thing to do, she took his arm. "On the contrary, I love a good mystery."

. . .

Bucyk was waiting when she came out onto the stoop, grinning like he had her in his pocket. Gone was the station wagon, and in its place a midnight-blue van with running boards and picture windows along the side panels, a Monument Valley sunset splashed across the rear doors. He fiddled with the air conditioning and gave her a hint of the big Blaupunkt speakers, then took her for a spin to Riverside Park. "How'd it go?" he asked.

"Before we start, let's get one thing straight," she said. "I'm not taking money for this."

It didn't seem to surprise him. "You might change your mind. How about we keep your payments in an escrow account? You decide you want at it, it's waiting for you. How about that?"

"If you do," she said, "get yourself another girl."

"Your choice," he told her. "We can always find something else to keep the money busy. Now let's take it from the top again. How'd it go?"

She shrugged him off. "You promised me more information. Let me out now if you're not giving everything you have."

He pulled off the Henry Hudson into a cobbled turnout below the Cloisters. There was a totaled Volkswagen upside down in the weeds and a couple of Puerto Ricans stripping it. They were about fifty, in cutoffs and tank tops, drinking malt liquor out of the can through straws. Their women were huddled in the shade of a linden tree, fanning themselves with movie magazines. No one paid attention to the van.

Bucyk killed the engine and reached back for a manila folder on a narrow bed covered in crushed velvet. "His real name's Mikhail Nikolaevich Kunavin," he said, not reading. "Thirty-six years old."

"He said thirty-two."

"He would. His home town's Stalingrad, or whatever

they call it now. He turned down a cushy job as a government interpreter to do a few years as a political officer with a Red Army tank unit on the Czech-German frontier. Came back home and married a niece of the Leningrad party chief. Had two kids, two little girls."

"Why didn't you tell me?"

"Did *he*?"

She had no answer for that.

"What the hell, it's a cinch they're not living together." He looked inside the folder and shuffled some papers. "He's here as a rep for a state-owned trading company, SOVTORG, distributing vodka, Caspian Sea caviar. At least that's what he's supposed to be doing. Where those icons are coming from, we haven't got a clue. We want you to find out if he's moving them with the knowledge of the government, or if he's freebooting."

"He's very cautious. He'll talk all afternoon, but he won't say a word about himself."

Bucyk switched on the radio and the power antenna telescoped above the roof. A ball game came on so low Kate could hardly hear it. "Give it a while," he said. "It'll come."

"He's extremely defensive. Whenever I ask anything about him, he turns the conversation around so we're talking about me."

"Like I say, it takes time. You didn't think this was a one-day job?"

"I don't know what I was thinking."

Bucyk tossed the folder on the bed. "When you seeing him again?"

"This evening. He's taking me to Lincoln Center."

"You work fast."

"He does. He wouldn't take no for an answer."

"You're not supposed to say no." He scowled.

She looked away, focusing on a tugboat nudging a couple of barges into the harbor under a swarm of gulls.

"You worried your boyfriend's gonna know? Screw him, the way he runs around."

"I told Nathan I need some time off and want him to keep an eye on the club tonight. I don't think the responsibility will kill him and I'm paying him out of my own pocket." She sighed. "So why do I feel guilty?"

"Probably a habit." He turned up the radio. "This is working out better than I thought. You're something to Nicholas already. If you weren't, you wouldn't be going to Lincoln Center. He'd be taking you to the Soviet-American Friendship Committee Anti-Zionist Cotillion, like that."

"That would be fun," Kate said. "All I'd have to do is open my mouth and—"

"Yeah."

"Oh," she said. "I think I see what you mean."

The sleek Lincoln cabriolet looked about ninety feet long, so impossibly luxurious that she'd never get used to it. There was a boomerang antenna over the rear and a VCR and phone inside, a refrigerator and a bar. The silver shag felt ankle-deep. She kicked off her shoes as the chauffeur put them on course for Queens.

Nicholas couldn't have been more at home. He fixed two highballs and wound down the smoked-glass window, letting some street light inside. He saw it sparkling in both glasses and rolled up quickly, as if he had all he could use. He handed her a drink. "Did you ever hear anything like them?" he asked.

"When you said we were going to a jazz concert, to a New Orleans jazz concert, I almost backed out. I thought it would be like Dixieland, but those old men can play."

"There's nothing old about their music," he said. "I've been in love with it since I was a child. Because I wasn't allowed to listen to it, I suspect."

"Why was that?"

"My parents wouldn't let me waste my time on anything as . . . as decadent as jazz."

"Why?" she tried again. Wondering how hard she could press him, what invention he'd fall back on.

"They were spending their hard-earned money on violin lessons for me. They said I'd become a jazz musician all right, over their dead bodies."

"Do you still have your violin?"

"Under glass," he said. "I gave it up when I was thirteen and never went near it again."

"You'll have to play for me sometime."

"Over my dead body," he said.

They left the Midtown Tunnel, arcing over SRO cemeteries whose blunt skyline mimicked the one at their back, past hazy flatlands of deserted factories and twenty-four-hour chop shops. Then Queens Boulevard funneled them into sturdy, residential Forest Hills. Through the stone proscenium of a railroad trestle Kate saw a gothic tower. The streets were paved in red brick. "Where are we?" she asked.

"Forest Gardens."

"It looks like England."

"It's supposed to," he said, "to people who know England from picture postcards. It was put up before the First World War by a visionary architect trying to create the ideal urban environment." He pointed into the shadow of a concrete grandstand varicose with naked vines. "There's the West Side Tennis Club, which used to host all the major tourneys."

"It's hard to believe we're still in the city."

"That's what attracted me to the area. It combines the best of two worlds."

"Which two?" She felt light-headed, a drink away from trouble.

"The world of the rich," he said. "That's one."

"And the other?"

He seemed to be making up his mind. "Of the very rich," he decided after a while.

They turned onto an avenue curling around prim flower gardens leaching color in the moonlight. Two lefts brought them inside a flawed cathedral of elms, the stout trunks pushing up sprays of barren limbs. Nicholas guided the chauffeur between Tudor mansions set on postage-stamp lawns. At a home hidden behind a stone wall shimmering with broken glass Kate noticed a black Porsche 944 in the drive. The vanity plate spelled NICK.

"Park at the curb," Nicholas said.

Kate squeezed into her shoes and tested one on the sidewalk, then the other. Her legs felt like jelly. Leaning on Nicholas's shoulder, she asked, "What were we drinking?"

He mumbled something she didn't hear. He dismissed the driver and helped her up the walk to the big house. She squirmed from under his arm and dashed off the flagstones, kicked off her heels again, sinking her toes into the cool grass.

"You don't live here," she said. "You're just trying to make an impression on me."

"Do you want to hear something funny? That's the same thing I tell myself every morning."

He pushed open the door into an ambush of blinding light. Kate twisted away. She heard a siren.

"Damn," Nicholas stepped back outside and punched a four-digit number into a metal box on the doorframe.

"What was that all about?" Kate asked. "I thought someone was about to open fire."

"For another five thousand dollars someone would. It's a burglar alarm, and it set me back more than I'll ever lose in a robbery."

The floor came level and some of the cobwebs cleared. She tried not to show it. "What's so valuable you need to protect it like that?"

He switched on a lamp and a room glutted on antique furniture took form. She wobbled down stone stairs to the closest seat and plopped down hard. "I'm starting to see," she said.

"Do you?" he asked in a tone it took some time to recognize wasn't condescending. "Most people on their first visit tell me how beautiful all this is, but what they experience is a museum. To recognize that it's not just for looking, that the priceless Victorian slipper chair you're sitting in is meant just for that, requires rare intuition."

Or guts, Kate wanted to say, or to be awfully dumb or crocked. She sat a little straighter. "Are you a dealer?"

"Would you believe this is a furnished room?"

Ten different ways of laughing in his face came to mind. She selected a silent one. "Why not?" Slurring the words intentionally.

"Most of these pieces came from a Southampton estate where they'd been assembled over seven decades. I bought the collection at auction and added to it as I saw fit."

"That gold clock, that Russian clock," Kate said. "You bought that."

"Gilt bronze," he corrected her. "And it's French, by Japy-Frères, around 1880."

She surveyed the room as if she were making an appraisal. "Tell me about everything."

He came down the steps and opened a mahogany breakfront, removed a cut-glass flagon and two Jacobite air-twist glasses. Kate brought hers into the yellow glow strained through a wall lamp's parchment shade. She twisted the slender stem in her fingers. "They're beautiful," she said. "What are they?"

"Imitations," he told her, working out the cork. "The real ones are quite rare and fragile. We don't want that kind of responsibility."

"No, not now," she agreed. "If I have another drop, you can't hold me accountable for anything."

"I won't."

Some light spilled across his eyes, betraying an eager-ness his voice hadn't given away. She was in the driver's seat now, but found it strange and uncomfortable. Well, what did she expect after letting Nathan use her so long as a Band-Aid for his ego? She wondered if she was a hopeless pushover. Nicholas was going to help her find out. He was the best-looking man she'd ever known and possi-bly he'd learned to kiss. More than that didn't interest her. If she kept her feet on the floor, she could be in bed with Nathan by four.

She took the bottle and tilted it toward her glass. She took a sip and then a smaller one and then filled his to the top. "On second thought," she said, brushing up against him, "I insist you do."

9

TWO THINGS that ticked Nathan off—a girl with a pretty face who let her body go and the same girl who wasn't ashamed to show it. Worse were the exhibitionists, who flaunted it at a defenseless public. One was onstage now, doing a pathetic breathless hula, ruining his meal. He rubbed his hands along his thighs, confirming the tight fabric of new muscle. If he'd been put in charge for more than one night, the girl would be scraping plates in the kitchen.

His thoughts were interrupted by the waiter, a Sephardic Jew with gray Harpo Marx hair pouring from a dented fez. He dealt a cold dish off his towel-draped arm and set it in front of Nathan. "The house specialty," he announced.

Nathan juggled the flavor on his tongue like a judge at a wine-tasting. "Balyk," he said. "What do Arabs know from sturgeon?"

The waiter had trailed at Lindy's and considered himself a certified Broadway character. "Not so loud," he winked. "They think it's gefilte fish."

Nathan yawned and looked at his watch. Five hours till closing and he was starting on his second supper. If he didn't push the table away, a week in the Nautilus room would be shot to hell. He'd nosh a little, then go upstairs and stretch out in one of the reclining chairs that seemed to be everywhere. You had to hand it to Kate—the staff was drilled so well, he'd never be missed.

He went to the office. He lay back in a gray Barcalounger and shut his eyes, but already was getting hungry again. He called the kitchen to tell the cook to put together a doggie bag and to close without him. The restaurant business was definitely not all it was cracked up to be, not for him. Kate would understand.

In the smudged moonlight of a night threatening rain, Seventy-sixth Street glowed with Victorian charm. A police car rolled by, the officers eyeing Nathan until he fished the key from a pocket and measured it against his palm. He paused outside the brownstone and took another look around. He loved it here, far from drab, utilitarian Brighton Beach—the beginner's America. It occurred to him that if the house were his, he and Kate would have been married years ago. Married and no doubt divorced.

As he went up the stoop he saw light seeping from the door. What was Kate doing back so early? The way she'd taken off, he would have laid odds she was seeing another man. He'd surprise her—and she'd help him do a J and polish off the food and then he'd find something silly to fight about so they could play kiss and make up, jump in bed and maybe not get to sleep before dawn. He nudged open the door and went in as quietly as he could.

The light was on in the anteroom and a stocky man in a twill jacket crouched on the steps with his back to the door. Some kind of repairman, Nathan decided. His smile melted into lopsided disappointment. He put down his bag and watched the man rip into the staircase. Then he cleared his throat. Stanley Bucyk stood up and whirled around.

"Short circuit?" Nathan asked.

"What the fuck are you doing here?"

A forty-dollar-an-hour union stiff with a monkey wrench up his ass. Nathan knew the type. Once he'd helped his uncle renovate a Sea Gate bungalow and the nonunion guys were almost civil as a rule, even when you had to call them back on the job to try and get it right. "I live here," Nathan said. "Miss Shapiro upstairs?"

Bucyk didn't know what to say. His hand went inside his

jacket for his shield, but he didn't have a shield. He felt for the .357 Magnum he'd taken off an East Fifties pimp. "This answer the question?"

The burglar! Nathan's chest began hammering, but he felt strangely in control of himself. He could see why Kate was so freaked out. This was a real thug, hard and vicious. Not real bright-looking either. Kate would have been smart kissing the dog good-bye.

Nathan nodded.

"Sit down on the bottom step." As Nathan shuffled his feet in a compact circle, Bucyk called down, "I changed my mind. I want you here where I can see you, on the landing."

Nathan walked slowly up the stairs. The man with the gun was close enough to smell. Nathan saw a dark semicircle under the outstretched arm. His own shirt was sticking to his skin.

Where the middle steps should have been, the runner was rolled up and the wood removed. Nathan stared into an open vault lined with packages wrapped in paper. Two steps above, piled beside a valise, were some torn envelopes and stacks of currency held together by bank wrappers—fifties and hundreds.

"You can put your eyes back in your head," Bucyk sneered.

Nathan leaped over the missing stairs and kept on going. When he got to the landing, Bucyk motioned him onto a bench seat. It wobbled beneath him as he perched on the edge looking down at the gun and the man holding it.

"Now lean back and stay like that," Bucyk ordered. "You feel a twitch coming on, you tell me in advance. Got it?"

Nathan raised his hand like a first-grader asking for permission to leave the room. He scrunched up his nose.

Bucyk angled the heavy gun upward. "Your funeral," he shrugged.

Nathan stopped clowning and sat rigidly with his hands

on his knees. It was one thing to show he wasn't scared, another to get his head blown off. But he was scared. He could feel his bladder contracting. "It won't happen again," he said.

Bucyk stuffed the gun inside his pants. He tore the wrapper from one of the paper bundles and examined an object that reminded him of an immense tube from an old television. "Know what this is?"

Nathan's thighs, still sore from his afternoon workout, were cramping with nervous tension. He shifted his weight and didn't answer.

"Me neither," Bucyk said. "But it's a cinch it's worth something to somebody." He scooped out the rest and put them into the valise with the money.

Then he reached blindly into the vault and came out with a package held together in the color comics from the Sunday *Newsday*. He peeled the newsprint away from two small mounds of white powder wrapped separately in clear plastic. Nathan saw them, too, and began sweating again.

"Know what *this* is?" Bucyk said.

"Rat poison."

"Yeah, right." Bucyk hugged the package against his chest as he made room inside the valise. He got down on his knees and swept his hand around the vault. "What else we got in here?"

"Rats," Nathan said.

Bucyk lurched away involuntarily. "Funny," he said, making clear that was the last thing he thought it was.

One kick, Nathan was thinking, one good kick in the ass and the fucker wouldn't walk for a week. "Why don't you stick your head in and make sure you're not missing anything," he said, wishing right away that for once he hadn't opened his big mouth.

Bucyk reached in up to the shoulder, but came out empty. He zipped the valise and tested the weight in his left hand, shifting it to the other when he barely could lift it. "What'd you say?"

Nathan dried his palms on his sore thighs. "Nothing."

"You said something," Bucyk insisted. He dropped the bag and yanked the gun from his pants. "What was it?"

The aching in his legs was becoming more than Nathan could stand. He raked the knotted muscles with his fingers, but got no relief. "I said, 'Go in for a look.' "

"You bet you did." Bucyk couldn't have looked more pleased. "You first."

Nathan froze.

"I'm not leaving you here to call the cops," Bucyk said, "so either I shoot you in the knee and cut the phone wires, or you get in the hole and I nail you in. It's up to you." He waved the gun for emphasis. "Me, I have my own idea on this. But I don't vote."

Nathan said, "I think I have claustrophobia."

"Your choice." Bucyk leveled the revolver at Nathan's leg.

"On the other hand, it's a problem I have to face up to sooner or later."

Nathan's thighs were on fire. He stamped his feet and leaned forward and the bench seat tilted beneath him. Bucyk, grappling with the valise as he backed down the stairs, was too busy to notice.

"You'll go in the hole, then," Bucyk said. "Make enough noise when your girlfriend comes home and she'll hear." He lowered the bag two steps, then paused. "Catch her in a good mood, she might let you out."

"She told you about me?" Nathan asked. "The last time?"

Bucyk spit in his hand and adjusted his grip. "What last time?"

Nathan's legs were killing him. He stood up shakily and the bench fell apart. He held onto the seat and then brought it up to his chest and charged down the stairs behind it. Bucyk let go of the valise, fumbling for his gun. Nathan was leaping over the missing steps when a bullet splintered the mahogany shield and entered his left side. It caromed around his rib cage like a pinball, nicking the aorta. His heart already had stopped beating when both men crashed headlong down the stairs and Bucyk was pinned underneath the wooden slab.

When the pain began to subside, Bucyk was tracing the outline of a welt that was spreading across his forehead. His hand came away damp and gummy and he tasted blood on his fingertips. He tightened his stomach muscles, drawing strength into the center of his body, directed it toward his shoulders and pushed against the dark wood. The mahogany pressed down just as hard.

He opened his eyes then. He was sprawled on his back with his head on the floor, dizzy from the impact and the rush of events. His torso was full of a throbbing which radiated from his lower spine where the edge of a step cut across it. As he inched out from under the wood, wetness dribbled in his eyes. He followed its source with his hand, wanting to gag as he explored a warm face slippery with blood.

Nathan lay face down on the bench seat, crimson bubbling from both nostrils. Bucyk pushed the bloody face aside as he slithered out from under. The slab skidded down the stairs toppling Nathan onto his side.

Bucyk snatched up the revolver, keeping an eye on Nathan as though he might have to use it again. "Happy now, hero?" he said. He adjusted a small holster under his arm and threaded the barrel inside. "Get what you want?"

His nose hurt. He touched the tip and maneuvered it from side to side, and the pain traveled across both cheeks and came together again in the back of his head. The room began wobbling, then picked up speed, and he squatted down beside Nathan, searched the filmy eyes for a flicker of life.

"You had to be a fucking hero," he said. "Had to screw things up." He slapped the vacant face and examined his bloody palm. "Think I give a shit about you? Fuck you, what you did to me. I'm talking twenty-five to life, hero, anybody connects me to this."

He went looking for a bathroom to wash off the blood, tugging at his nose, pretty sure that it was broken. The medicine-cabinet mirror showed the bridge listing slightly to the left. But he wasn't positive it hadn't been that way before. Thirty-four years he'd been living with that face, and now he couldn't say where the pieces went. He heard a slapping sound behind him and pulled out the gun again, ran through the house till he spotted venetian blinds fluttering against an open window and ripped them down.

He went back to the anteroom and set the valise upright. But when he tried lifting it, he couldn't get it off the floor using two hands. He shut off the light and stepped outside, tilting his face toward misting rain. Then he dragged out the valise and kicked it off the stoop. He ran to the corner and came back in a cab, brought the valise around the block where his van was parked, leaving ten dollars for a ninety-second ride.

If she didn't quit laughing, Nathan was going to have a lot of questions. And if Nathan started digging the way only he could, he'd have the whole story out of her before she could come up with a safe one. She pinched her lips together, trying on a serious expression, but had to give it up when she remembered Nicholas's dumb astonishment as she told him she was going home. Nathan would get a kick out of that. Only, how do you tell your boyfriend about a narrow escape from another man's bed?

She touched the knob and the door swung open. Christ,

the older Nathan got, the more irresponsible he became. She was praying that someone had reminded him to lock up at the Knights. It was too much to hope he had pulled the steel gate across the storefront like she'd told him.

She paused on the doorstep. In the feeble light from the street she made out a shadowy form on the stairs, and she ran to Nathan and put a hand on his shoulder and he fell onto his back. A red-black mass of gore had congealed under his nose. She saw another on his shirt. Then her whole world went red and black and hazy. She felt moisture welling in her eyes and fought it as she had fought her laughter a moment ago. Dropping to her knees, she pressed her lips against Nathan's forehead. The skin was cool and clammy, and as she pulled away she noticed that it was gray.

"Nathan, say something." Then she began sobbing. "Please, Nathan . . ." Offering him the chance to prove this was just another of his jokes. "Please, no."

She ran to the kitchen, turning on all the lights. She called 911 and slammed the receiver before anyone asked what the hurry was for a dead man. She dialed Bucyk's number from memory. Above a smoky cocktail piano somebody was doing a godawful Bogart.

"This is Marlowe," he lisped. "My buddy Stan . . ."

Kate said, "Shit."

". . . is out right now, but if you leave your name and number, I'll see he . . ."

As she waited for the tone, a man doing a credible Bucyk said, "Yeah?" The voice was dull and thick, as though he was coming down with a cold.

"Detective?" she said over him.

"How'd you like the Bogie?" He knew better than to let her answer. "I was getting ready to turn in, but . . . How'd it go?"

She didn't hear him. "My boyfriend . . . he's been shot, I think. He isn't breathing."

"What's this?" Wondering if he sounded surprised enough, deciding she wouldn't notice either way.

"He was here again—"

"Who was? You're getting ahead of yourself."

"The stairs, they're all torn apart. The burglar—" She broke down. Bucyk listened for a while and then put the receiver quietly on a table and went into the kitchen for his cigarettes. The apartment, three rooms in a middle-income project in the West Nineties where police and firemen jumped the waiting list, had been his for six years and still he had no ashtrays. He went through two bags of garbage for a jar lid and when he came back he heard her sniffling, trying to gasp out the words. She blew her nose and began sobbing again.

"Cry if you want," he said. "We're gonna get you through this in fine shape." He lit up and took a long drag and forced the smoke out quickly. "Feel better now? You sure he's dead?"

Her sobs were coming more softly, spaced farther apart. "I'm no doctor . . . Oh, what's the use of wishing? Yes."

"You called the police?"

"No, I thought you should know first."

"That was smart," he told her. "I'll pull some strings to, you know, smooth the way."

"You'll be here when they come?"

"I'd like to," he said, "but we can't drag the Bureau into a murder. I'll tip Infante to what happened and he'll put in a call for a meat—. . . for an ambulance and homicide detectives."

"Please hurry. I'm so nervous."

"There's something I got to tell you first," he said. "The dicks are gonna have a prime suspect before they even get there and it isn't gonna be the guy who stole your dog. It's gonna be you."

"Me?" She screamed it. A little hysterical. "Why me?"

"Because you've been living with the deceased. It's how

they teach it at the academy. Come down hard on the spouse, on the girlfriend. Usually pays off, too."

"But all they have to do is look at me and they'll know I could never—"

"Be nice if it worked that way," he told her. "But these are parochial-school boys, a lot of them, and they got a complex about gals like you giving it away while they were doing push-ups with only the gym floor underneath. Their whole life they're looking to catch up. They find out you didn't show at the club tonight, they run your name through records and see where you've been collared, they finally got a chance to do some serious screwing."

"But that arrest was nothing. You told me so yourself."

"Till now," Bucyk said. "In a case like this a simple assault beef becomes something, a big something."

He thought she would start crying again. Instead her voice steadied and she asked, "What do I have to do?"

"You be very careful when they're asking you questions. Keep your answers short and don't volunteer anything. That's the safest way to go."

"Do you know a lawyer I can call?"

"Do that and they'll never leave you alone. Innocent people don't ask for lawyers. They teach that at the academy, too."

"Why must I go through this?" she asked him. "You can tell them where I was. And Mike can back it up."

"No way you mention Nicholas. His name comes up, it'll have repercussions all the way to Washington, hell to Moscow, and everybody in between looking to sell you down the river. You don't really think you can use a Soviet spy as an alibi witness? You try, we'll have to cut you loose."

Kate stuck her head into the corridor, craning for a glimpse of Nathan, and was relieved when she couldn't see him. "What *do* I say, then?"

"I don't know yet. What's it look like happened?"

"I found Nathan on the stairs. And the place is a mess. He must have let the burglar in like I did."

"Every bored housewife tips the delivery boy something extra to knock off the old man, they get the idea it should look like a burglary," Bucyk said. "You hand them a story like that, the dicks'll try and break you down for a better one, never leave you alone till they see your initials on a ten-page statement."

"But it's the truth."

"Doesn't mean a thing. Let 'em figure it out themselves. I think you're right about needing an alibi."

"You just said I shouldn't involve Mike in this."

"Do you a favor," Bucyk said. "You can say you were spending the night with me." He coughed and then he cleared his throat and Kate thought he was being sarcastic until he said, " 'Scuse. This is a personal relationship you'll tell them about."

Kate could see him choking on his own laughter, gloating. "Are you sure you want to get involved?"

"Long as we don't bring in the Bureau, I don't see there's any harm. We'll get our story straight and no one'll crack us. Whaddaya say?"

"If you think it's a good idea . . ."

"It's the best we've got. They ask, tell 'em we were out in Jersey. They want more, say you were tight, you don't remember exactly. A Holiday Inn somewhere. Details make 'em suspicious. They feel better about you when you're vague, kind of confused. Tell 'em we had a fight and I dropped you off at home and this is what you found. They want more, they have to come to me."

"You'll call them now?" Her voice had become a worn monotone.

"And we can talk about Nicholas later, huh?"

"Later," she said.

"One more thing. The dead . . . your boyfriend, what was his name? For my own information."

"Nathan Metrevelli. Why?"

"It's a shame," Bucyk said. "It's a shame this had to happen to everybody."

10

AT EAST Houston and the river, by the handball courts in the park that didn't have a name, Harry Lema was looking for money or grass, whichever came first. He was looking in a purple satin windbreaker with THE JACKSONS VICTORY TOUR in felt script across the back, tearing it inside out. A black kid eighteen years old was wearing it over gray sweats, new Air Jordans with the laces untied and pulled loose and a knit rainbow tam corraling his rubbery dreadlocks like a cat in a bag. Stretched out on his belly the kid was six-two, two and a half, with rippling muscles tapering into a twenty-nine-inch waist, sinewy arms like a young Thomas Hearns, and if the scraggly-ass bastard climbing up his back ever wore out he wouldn't bother with the gravity blade taped inside his thigh, just pound his pasty face into the wall. The kid's name was Nestor Little, Jr., and he was from Sixty-eighth and Lex, where his father was a urologist. Not twenty minutes ago Harry had given him two hundred dollars for a lid of Colombian that was all seeds and stems, hydroponic compost from a greenhouse in the Bronx, it smelled like.

Harry dug his knee in the small of Nestor's back, enjoying the pained whoosh of air that resulted. When he caught his breath, Nestor said, "You crazy, man. You got your shit. You wanna make trouble for?"

"Shit's all it is."

"You didn't like it? I got some nice *sess.*"

Harry shifted his weight, forcing Nestor's chin down where the city's pooper-scooper legislation was not strictly enforced.

"Oof," Nestor said. "Didn't nobody ever tell you caveat emptor?"

"Where's the two bills?"

"You breakin' my neck."

Harry slipped his hand inside Nestor's shirt. He pulled out six baggies stuffed with dry stalks, a couple of vials of red capsules and a foil packet which he put in his pants and then gave back to Nestor. There was no wallet and only six dollars. "Where is it?"

"Can't think," Nestor said. "I got a low threshhold of pain. You killin' me."

"It's an idea. Where?"

"Ow, ow, ow, ow, ow," Nestor said.

Harry tore off the tam and shook out a butane lighter and two packets of rolling papers, sailed it into the wall like a rainbow Frisbee and watched it crash.

"Ow," Nestor said again. "My partner have it."

"Don't give me any more of your shit," Harry said.

"Ain't shit," Nestor said. "Name Little Peter. Fat dude, carry an umbrella all the time, with an antenna inside like fuckin' Zorro. Stand round the corner and keep an eye out while I do business."

"Never saw him."

"He seen you," Nestor warned.

"You live through this," Harry said, "tell him he still owes two bills."

"Peter hear what you done, be lookin' for you first. The dude have a problem with his temper. Now you do, too."

"It's not like I don't want to believe you," Harry said sympathetically, "but the only Little Peter you ever saw was hanging between—"

"Not funny, man."

Then the kid's body was steeped in shadow and Harry felt a chill across his back. It had nothing to do with the weather, which was sunny and in the low seventies. In the split second of consciousness remaining it occurred to him that the voice had been deeper than Nestor Little, Jr.'s, and seemed to be coming from behind and above.

Drifting out from under the anaesthetic, Harry dreamed he was zipped in a sleeping bag with a girl in a white nightie. She had small-to-medium boobs, which was the way he liked them now, and he could feel their heat on his skin. But there was no room to move his hands. Soon he got tired of trying and lay quietly, so that she would think he was asleep and stay where she was. When he opened his eyes, dizziness arrived with the light. A woman was pressing her face close to his and he smiled back, still feeling warmth. As she came into focus he saw that she was around fifty, with a crisp doily in her mousy hair. She was saying, "How are you going to pay? Do you have Blue Cross–Blue Shield or HIP . . . ?"

Harry stopped smiling, hoping she would go away.

"Or are you on Medicaid?"

Then the pain hit. It had been hibernating in the back of his head and now she'd gone and woke it up. Lasers shot across his forehead and down his cheeks and into his neck. His skull felt like only the scalp was holding it intact. He wanted to squeeze the pieces together, but his hand wouldn't move. In a panic he looked down and saw his arm sheathed in white from elbow to wrist. He touched the other hand to his temples and felt cloth all around.

"Wha' happened?" he asked.

"Sir, we must have this information."

"Isaac," Harry screamed. "The fuck were you when I was gettin' killed?"

"*Sir,*" the woman was saying, "we must have . . ."

The doctor said, You won't be using that arm for a while. We had to insert a pin in the ulna and the radius is fractured, too. The cast won't be coming off for at least eight weeks. You took nine stitches in your scalp, but fortunately you have a hard head, no telling how long you were unconscious before the park attendant found you. One thing we don't understand—your back, the area around your buttocks is covered with welts. We thought it might be some kind of rash, but they're too pronounced. It looks almost as if you'd been horse-whipped.

Harry said, It must be something I'm allergic to.

An ambulette brought him back to Inwood. There were three other passengers, a dried-up Chinese woman with no feet and two men who didn't say anything or move on their right sides. The driver was employed by the Vera Institute of Justice. On the knuckles of his left hand Harry saw L-O-V-E in a crude tattoo. On the right was H-A-T-E. He told Harry he was from Hell's Kitchen before they called it Clinton, on work-release from Greenhaven on a skin beef he didn't care to get into.

"What's it like, the driving?" Harry asked. "You wanna scream, takin' the old farts around in traffic like a fuckin' chauffeur?"

The driver said it wasn't so bad, he was making out dealing dimes all over Manhattan. "Mexican brown," he offered. "Help you with the pain."

Harry dipped his good hand into a pocket and fished out his wallet.

"Got works," the driver said.

Harry let go of the wallet. He knew four guys dead from AIDS and only one he was sure was queer. "Maybe next time," he said.

"Next time," the driver told him, "you could be in the joint."

"Where it hurts most," Harry said.

The apartment looked like shit. The kitchen table was down on two legs and the shades were shredded on the floor. The couch was torn apart, the batting all over the place in balls of white fluff. Smelled like shit, too. Harry ran to the window and something hit him behind the knees, nearly knocking him over. He heard a low growl.

"Isaac, that you?" He reached down to pet the dog. The growling got louder. "I'm sorry," he said. "Really, I am." He withdrew his hand slowly. ". . . Sorry."

He backed into the kitchen. The food bowl was empty, the other one dry. He ran some water and put it on the floor and the big dog went straight for it. Harry looked in the refrigerator, but saw nothing from Coddled Canines.

"I gotta go to the store now, Isaac," he said, "but I'll be back in a couple minutes."

He hurried to the door. The wolfhound got there first. "Right back. I swear."

Isaac growled again, baring shiny teeth.

"Okay, fella," Harry said, smiling nervously. "You win."

Harry went into the kitchen again looking over his shoulder. He chipped a large steak from the freezer and threw it on a burner, turned on the gas. "Soon's this loosens up, it's yours," he said. "Then we can talk about goin' to the store."

While Isaac attacked the meat, Harry pushed dog crap around with a broom. He tried scooping it up in a shirt cardboard, but with one hand it was impossible. He was on his knees trying, when Isaac jumped on his back. Harry shut his eyes, wanting only that what was coming should be quick and relatively painless. He felt the dog's mouth on his throat, then hot stickiness, the big tongue. No teeth. He opened his eyes again. "You wanna go for a walk, that what you're tryin' to tell me? Soon's I finish havin' my heart attack."

Kate was pacing the stoop, waiting for the detectives, when the phone rang. No way she was going for it, not with Nathan still on the stairs. She listened to it ring twice more and then looked the other way and ran for the kitchen, hoping it wasn't Bucyk with a last-second change in plan.

"Hello?"

Silence.

What a time for a breather, a breather holding his breath. She looked for a police whistle Howard had given her, one he said was guaranteed to melt eardrums, and remembered that she had left it by the upstairs phone. "Hello?" she said again, louder.

"Hey, how we doin'?"

Her ear didn't place the voice right away. Her stomach did, putting an extra loop in the knot it was tied in. "Who is this?"

"You forgot already? How long's it been, been two weeks?"

"Oh my God," Kate screamed.

"Yeah, me," Harry said.

In the instant before the receiver crashed he heard her scream again. It reminded him of a wounded animal, though which kind he couldn't say. He didn't hang up right away. He said, "Fine thanks . . . and you? Just wanted to find out if you were receiving. I'm comin' by with your dog."

The Olds was still in one piece, still on the street where he'd left it when he got caught downtown. Some kind of record. There were six tickets on the windshield, which he added to the collection in the glove compartment. He unlocked a case-hardened steel chain that was looped around the steering wheel and brake pedal and then jabbed a key at the ignition. It went in up to his fingers. Son of a bitch . . . someone had gotten in and reamed out the switch. He found the broken parts on the seat under Isaac's tail. He pushed open the door and the dome light revealed grooves in the chain where a bolt cutter had gone up against it.

He felt under the seat for a few scraps of unshielded wire that he kept there for emergencies, such emergencies as unattended Benzes and BMWs. Then he got out and unlocked a short chain running through the hood latch and the grille. Using his good hand he wrapped one end of a wire around a battery clamp and the other around the ignition coil. He connected a second wire to the other clamp. As he made contact with the solenoid activator, the starter croaked and died.

Some slimeball pushing a shopping cart filled with hubcaps had let him have the battery for eight black beauties, and he had to charge the goddamn piece of crap every other week. At best, there were three more tries left in it. He touched the wire to the solenoid twice more before the engine sputtered and caught. He pressed down on the carburetor linkage and a greasy cloud shot out of the exhaust. Then he slammed the hood and hurried behind the wheel, gunning the motor till the idiot lights went out.

"Fine state of affairs," he said, "you gotta hot-wire your own car."

Two lanes of the Henry Hudson were shut for repairs and traffic was permanently backed up off the bridge. He wove along the shoulder till he had skirted the mess and was in the West Seventies in half an hour. Another record. The dark side streets were deserted except for a few derelicts nodding on the steps of a community church, first in line for a free feed and a shower. He turned onto Seventy-sixth and slammed the brakes.

The block was alive with cops. He flashed his high beam and counted five unmarked cars mixed in with at least as many cruisers. Nose-to-nose at the hydrant were a truck from the medical examiner's office and a Roosevelt Hospital ambulance.

Harry reached over and scratched Isaac's ears. "I gotta admit she didn't sound real pleased to be hearin' from us. But I didn't think she'd circle the wagons."

LITTLE ODESSA · 127

The dog dropped a paw on Harry's shoulder and licked his face.

"Can't wait to sleep in your own bed, huh? I know, only I'm not so sure tonight's the time to try."

Isaac raised the other paw and scratched at the window. Harry pulled away and frowned. "Whyn't you say so in the first place?"

He cut the engine and opened the door and Isaac went straight for a parking meter. Harry clipped a metal leash to his collar and walked the big dog down the block. A uniformed officer was standing guard over the brownstone, protecting it from three men in warm-up suits and a paperboy huddled under a street lamp.

The dog lunged ahead and Harry had to plant his feet to keep his balance. "Tell you the truth, Isaac, this is a hell of a time to be callin'. How's a couple of beers and some liver sound to you?"

A man in a white surgical gown backed out of the house wheeling a stretcher cloaked in a soiled sheet. A detective was at the other end. Together they carried the cart off the stoop and loaded it into the ME's truck.

Harry yanked off his glacier glasses and stared. "This could be a fuckin' tragedy. We gotta go home and figure out what it means."

The dog was yelping as Harry wrestled him back to the Oldsmobile and pushed him onto the seat. Harry put the key in the ignition automatically, and lost it in the steering column.

"You just can't say enough for this town," he told Isaac, and reached under the seat for his wires.

The homicide cop couldn't have been more than thirty-five, forty at the most, and already his nose had gone doughy, purple capillaries tangled in the rough skin like highways on a relief map. He had shaggy, silver-gray hair, and big horse teeth which he used to break open the red pistachio nuts Kate had put out on the piano. If he mentioned his name, she had forgotten it. He got up off the Barcalounger and said, "Let's hear it again."

"But I've already told you six times."

"Seven," he said, cracking a nut with the big teeth and rubbing the red dye from his fingers fussily. "Seven's a lucky one."

"Not for me."

"So's eleven," he said. "It doesn't make any difference to us."

Kate twisted a furry braid of tissues and looked at the window where Infante was leaning on the sill. "There's no need for this," she said. "If you want to believe I could have anything to do with what happened to Nathan, go ahead. I'm too tired to argue any more."

"It's for your own good." The detective sneaked one more pistachio and pushed away the bowl. His face had lost some of its unpleasantness. "The last part," he said. "Start there."

Kate shook her head sadly but firmly. "If you're not going to arrest me, I'd like to try to get some sleep."

"Please," the detective said.

She wiped her eyes again. "Just the last?"

He nodded. "After you had the squabble with your date."

She took a deep breath. "I didn't want him near the house," she said. "If Nathan saw him, he'd have gotten the wrong idea." She looked up at the detective. "That sounds bad, doesn't it?"

"Go on."

"He dropped me off and I went up, and the door was open. I—"

Infante broke his silence. "What time is this?"

"You know the time. I told you half a doz—"

"Tell us once more."

"About two and a half hours ago," she said. "What time is it now?"

Without looking at his watch the shaggy detective said, "Twenty to six."

"Three hours, then."

"And you didn't go out again?"

"How could I, with Nathan . . . ?"

"You're sure?"

"Yes," she said. "Why is this so important to you?"

"Not to me. We've been talking to someone, a jogger, who saw you go in. He said he noticed you because he never sees a woman alone on the street at that hour. He told us he'd stretched a hamstring and was still working out the kinks when the first cars arrived. He watched for a while and then went back home. He just came out again."

"So?" Kate asked.

"So, he didn't hear a gunshot and no one else we've spoken to did either. And since Mr. Metrevelli appears to have died a while before that time and we haven't found a gun . . . What I'm saying is, we have to buy your story."

"Does that mean I can go to bed now?"

"Soon," the detective said. "We want you downtown."

"No," Kate yelled at him. "I won't let you lock me up. I want to see a lawyer."

"Who said anything about . . . ? We need you to take a gunshot-residue test."

"What's that?"

"To help determine if you've fired a gun recently."

Kate laughed bitterly. "I wouldn't know how to hold one."

"If you test negative, you have nothing to worry about."

"But I am worried," she said. The detective stopped rubbing his fingers. "I'm worried about everything."

"Can I get a word in here?" Infante asked. "I don't believe a thing she said."

The shaggy detective shrugged. "We want you down-town."

Kate ducked inside a phone booth and unfolded the door, sliding it open again until the light went off. "Damn it, why are you out when you know what I'm going through? They made me come to police headquarters for a test to see if I shot Nathan. Now they want to talk again. I've been giving them the story like you told me and they're going to check it with you. I still haven't gotten any sleep, or found someone to open the club, and whenever I get a second to myself, I think about . . . about the way Nathan looked and, God, I feel so terrible I wish it had been me instead." Without warning the connection was broken. "Damn it," she said again.

She was fighting back tears without success. She found more change inside her bag and dialed the number, waited for the tone.

"This is Marlowe. My buddy Stan is out right now . . ."

"Oh, fuck you, too," Kate said. Then: "The funeral is tomorrow morning."

The gawkers at the lamppost had given way to men in business suits and running shoes, thirty-fivish mothers pushing high-tech strollers. They stared earnestly at the brownstone and then moved on as others took their place. Kate went up the stoop pretending they weren't there. The house looked like a bomb had hit and she was ground zero. She felt tears welling up again, but was cried out a long time ago.

The middle steps were gone from the staircase, seized by crime-scene technicians with a section of the runner and the bench seat. In yellow chalk at the bottom of the flight was the rough outline of a man and, over the chest, like the target on a fencer's vest, a splotch of dried blood. The anteroom was littered with strips of tape and plastic bags, glass vials that had been emptied into Nathan's still veins. The banister was gray with fine powder, as if the house had been sealed for ages. Kate dipped her thumb in the dust and examined a smear of loops and whorls against the dark wood.

She climbed the stairs without passing over the chalk marks, squeezing away from the yellow drawing as though it delineated holy ground. She paused before the empty space and peered into the vault. How much could the envelopes have contained? How much for Nathan's life? She jumped to the landing and ran into the bedroom, sprawling on the mattress in all her clothes.

She pulled the telephone receiver off the hook and buried it under the pillow. The shrill pulsing of the warning signal startled her and she hung up again. She zipped off her jacket and tossed it on a chair and by the time her head touched the pillow she was asleep, dreaming that she was a little girl seeing Coney Island for the first time.

A man with powerful hands was dragging her into the skeletal shadow of the Typhoon. She was terrified of the roller coaster and couldn't stop crying. She wanted to run away, but the man was too fast for her and caught her every time she tried. He kissed her on the mouth. It was Nathan, looking happier than she ever had seen him.

They sat in the first car climbing over a beach dark with people. She held the bar so tightly that her hands hurt. Nathan's arms were high over his head, but she could tell that he was scared. Then the car plummeted off the track and they soared over green water lapping against the horizon. The wind was ringing in her ears. She let go of the bar to cover her head and her hand hit something hard. She woke with the phone in her fist. "Hello?" she said.

"Kate, where were you?"

"Nathan?"

"What?"

"Oh," Kate said. "Oh, it's you." Bluffing, trying to collect her wits. "I didn't recognize your voice."

"I've been calling all morning. Here . . . at the club. Even Brooklyn."

"Howard?"

"Who did you think it was?"

"No one," Kate said sadly. "No one at all. How is everything?"

What she expected was a five-minute monologue, his adventures embellished. Instead he said, "Not so good."

How did he know?

"In fact, it couldn't get much worse."

Things were coming into focus. She was afraid to say anything.

"I'm in trouble with the police, Kate."

You too? she almost asked.

"Kate . . . ?"

"Yes."

"I'm calling from prison."

"Where? Were you hijacked?"

"No such luck," he said. "I'm still in Israel. Small world. They put me in a cell across from a man from Glukhov, my hometown in Russia."

"At least you have someone to talk with about old times," she told him. Not believing a word of what he'd said, waiting for the punch line.

"A war criminal. A guard at Maidanek. He's here awaiting trial for crimes against humanity."

Kate said, "You're at the airport, aren't you? You want someone to pick you up."

"I want you to get me out of this terrible place."

Another bad dream, Kate thought. Better yet, Howard and Nathan had gotten together somehow to plot a morbid joke at her expense. She forgave them, though. God, if only she could. "You're not in New York?" she said cautiously.

"In Ayalon Prison. Between Tel Aviv and Jerusalem. In maximum security."

"But how . . . ? I don't understand."

"It's a long story."

"You have to tell me every last detail when you get back," she said. "No excuses."

"I'll tell you now. But first, did you look under the stairs yet, like I told you?"

He knew, damn it. He knew everything and was drawing it out of her as cruelly as he could. "I was going to," she said.

"When you do," he warned her, "you will find more than money there. Didn't you wonder about the house, how I am able to indulge in such luxury on what I take out of the Knights?"

"I happen to know you're doing very well."

"Not that well. To maintain my standard of living it is necessary that I acquire another trade. So I am a dealer in hard-to-obtain goods. Two, three times a year I move a *bissel* cocaine from my second adopted land to the first."

"Howard, you?" Any other time, she would have had to laugh. "You got caught smuggling dope?"

"It's more complicated than that," he told her. "It is also my pleasure to provide Israel with such military equipment as the United States government is not keen its most loyal ally should have. This is what brought me to New York in the first place."

"I don't believe you."

"Believe it," he said wearily. "Believe it." In the background Kate heard someone speaking Hebrew too fast for her to pick out more than an occasional word. "They are telling me to get to the point," Howard said. "But the point is that I am here."

"Who's telling you?"

"What I'm trying to explain," he went on, "is that sneaking electronics gear out of the U.S. is not so different from bringing cocaine into Israel. For me, exactly the same. I transported both in parcels the customs inspectors at Lod Airport were under orders not to look into."

Kate asked, "Then how did you wind up in jail?"

"Politics. A new bunch came in at the defense ministry and no one told the customs people not to peek. The result is I share a television with a Nazi. If you won't help, for a very, very long time."

"What can I do?"

"Go to the stairs when you hang up and look in the vault."

Kate sighed deeply.

". . . Did you hear?"

"Yes, Howard. But there's—"

"You must do this for me," he said sternly. "Next to the cocaine you'll see smaller packages. Last time, I told you not to touch. Today I'm telling the opposite. Inside are electrical devices called krytrons, which come in handy if you are looking to construct a trigger for a medium-size nuclear device—like my friends here are doing. Doing so openly, I might add. They don't care if you or the whole world finds out, so long as they get them. They want these krytrons immediately, not when I planned to bring them with the next shipment of cocaine. They will be delighted to let me free when I . . . when we turn them over. Not one second before."

"I'm afraid I have some awful news," Kate began.

"Tell me some other time. What is happening to me is all the bad news I can take for now. I am asking you to bring these devices I have to Tel Aviv. Tomorrow is not too soon. Do you understand?"

"I can't, Howard. I just can't."

"Do you want me to rot away in this miserable cell?" he screamed at her. It was the first time she had heard him raise his voice and the effect was paralyzing. "Kate," he said more calmly, "You can't imagine what it's like. All these crazy Arabs, the noise. And the food. It isn't even kosher."

"Are you sitting down?" Words were arranging themselves on her tongue, but she hadn't the heart to get them out. Not the way Howard sounded. If she did, that would make two men dead because of her. "Are you?"

"What is it?" he asked.

"I can't come . . ." She stopped. "I mean I can't come right away."

"What is more important than getting me out of here?"

"Nothing," Kate said. "It's . . . uh, you see, it's . . . because I don't have a passport."

Howard exhaled deeply. "You had me scared for a moment. I thought you didn't care enough to be bothered."

"Howard! How can you say such a thing?"

"Prison puts crazy ideas in a man's head sometimes. Even after only two days."

"I can understand."

"Not unless you've been in a place like this," he told her. ". . . So how soon can I tell them you will be here?"

"I'll go to the passport office right away. At this time of year, it shouldn't take long."

"You're the only one who could do this for me. I knew I could count on you."

"Don't mention it," Kate said.

Bucyk stood at the candy display, watching a counterman whip up an egg cream in a glass etched with a Fresca logo. "Not so much milk," he said. "I don't have ulcers, not yet."

The counterman dried his fingers on a linen apron. For thirty-five years he had been talking about selling the luncheonette and getting into a dry business, something where his hands wouldn't be chapped all the time. He pushed the glass across the chipped marble with the seltzer and a spoon. "Make it yourself, you know so much."

Bucyk sucked at the foam as he went to a table at the window. Across Coney Island Avenue was a yellow brick mortuary with a white Star of David under a fading swastika on the awning. Parked at the curb were a black Caddy limo and a stubby gray hearse. It was the smallest, plainest, no doubt highest mpg hearse Bucyk had seen. Without flowers, he thought, it looked stripped. The Jews, even the ones right off the boat, had an attitude they carried all the way to the grave.

Men in dark suits were milling on the sidewalk smoking cigarettes down to the end in the European fashion. One by one they stubbed the tiny butts in a bowl of white sand and filed solemnly inside the building. Bucyk brought his egg cream to the counter for another squirt of chocolate. What was going on across the street was not like a Yankees game, where he could kick himself if he missed the first pitch. He stood at the door thrashing the drink with a spoon. When the seltzer and milk were gone and about two inches of syrup stood at the bottom, he left the glass on the counter and stepped into traffic.

A tray piled with black skullcaps sat on a table in the empty lobby. Bucyk played his hand over the cool silk, then tugged his fedora over his eyes. He picked up a prayer card and studied the Hebrew characters until he noticed phonetic lettering upside down on the opposite page. He inched open the chapel door and saw four men bringing in a plain pine box. A fucking orange crate. An attitude they carried all the way to the grave—and into it.

As the rabbi intoned a blessing, Bucyk slipped inside. He had the last six rows of chairs to himself. About twenty men and women were clustered up front and off to one side three boys not much younger than Nathan, with the same bony cheeks and gray eyes. Kate sat in the second row between two women who looked like she would with another thirty pounds. When she lifted her head from a black book, the big lenses magnified red-rimmed eyes.

Bucyk put an arm over the next two seats. He felt comfortable, buoyant in the drone of prayer. In a way, he thought, this was his party, his and Nathan's. Already he had made peace with his conscience, though he hoped he wouldn't have to do the same for a jury.

The rabbi was middle-aged, with a manicured black beard. He finished with his prayers and addressed the mourners in Russian. Probably telling them that what had happened was God's will. He took off metal-rimmed glasses and put them carefully on the maple lectern, pushed his yarmulke on the back of his head.

"*A klug tzu Columbus,*" he said in Yiddish.

"A curse on Columbus. Shame on America for allowing our beloved Nathan to be taken so senselessly and violently from us."

Bucyk put his hand in his lap and slouched down. He kept his eyes on his shoes till the coffin had been carried out and the mourners were streaming to the door.

Kate went across the aisle to hug a stout woman in a silver wig who was leaning for support on two of the boys. Then she followed the family to the rear of the chapel. As she walked past his row, Bucyk touched her elbow. "Can I talk to you a minute?" he asked.

Kate looked at him as if she didn't recognize the face, and his hand went to his nose and jiggled it. To one of the other women she said, "I'll be right out." She went with Bucyk into a corner. "What are you doing here?" she asked.

"First of all," he said, "I want to extend my, you know, condolences, to you and to the family. I know how much he meant to you."

Kate waved her hands in frustration. "What are you doing here?"

"Still working for you," he told her.

"Now?"

"You always hear about criminals returning to the scene of the crime. Forget it, it hardly happens. What they sometimes do, they go to the funeral. Gives them a sense of accomplishment. I thought it would be nice if I paid my respects and checked for strangers at the same time. You didn't see anyone looks like they don't belong here?"

Kate shook her head.

"I didn't think so."

"Is that all? The car is leaving for the cemetery."

He put a hand on her shoulder and held her there. "I'll try and be quick," he said. "Homicide dicks stopped by last night. From what I get from them, you're not sticking to the story."

Kate's eyes widened. "But I told them everything just the way we discussed it."

"You certain? This is important."

"Shhh." She glanced at the last of the mourners moving into the lobby. "Of course I'm certain."

"These guys are cagier than I gave them credit for." He toyed with the second button on his jacket. "They're trying to turn us on each other."

"The detectives I talked to seemed to believe me. They said I passed the residue test."

"They don't put a lot of currency in that," he told her. "It doesn't prove you weren't wearing gloves. And it doesn't tell them you didn't pay somebody to hit him."

Kate started to say something. Bucyk shook her off. "I know, I know," he said. "But that's the way these guys think."

"Does that mean I can expect more of a hard time?"

"Not if you keep reminding them we were together. Do that, and eventually the idea will penetrate their thick skulls."

"To think they believe I could actually—"

"You didn't tell me yet," he said. "What happened with you and Nicholas?"

One of the heavyset women came back into the chapel. "We're waiting," she said.

"I've got to go now."

"I know this isn't the ideal time to be asking," Bucyk said, "but I have to find out."

Kate looked at the other woman. "Hold the car," she said. When they were alone again she told Bucyk, "*Nothing* happened. Okay?"

"Fine by me." He took his hand away and Kate went quickly into the lobby. "Fine by Nicholas, too. At least that's what we're hearing from his friends. Whatever it is you're putting out, the guy can't get enough. He wants to see you again."

Kate stopped and turned around. She took off her glasses and squinted at him. "I really don't want to talk about it now, Detective."

He stood at the door, watching her slide into the limousine. "Don't call us . . ."

SHE PINCHED the metal teeth together, tugging at the tab. A stitch popped and she pulled the black dress over her head and stepped out from under it. She hated that dress, her funeral dress, snatched off the bargain rack while her father lay dying in a Caledonian Hospital cancer ward. She toed the dark puddle of cloth, then bent down and fit it on a hanger. In a couple of hours she'd want the dress again. Infante had asked to see her at the Knights and she was looking forward to it like another funeral—her own.

She sagged against the bed and forced her eyes shut. Though she had been up for most of two nights, she was too edgy to relax. After a while she gave up trying and toyed with the venetian blind, guiding a block of shadow over the pillow. She reached for the clock and she was amazed to see that it was already after three o'clock. Impossible, but she must have been out for close to ninety minutes. She felt more used up than before.

She found Infante filling an ashtray at a booth near the kitchen. He was a pear-shaped man in his early forties with shadowy crevices like dotted lines in his hollow cheeks. "I was beginning to think I'd been stood up," he said. His sloppy frown repulsed her.

"I was at the cemetery." She kept her chair pushed away from the table. "What did you want to talk about? Is there anything new on the investigation?" she asked, knowing she was the last person he would tell.

Infante placed his hands on the table palms up, as if he was showing all his cards and none were aces.

"What, then?" She was trying to sound annoyed, not having to work at it.

"I've been running down your story," he said, "and there's parts that don't hang together. Frankly . . ." He scraped the torn edge of a fingernail along a furrow extending from the point of his cheekbone to his chin, rooting at a cluster of stubby hairs. "What you gave us is a load of crap, if you don't mind my saying so."

Kate moved her chair back another few inches. "You're entitled to your opinion, I suppose."

He focused between her eyes, trying to unsettle her. "That's all you've got to say?"

A broom handle slapped against the dance floor and Kate started. She saw the afternoon porter pounce on a dime and three pennies like they were gold nuggets. As he scrambled for more treasure on his hands and knees, it occurred to her that she had forgotten to book a dancer for the weekend and she made a note to give the musicians the time off with pay. No way she was going to pinch-hit again, feeling the way she did.

"Am I boring you?" Infante was asking. "Because if I am, you're in for plenty of excitement before you know it. Homicide's all for locking you up till they get what they want out of you." He paused again and his face softened. "It wouldn't hurt if you leveled with one cop, put him on your side."

It was either a come-on or a trap, and each possibility was as appealing as the other. She didn't trust him in spite of his concern, or perhaps because of it. "I have a cop on my side," she said. "I have him all over me."

A waiter was setting tables along the wall near the windows and she got his attention and mouthed the word *seltzer.* "Why are you so worried about my welfare?" she asked Infante. "Last winter, you couldn't wait to put me in jail."

"Every girl who airs it out on Times Square ought to

have the pleasure. The smart ones might take the hint and go back home to mom."

"Please don't do me any more favors," Kate said.

"This is murder two we're talking about. If we have to lock you up again, it'll be as a material witness or even accessory, till something better comes along. If I was you, I'd be stockpiling favors. All they cost is the truth." He took a fresh pack of Camels from his jacket. "You could start by telling me where you were the other night."

"How many times do I have to repeat it? Stan's been very good to me since the burglary and he asked me out to Jersey to eat."

"There's not enough restaurants in New York?"

Kate shrugged. "There's a place he likes, it's his favorite."

"He never mentioned it. What's it called?"

"I forget . . . a fish house."

Infante used a brief silence to arch his eyebrows.

"And after, it was getting late and . . . well, we couldn't go to the brownstone because I'd asked Nathan to stay there in case there was trouble again."

"Why didn't Bucyk invite you to his apartment?"

"He says it's a pigsty."

"That's the first honest statement you've made."

Kate looked at him unpleasantly until he said, "Go on."

"And then we drove around till we had a silly argument and I asked him to bring me home."

"But you were going to spend the night with him?"

"I don't see where that's any of your—"

"You have a mirror handy?" Infante asked.

"What?"

"A mirror, you know."

"I don't think so, why?"

"You ought to see your face," he told her. "You look like you're going to retch, thinking about it."

Her hand went automatically to her mouth. She caught herself and ran her fingers through her hair. "Do I?" she asked coldly.

"Out of the question you'd let him get close to you, not if he didn't have a gun to your head."

"So he had a gun."

Infante said, "You're a terrible liar, about the worst I've heard. Don't you practice?"

"It wouldn't be that you're the least little bit jealous of Stan, would it?"

Infante's face didn't change, but his voice did. "What's he got that I want?" he asked quickly. "You, you think? Don't flatter yourself. He doesn't have anything."

"Because you're still stuck in a West Side station house, cuing up chest pains for early retirement while Stan is doing important work for the FBI."

Infante grinned as though his face was going to tear along the dotted lines. "Is that what he told you? That's worse than the crap you're handing us."

Kate sat rigidly, showing nothing.

Infante began laughing. He laughed so hard that he began to cough, and Kate thought it was an act till the waiter brought her seltzer and Infante emptied the glass before he could gasp out another word.

"I don't see what's so funny," Kate said. Her stomach felt queasy.

"You are, you and Bucyk both. He told me, the night he ran you in from the Starlight, he said, 'Paul, you got to see her. And brains as big as her melons. Brains,' he said. A lot he knows, you can't see through a guy like that." Infante was laughing again. "Stash Bucyk a federal agent?"

"I didn't say he was an agent," Kate told him, the queasiness intensifying as it spread through her body. "He's a . . . like a consultant. He does jobs the FBI wouldn't normally assign its regular agents."

"I'll bet," Infante laughed, and Kate thought he was

going to start choking again. Instead he asked, "That's what he told you? Why, what's he up to?"

"I . . . I'm not at liberty to tell you," she said stiffly.

Infante's eyebrows arched higher. "Would you be more inclined to if I told you the FBI never has and never will have anything to do with a Stash Bucyk, the exception being if they haul him in on a federal rap?" He tore the cellophane from the Camels and crumpled it into a clean ashtray from another table. Then he nudged the pack just out of reach and glared at it like it was the enemy.

Kate was looking at Infante with the same icy stare. "Is that why you were so secretive when I tried to reach him after the burglary?"

"What I was doing was trying to save face for the poor slob and maybe keep him out of more trouble. In case he didn't mention it, Bucyk was cashiered out of the department last spring. He's such a greedy bastard, he was even an embarrassment to the men he was collecting for. You didn't see him at your restaurant every month with his hand out, the one you grease so it doesn't ticket all the cars on the block, so he doesn't chase your customers away?"

"Here? He was squeezing Howard?"

"More like a bear hug."

She didn't want to hear more. Why didn't he cadge a meal and stuff his face, or just go away? "That's your problem, then," she said unconvincingly. "He wasn't stealing for me."

"It's not the issue. If a few bills have to change hands so the precinct doesn't come down with writer's cramp, who's being hurt? The Broadway Merchants Association isn't squawking." He brought out a disposable lighter and arranged it on the table beside the cigarettes. "With Bucyk, though, the pad came first. Police work was just a sideline till he figured why not sell out altogether. It almost brought the whole West Side down."

"I didn't see anything on the news."

"Damn right, you didn't. Another major scandal hits the

NYPD and the vultures'll have the commissioner's heart on a platter. There was an internal affairs investigation and the only ones holding their breath were every cop this side of the park."

"If everyone looks the other way, why bother about Stan? You're contradicting yourself."

"He went too far. He bent over for a big-time drug dealer from Queens, a disbarred international lawyer with his finger in lots of pies, and torpedoed six months' work by the DEA and the narcotics task force. If the brass wasn't so worried about covering their hide, he'd be doing hard time. Instead they whacked him on the knuckles and now I hear he's henching full time for this guy."

"In Queens?" Kate asked, as if those were the only words she heard. "The pusher is in Queens?"

"He's wherever you find noses," Infante said, "but Queens is where he lives, in an exclusive neighborhood called Forest Gardens, though you have to wonder how exclusive if they let in scum like that."

"I don't believe anything you're saying." She was kidding herself, not fooling either of them. "You just want to turn me against Stan."

Infante reached for the cigarettes, but pulled his hand back. "It'd be a waste of time putting in a bad word for Bucyk when it's the thing he does best himself."

The bottom had dropped out of Kate's stomach, the feeling more unsettling than anything she had experienced on the Typhoon. "You're lying," she said without conviction. "You're lying or you're wrong, about everything. Stan knows someone there, but he's no drug pusher, he's in the import-export business."

Infante smiled condescendingly. "Same thing, isn't it?"

"Not at all." Her voice was rising, breaking against the steely edge of his sarcasm. "He's Russian. He trades in artifacts from the Soviet Union."

"What would someone like that want with Bucyk?"

"He's not just in antiques. He's a . . ."

"Yes?"

"Never mind," Kate said, and stopped to regroup. "What I told you about Stan and me, is that so impossible to believe?"

"It wouldn't be—if a man wasn't dead and you weren't in deep trouble."

"I'm sorry," she said, "but it's the best I can do."

"I'm sorry, too. Sorry for you, what's going to happen."

Kate's eyes flickered and Infante thought she was going to say something. But then she looked away and the moment was lost.

"I guess there's nothing more." He scooped up the unopened Camels and stuffed them in his pocket. "Trying to give up the coffin nails," he told her self-consciously, eyeing the full ashtray. "Life's too short to be your own worst enemy."

"Save it," Kate said. "For all the good it will do."

She saw him to the door. A thunder squall trapped him under the awning and he turned up his collar and dashed toward a gray Dodge at a meter. Watching him go, she regretted not getting more out of him. But as it was there was too much for her to sort out by herself. She went to the office and rang Bucyk's number, hanging up on the recording without leaving a message, then rummaged through the closet which doubled as the Knights' lost and found.

She hurried outside under a rice-paper parasol wishing someone had left a raincoat her size instead. Broadway was a river of off-duty cabs dammed at a red light. She jabbed the parasol at the wind and pushed toward the subway arcade on the Seventy-second Street traffic island. A couple of winos were sprawled on the first dry stair. She shut her ears as she stepped smartly over their outstretched legs.

She waited twenty minutes for a local and took it two stops to Columbus Circle. Under clearing skies she thought the city looked dingier than it had before the rain, as though the grime had been washed away to reveal underlying decay. She walked east on Fifty-seventh Street homing in on a gray tower that looked down on Carnegie Hall. The art gallery was closed, large sheets of brown paper taped over the glass doors. She tapped her ring on the glass and a blond girl stuck her head out and said, "The opening is on Saturday."

Kate put her foot in the door. "I'd like some information about the last show you had."

"The Condoli? I'm afraid it's already been taken down."

"No, the Russian icons."

The door opened wider and Kate caught a spoor of fine French perfume tainted with nail-polish remover. "The gallery is closed to the public until the weekend, while we're hanging," the blonde said.

"It might be too late then."

The blonde understood, or thought she did. "Are you representing a foreign buyer?"

Because it was the first thing to come to mind, Kate said, "I'm not at liberty to tell you."

The key to the city. "No problem," the blonde said. She stood aside, nodding toward an elephant's foot on the floor and Kate grimaced and dropped the wet parasol inside.

The front room was awash in gray light entering through floor-to-ceiling windows. Brawny women were moving large canvases around the walls under the direction of a barefoot girl in a man's suit with padded shoulders. A frustrated symphony conductor, Kate decided, watching her darting hands.

"The icons will be on exhibit till the end of the month," the blonde said as they walked into the rear gallery. "Is there anything in particular that you're interested in?"

"The man who put them up for sale," Kate told her. "If you can tell me where I can reach him . . ."

"We're his authorized agent. He demands anonymity."

That sounded like Nicholas. Maybe Infante *was* toying

with her. "You mean, because of all the trouble he has in getting them out of the USSR?"

"It's not our business why," the blonde said, examining her nails. "If he doesn't want his name—"

"Marissa?" someone called from the office.

"Excuse me," she said and went out of the gallery.

Kate heard her in conversation with a man with a husky voice. She strained to catch a few words, but someone in the other gallery had begun hammering. Then the blonde stepped out of the office and said, "Come with me, please. He's here now. And he'll see you."

"Who will?"

A man with glossy black hair was leafing through an art catalogue with his back to her. Looking over his shoulder was a stern figure in the dark cassock of a Russian Orthodox priest.

"Miss . . . ?" the blond girl said.

"Shapiro."

"Miss Shapiro," she said, and both men turned around. "This is Metropolitan Nikodim, who brought these beautiful icons from basilicas in Belgorod-Dnestrovsky."

The man with the glossy hair was about twenty-five, with a soup strainer mustache hiding a harelip. He turned another page as the cleric smiled and clasped Kate's hand. "You are admirer of holy art? What may I help?"

"Oh," Kate said softly and pulled back her hand. "Oh, shit."

There was a phone booth in the lobby and it took two quarters to find out that it wasn't working. There was another near a bus stop at the corner. Above the drone of seven-mile-an-hour crosstown traffic Kate listened for a dial tone and tried Bucyk's number once more.

"Yeah?"

"We have to talk," she said firmly. "Where can we get together?"

"Who's this . . . ? It's you? What's up?"

"I need to see you."

"That's not such a hot idea," he said. "It doesn't look good . . ."

A bus pulled toward the curb, the engine winding down through a faulty muffler. Kate slapped a hand over her other ear. "What, I didn't hear?"

"I said let's do our talking on the phone. What's so important, anyway?"

"You lied to me."

"About what?"

"About everything, damn it."

"You've been talking to the dicks again." He kept his voice low, but with a sharpness to it, as though he was reprimanding a prize pupil who had failed a simple test. "They're putting ideas in your head?"

"Opening my eyes is more like it," she said. "I must have been blind. You're not working for the FBI any more than . . . than I am. You weren't even a good cop. They said you were taking payoffs all over the West Side."

"That's it? That's the worst they could say about me? Since when's that a crime? Did you ask them that?"

She didn't want to get into it; the illogic was on his side. "I found out on my own. I just came from the art gallery. No one there has ever heard of your Mike Nicholas, or Mikhail Kunavin."

"You don't think he uses his real name?"

"Enough, already," she screamed above the traffic. "How stupid do you think I am?"

Bucyk's tone changed to something close to pity. "I've got to wonder," he said, "the way you're letting them jerk you around, cutting your own throat. I warned you this would happen."

"The only one who's manipulating me, who *was*, is you. If you don't tell me what you're up to, I'm going to the detectives with everything I know."

"You do that," Bucyk said. "Tell them you were with

Nicholas and I'll be glad to back you up. See where that gets you—but don't be surprised if it's Bedford Hills."

"Where?"

"In the tony part of Westchester, a country club for bright ladies like yourself, with inch-thick grillwork on the windows. But what do I know, maybe you'd like it there?" He paused to laugh to himself. "There's things I haven't been entirely up-front about. I admit it. But these are secrets you don't want to have to keep. Trust me a little longer and you'll find out everything, then make up your mind who your friends are."

"I don't trust you now," she said.

"Well, that's your problem."

"No, it's—"

Then a voice she didn't recognize at first, an androgynous monotone, was reciting, "Please deposit five cents more for the next five minutes or your call will be . . ."

"Hang on," Kate said, fumbling in her purse for more change. "Shit, all I have is a half-dollar and some pennies."

"We talked enough already."

"Call me back," she demanded. "Two-five-four . . ."

The recording came on again, and then silence, and Kate backed out of the booth into driving rain. She peered up at a heavy sky convinced that hovering overhead was a dark cloud with her name on it. Bucyk had seen right through her bluff. The thing she had to do was to call his by going to the police. Only what was she going to tell them? That her boyfriend had been murdered at her place while she was out on the town with a Soviet spy who was actually a cocaine dealer? That a burglar and a crooked cop and an Israeli agent had been drawn to her like bees to honey? More like flies to shit, they'd say, and throw away the key. The only decision left was whether to laugh or to cry out loud, but a beat cop glaring from the shelter of a storefront chased the beginnings of a smile from her lips. In other cities she had heard that padded cells were reserved for unfortunates found weeping on the sidewalks. In New York, for reasons she was only starting to understand, it was the laughers who had to be out of their minds.

She turned uptown on Broadway measuring the slick streets with long strides. Her shoes were squishing against the pavement by the time she came to Seventy-sixth and she ran down the block with her key already in her fist. Mounting the stoop she noticed a glow in an upstairs bedroom. With everything else on her mind, she must have forgotten to turn out the lights. She'd forget her dress, if she wasn't locked into it.

As she slid the bolt behind her, she thought she heard light footsteps on the stairs, but decided it was the pounding of her heart. Jesus, how she still felt jumpy each time she came back to the house! The sound was too soft to be footsteps, more like water dripping onto a carpeted floor. She tried not to think of what else she could have forgotten.

She walked out of her shoes and pulled the black dress over her head and looked up broken stairs to a landing where a large white dog stood poised with a rawhide bone in its jaws. Kate's breath came quickly in deep gulps and the more of them she took the less good they seemed to do. The animal barked twice and bounded toward her, his long tail slapping like a metronome gone haywire. In his place on the landing was a bearded man whose right arm was wrapped in a sling.

"Long time no see," the man said.

Kate felt the doorknob press into her back. Her knees buckled and the cold metal traveled the length of her spine. It collided with the base of her skull and she slumped unconscious to the floor.

She rolled onto her side and tucked the blanket under her chin, relieved to be safe in bed. It was another of her crazy nightmares, the most vivid ever. The pain in the back of her head was real, though, and she explored for its source with her fingers. An inch above the hairline they stumbled over a swelling that was agony to touch.

"Yeah, you took a good one."

Her heart began hammering again as she opened her eyes. She was in Howard's room wondering how she got there. Sprawled at her feet as if he had never been gone was Isaac Grynzpun, chewing on his rawhide. She sensed motion behind her, but more pain in her head was too high a price to investigate it.

"Lay still. Anything you need, ask."

She saw him as he came around the bed looking rattier than she remembered in a rain-spattered field jacket. The dizziness returned and she thought she was going to black out, but she fought off the feeling with short breaths.

"You look like you seen a ghost," he smirked. "No ghosts here, huh Isaac?"

Kate tried raising herself on an elbow. "What do you want? Haven't you done enough already?"

"Let's begin with what I *don't* want, which is your dog," Harry said.

Kate glared at Isaac as though he had joined a conspiracy against her. She patted her scalp and checked her hand for blood. "What happened to my head?"

"Not my department. You were so happy to see Isaac here, you fainted. You hit the door on the way down."

Kate was trying to appear in command, not having much success. She studied his face, but what he had in mind for her was hidden behind his beard. It had come in fuller, so that the thin spots which remained seemed white and shiny and heightened the moth-eaten effect. "Will you go now?" she asked.

"That's all you got to say? Isn't there something you're forgetting?"

"What else could I possibly have to tell *you*?"

"Thank you," Harry said. "Thank you for returning my dog and for putting me in bed after I knocked myself out like such a jerk."

"Just go."

"If that's the way you feel . . ." He backed off from the bed, but stopped after two steps. "Soon as I get what I came for."

Kate turned away but kept an eye on him, like she did to the creeps who never failed to find her in a crowded subway.

"You remember," Harry was saying, "what brought me here in the first place."

"You have everything. What more do you want?" She saw him looking at her curiously and clutched the blanket around her shoulders.

Harry said, "I got here ten minutes ahead of you. I didn't get a chance to start looking."

"The night you shot Nathan."

"The f— . . . What?" He took a quick step back, as if he had been thrown off balance. "It must've slipped my mind," he said. "Who's Nathan?"

Kate cursed and rolled onto her other side. Harry grabbed her arm and put her on her back. She swatted at him, and as he twisted away with a startled laugh she skinned her knuckles on the hard cast.

"God damn it," she cried.

Harry clamped her wrist in his hand and stuffed it under the covers. Then he sat on her legs. "Who?" he asked when she had stopped struggling.

"He was my boyfriend."

"He got shot? When did this happen, two nights ago? That why everything's so neat downstairs?"

"Do I have to tell you?"

"No," Harry said. "Not really."

"I'm glad he broke your arm. I wish it had been your head."

Harry used his good hand to maneuver the cast tenderly onto his lap. "It wasn't any Nathan that did this."

"You can't deny it. The house was torn apart just like the other time . . . Nathan got you good before you . . ."

"Yeah, I came by," Harry admitted, "but the block was crawling with cops." He slid off her legs and sat beside her on the edge of the mattress. "The closest I got was across the street."

Kate tried to edge away, but Harry tugged at the blanket, holding her there. "I wouldn't believe anything you said," she told him.

"Same here. Where's the dough?"

"How many times must I tell you? You have it all."

"Then what the hell you think I came back for?"

You're here to rape me and then shoot me like Nathan, Kate wanted to say, to make sure you didn't leave anything that isn't nailed down. You're here because you're thoroughly demented, a maniac. She said nothing.

"You sure you never fell on your head before?" Harry was saying.

Humor him like the other time, Kate thought. Play to his vanity and his pretense of innocence. "If you didn't shoot Nathan, who did?"

"Lot of guys break inside houses and some of the amateurs carry loaded guns. They don't all report to me."

"But why here?"

Harry threw up his good hand in disgust. "We been through it a million times. A guy has a brownstone, a restaurant on Broadway, you got to figure he has some bucks on hand."

"It was more than *some* money," Kate said. "How did you find out?"

"To be honest," Harry began, and Kate looked at him sharply until his eyes backed hers down, "I heard a camel jockey talkin' about it once in a place I used to live."

"What jockey? What place?"

"It isn't important."

"It is to me."

"A place you never heard of called the Duffy-Lawes Residence on West Ninety-sixth Street, which is sort of a sleep-away camp for us unfortunates that are society's victims and vice-versa."

"Like other burglars, you mean?"

"The beginners, yes. The point is that I was there learnin' all about good grooming and such job-market skills when one of the other antisocial elements brought up Ormont, and how he was beatin' the IRS for a nice piece of change and rollin' it over into cocaine, which from time to time is something I'm also interested in."

"And he was a jockey?"

"A towelhead," Harry said. "An Arab. An Ali somebody."

"What else did he mention was in the safe?"

"The dough, the coke, it's enough for me. I'm not a greedy bastard."

"He didn't say anything about kry . . . about electronic devices?"

"He did, it didn't register. I'm not a TV repairman either." Harry reached down to stroke Isaac's head affectionately. "Now you tell me something."

"What?" Kate asked.

"Everything—and from the start."

12

"WHAT I can't get through this thick skull of mine is how if Ormont's such an operator, the whole world knows what's inside his vault. There's the towelhead—"

"Ali was Howard's partner," Kate said. She was sitting in the Barcalounger, still wrapped in her blanket, watching Harry squirm agoraphobically on the big double bed. "Howard pressed charges against him when he found out he was being swindled."

"And then there's me. And the guy who killed your boyfriend."

"That's not so many. Only two."

"No," Harry said patiently. "You're a little slow catching on, but that makes three. Who else would know?"

Kate gestured with hands spread apart. "Howard is very private. He kept me in the dark about so many things, the first I heard about the vault was from you. I thought you were out of your mind."

Harry stopped squirming. "Now what do you think?"

"He should have told me."

Harry took an unsharpened pencil from his pocket and dug under the cast urgently. "There's always the chance it was some jerk with a gun who lucked into the job. Only I don't believe in that kind of coincidence, not till I'm the party who makes out." It was still a contest between them, but with the money gone he wasn't trying for a quick knockout. The trick was to go the distance until she hadn't the strength to be hostile. ". . . Or Ormont's bookkeeper. He'd have an idea, at least."

"Keep dreaming," Kate said.

"Am I? How about the guy who sold him the coke?"

"You'd know more about that kind of person than I would. Anyway, Howard didn't say where he got it."

"Which brings us back to the leading suspect."

"Who's that?"

"You," Harry said. "Where were you the other night?"

Kate's jaw firmed. "I won't even respond to that."

Harry poked Isaac Grynzpun with his toe and the big dog scampered to the floor. "That won't do. I'm no cop, I never heard of your right to remain silent." Then Harry walked over to the Barcalounger projecting a sullen threat through the dark beard. "Starting now, the shoe's on the other foot," he said. "Answer the question."

"Homer might have known," Kate went on in a little girl's singsong. "Only Homer wouldn't have done such a thing."

"The fucking question," Harry said, "is where you were—"

"If you must know, I was on a date with a Russian spy. The FBI put me up to it." She giggled drunkenly. "Except it wasn't the FBI. It wasn't even a spy, just a crooked cop."

"Who, the Russian? What is all this shit?"

"The FBI man. He was working for the Russian. But the Russian is really a . . . a . . . Oh, my God," she cried. She got out of the Barcalounger holding her head at an angle as if she had a stiff neck, and plucked at a box of tissues on the nightstand. "I did it. I must have been blind . . ."

"This ain't Perry Mason," Harry said. "Start making sense."

"I killed Nathan," she sobbed, and staggered against the bed.

"Let's hear it from the top," Harry said. He had taken her place on the Barcalounger while she sat back in bed again with Isaac at her feet. Crumpled puffs of Kleenex lay scattered on the mattress like shriveled snowballs.

"Go away."

Harry said, "I'm tryin' to be friends."

"I have all the friends I need."

"Friends like those . . ."

"Just go." She reached for another tissue and blew her nose.

"You have to lay it off on somebody," Harry said. When she didn't tell him to go away again, he added, "It'll eat you up inside."

Kate wiped her nose and then cried some more and then she asked, "Did you ever hear of a cocaine dealer who calls himself Mike Nicholas?"

She said the name distastefully, so that Harry had to guess if it was the sound of it or having to ask him that rubbed her the wrong way. "Tell me more," he said.

"We went out just that one time. He wined me and dined me and then he brought me back to his mansion in Queens and—"

"You can leave the next part out," Harry said.

"And nothing happened. I went home and haven't heard from him since."

"He let you walk out the door, didn't slap you around or nothing first?"

"He insisted I take money for cab fare," Kate said.

"That doesn't sound like any dealer I know."

"What does it sound like?"

Harry was in no hurry to answer. Kate turned toward him anxiously, annoyed at the interruption. She welcomed his questions and was debating whether to ask if they came to him so easily because he'd had experience answering the same kind from the police.

"Like somebody who got turned off in a hurry," he told her after some thought. "Or who wasn't real hot to trot in the first place, you don't mind my suggesting it could be possible."

"In this case, I rather like the idea."

"Or somebody who wanted you out of the house for a few hours, say long enough to steal back his coke and whatever else he knew was in the safe."

"He was with me all evening."

"Not his line of work. He'd bring in a pro, somebody like me," Harry said.

"Are you saying that he did?"

"You got a one-track mind, know that?"

"There's something else . . . the policeman I was telling you about, it turned out he was working for Nicholas."

"You enjoy lettin' men dump all over you?" Harry said. "Or you just hate yourself in general?"

"Don't think I haven't spent hours thinking about it. But what it is, it's just rotten luck."

That was everyone's out, he wanted to tell her, everyone in the joint. Bring it up in group and even the shrink would have to laugh. No wonder the Mr. Rights were taking numbers to run her life. Well, he thought, at least the line was moving fast.

"Do I have the whole story now?" he asked. "What about those electric parts?"

"That's nothing."

"Must be, the way you drop the subject whenever it comes up."

"Let's drop it again."

Harry opened his hands and their eyes followed an imaginary object on a collision course with the floor. "What are you gonna do now?" he asked.

"Do I have a choice? I'll tell the detectives everything."

"You understand the kind of person you're droppin' a dime on? The odds are you're fish food before the DA can whip up a grand jury to hear you. Got any better ideas?"

What dime? Kate wanted to ask. What fish? But he was talking too excitedly for her to get a word in.

"I got one," he said, and Kate experienced a moment of reassurance until he added, "Let's do dinner tonight. I know a great little place in Chinatown, take your mind off your troubles."

"I have one that's even better," she said, smoothing the blanket with the side of her hand.

"Yeah?"

"Leave now, and I'll wait fifteen minutes before I call the police."

"That's gratitude? Here I been racking my brains for a way out of this pickle you got yourself in and you can't wait to give me the bum's rush."

"If you want to help, you'll go. Please," she said. "I have to think."

Harry stood up and zipped his jacket. He went over to the bed and Kate retreated to the edge of the mattress. "Well, Isaac," he said, and scratched the big dog's ears, "it's been a pleasure. You too, in a way," he told Kate, offering his other hand.

Kate hesitated, then squeezed his fingers where they protruded from the cast. "They're cold," she said. "What happened, were you robbing someone else's house?"

"This kid," Harry began uncomfortably, and then stopped. "These three kids were after my stash." He liked that better and gave her a little more. "Big kids, with baseball bats. I look worse for wear, just remember who took the decision."

"Are you good at that?" Kate wanted to know. "At beating people up?"

A muscle groupie, Harry was thinking, and opened his jacket again. "I can handle myself, the need arises. You should see me with two hands sometime."

"I doubt that," Kate said. "You're not very big at all."

"Dirty, though."

Kate didn't laugh. To Harry it looked as if she was taking notes. "I'm serious," she said. "Are you fast on your feet?"

"The footwork's so-so. What I got is a good left and a concrete jaw."

"I mean can you run?"

"Like a thief."

"And you have lots of experience?"

"In the amateurs," Harry lied. "I was thirteen and—"

"You're missing the point," Kate said in exasperation. "I'm trying to find out if you're a better housebreaker than you've shown so far."

"You kiddin'? It's a racket I know inside and out."

"One more thing." She inhaled deeply. "It occurred to me that maybe you'd be willing to do a job for me . . . uh, contract work."

A smile crossed Harry's face—darkened it, Kate thought. "Doin' what?" he asked. Then the smile was gone and he was saying, "I keep tellin' you I'm a burglar, not a hit man."

"I understand. I'm looking for a burglar . . . I think."

"Could've fooled me," Harry said, and sat down beside her on the bed.

"It's really very simple."

"Yes, that's true," Harry said. "I go out there, break in, and they shoot me dead on the spot."

"You say you're a professional. Why should this job be harder than any other?"

"Easy for you to say."

It was, Kate thought, surprised that he didn't bite. And so was this: "What are you afraid of?"

"You're forgettin' something, aren't you? They already killed somebody."

"Bucyk did," Kate said. "Nicholas was with me all evening. Anyway, he wouldn't dirty his hands."

"A major supplier," Harry said with a shudder. "The place is probably like a fort, cocaine cowboys with machine guns on the roof."

"I've been inside and there are no bodyguards, if that's

what's worrying you. He lives alone. And if he keeps any weapons, I didn't see them. There's just him," she said coyly, "and a house full of expensive antiques."

"Is that supposed to get me all hot and bothered? Antiques are not my line. You have to fence 'em for like twenty percent of what they're worth. The IRS gives John Q. Public a fairer shake than that."

"What *is* your line?"

"Coke's one of 'em," Harry admitted. "But it seems we have a conflict of interest there."

"I just need a little. What I'd really like to get my hands on are the electric parts."

"The ones you aren't interested in?"

"Those," she said. "Antiques, the money, the rest of the cocaine, whatever else you find, you can keep most of."

Harry poked a finger inside the cast and withdrew it quickly. He took the pencil from his pocket again and worked it under the plaster. "What if the electric stuff's not there?"

"Clean him out," Kate said bitterly. "Even if I don't get what I want, you should do very nicely for one day's work. The house is like a gold mine."

"I gotta think about it. I need to look at the setup, factor in the potential for profit against the odds I'm gonna get whacked out or go to the joint. This is not the kind of thing you want to make a spur-of-the-moment decision."

"When can you let me know?"

"Soon." He jabbed the pencil all the way in and left it there. "Meantime, since you're not hungry, you feel like goin' for a ride, kill a couple hours?"

"We buried Nathan today. I'm really not in the mood for—"

"A drive out to Queens?"

"Me?" Kate asked. "I mean, *me?*"

"You want I should die alone?"

"But what do I know about housebreaking?"

"More'n you let on. The rest, what it takes is on-the-job training."

Kate said, "I'll just be in the way."

"For cryin' out loud, we're not goin' in. All I want is for you to keep me company while I check out the place."

"How about taking Isaac?" she asked. "At least he can give you some protection."

Harry pulled out the pencil with satisfied smile. ". . . That, and somebody gotta show me the way."

"Oh," Kate said. "I hadn't thought of it."

"Lot of things you hadn't thought about. It's what worries me."

"Do we have a deal, then?" she asked.

Harry offered his hand again and Kate was surprised at how warm the fingers felt. "Great," she said. "There's just one more thing. I've never done anything like this before. What do I wear?"

Harry considered it with his eyes closed. "Your black dress," he said. "It goes with the job."

"Before we get there," Harry said, "you should call the house and make sure he isn't in. I don't want him lookin' out the window and seein' us lookin' back."

Kate pushed herself away from the mirror where she was applying her makeup. "Can you bring me the dress now? I hope it's dry."

Harry went out of the bedroom. When he came back, Kate was sitting on the edge of the bed with the phone in her lap, slapping the earpiece against the heel of her hand. "The line is dead," she told him.

"*Hey,*" he said, and tossed the dress at her. "Not now. You call when we get to Queens, when we're a couple of minutes from the house."

"I don't understand," she said. "It was just working . . ."

"You got to make the call there," he said, not looking at her, hurrying out of the room again.

Kate said, "I'll walk around the corner with you. It's quicker that way."

"I said wait right here."

"I can't see why. What are you trying to hide?"

"Don't see," Harry said. "Just wait."

He ran to Amsterdam, where he had left the green Cutlass in front of a church. He hot-wired it with a practiced hand and then circled the block, half-expecting her to be gone. As he came up to the brownstone she stepped off the curb and he set the parking brake and got out to open the door for her. "Our first date," he leered, "and we're goin' all the way."

He shifted into drive, touched the gas, and just as quickly tromped down on the brake. Kate braced herself against the dashboard. "What's wrong?" she asked.

"Remind me to pick up some batteries when we get out there. This is important."

"If I remember—"

"Don't give me any ifs," he said, putting the car in motion again. "And now that we're partners, I got a name in case you didn't know."

"Are you sure you can trust me with such a big secret?"

"I'm not tellin' you anything you wouldn't find out sooner or later," he said. "I saw you eyeballin' my license plate. Anybody ever tell you you move your lips when you read? Call me Harry."

"Harry what?"

A small boy on a bicycle pulling a younger child on a skateboard darted across the street from between parked cars and Kate yelled, "Look out!"

"Look out, *Harry*," he said, swerving easily around them. ". . . Just Harry."

He dropped down to Fifty-ninth Street, then cut across to the Queensboro Bridge, followed Queens Boulevard all the way out to Forest Hills. At Yellowstone Boulevard he pulled up to an appliance shop and turned to look at her. "Something you're forgettin'," he said.

"I didn't forget. But if you're not breaking in tonight, why do you need flashlight batteries?"

"They're not for a flashlight. What we want are 10.8-volt nickel-cadmium battery packs, got it?"

He was ducking beneath the lid of the trunk when she carried a small bag onto the street, watched him empty a cardboard box that might have been looted from the store she had just left. "What *is* all that stuff?" she asked.

Harry sorted through a collection of plastic objects that reminded her of TV remote controls. "This," he said, showing her a small radio with a stubby antenna, "is the finest portable police scanner ever hocked. A Motorola HT220. It just about lets us hear inside the cops' heads, there's anything goin' on there."

"Why should we care what they're thinking? We're not doing anything illegal . . . today."

"Some concerned citizen sics 'em on us, it'd be good if we were among the first to know. Which reminds me, it's time to make your call. There should be a pay phone in that drugstore there. Try him, then give him five minutes to get out of the craphouse and try him again. Someone answers, hang up. They don't, put the receiver down without breakin' the connection."

She went into the pharmacy reaching inside her purse for Nicholas's number. Through a window display of roach killers and calcium supplements she could see Harry bent over the trunk. He tucked a few items under his arm and brought them to the front seat, then walked back and slammed the lid. Working with just the one hand, his motions were deliberate and clumsy and seemed to require more effort than they were worth. No, she told herself, he was not her first choice in burglars. But where was she going to find anyone else crazy enough to help her? After ten rings she hung up and began watching the clock above the prescription counter. Seven minutes later, when she came back to the car, Harry was waiting behind the wheel.

"No one's home," she said.

"Let's put a move on and get it over with. The only thing worse than havin' him see us from the window is he drives up while we're still snoopin' around."

Kate slid onto the seat and her thigh collided with some of the radio gear. "Are these police scanners too?" she asked. "Why do we need so many?"

"They're walkie-talkies," Harry said as the Cutlass crept from the curb. "Top-of-the-line Maxon FM UHF CPO520s with mini-resonators and four-channel capability. I had 'em customized, put in my own crystals so we got a wide, secure band."

"That's nice," Kate said.

"What I'm sayin' is I had 'em fixed so the hams and CB operators who monitor the usual frequencies can't listen in on us." He pulled up to a red light at Continental Avenue and Kate indicated a right turn. "I'm not as dumb as I look."

"It's a load off—ouch," she screamed. "My ear. Put your hand back on the wheel."

He drove under the trestle without being told and they came into Forest Gardens. Some of the fragile English veneer had worn off against the dusk and the gritty sameness of Queens was closing in on all sides. Kate said she didn't remember the way and Harry slapped his forehead and they cruised the spiral grid for ten minutes before she pointed to a large house behind a stone wall. The driveway was empty.

Harry whistled between his teeth. "Where's the drawbridge?"

"It is impressive the first time you see it."

He drove around the block and parked a third of the way down the next street with the engine running. "There's no lights on," he said. "I'm goin' over and see if I can hear the phone. I do, no one's home." He switched on the scanner and leaned it upright against the seat between them. "You keep one ear on this all the time. You hear a call for anywhere in Forest Gardens, what you do is . . ." He installed batteries in both walkie-talkies, put one in her lap and hooked the other onto his belt. "You talk in here and let me know about it."

"Here?" she asked, tapping her nail against the raised plastic beneath the stubby antenna.

"Uh-huh. Couple of other things you should know, too. Number one, you don't kill the engine for any reason, no matter what. Got that?"

Kate nodded.

"The other is, stay inside the car. It's dark now and the streets are pretty deserted, but we don't want to take the chance on someone comin' along and gettin' a look at you and you make such a good impression he never forgets your face." He reached into his jacket and came out with a pencil flashlight.

"Do you always go around prepared to do this kind of thing?" she asked.

"I used to be in the Girl Scouts."

He slipped outside and went purposefully toward the big house. A couple of ash blondes in high heels and toreador pants came toward him behind a Lhasa apso with a pink ribbon between its ears and a chip on its shoulder. Harry kept his eyes straight ahead and the women paid him as much attention as they did to the dog's barking. He disappeared in the shadow of the stone wall, emerging for an instant at the gate. He rattled the black metal, then wedged a foot against the latch, boosted himself up over the top and was gone.

Kate held the scanner to her ear, and a burst of static

made her pull it away again. A woman with a rapid-fire delivery was ordering police units to a hit-and-run accident at Yellowstone and Weatherole Street. Kate fidgeted with the walkie-talkie and then tuned the car radio to a classical music station. Some Beethoven would be good for the nerves, for hers and Harry's both, she thought. As she placed the walkie-talkie near the speaker, the Cutlass sputtered and coughed and the idiot lights turned the front seat a watery pink. Kate pointed her toe over the transmission hump and fed some gas till the engine evened out. She put down the walkie-talkie and adjusted the rearview mirror so that she could see the other block without having to look over her shoulder.

The house was dead center in the glass, a picture postcard floating over the windshield, when a veil of darkness fell across the mirror. Kate froze. And Harry pulled open the door and sat beside her.

"He doesn't care for unannounced visitors," Harry said. "He's got a SafeTech electronic lock on the door. It has a ten-digit keyboard and four-digit code, which means there's five thousand possible combinations to play with. There's also a lockout timer, so if the whole code isn't entered in sequence in less than five seconds, the thing shuts off and you have to start all over again. The place is as easy to get into as the Dallas Cowgirls' locker room."

"Damn," Kate said. "I should have known this would never work."

"Hey, I'm just tryin' to give you the lay of the land."

"You can defeat a burglar alarm like that? You're that good?"

Harry's voice flattened out. "It's the most sophisticated I've ever seen, about one hundred times smarter than I am. I wouldn't know where to begin to beat a work of art like this. Once you get inside there's probably motion sensors and heat detectors like the fuckin' Ho Chi Minh Trail, and the setup's plugged into the Walker SafeTech

office on Queens Boulevard somewhere. Anyone breathes
heavy on a door or window, or tries cuttin' the juice,
Walker'll have a couple of rent-a-cops over in two minutes
tops."

"You've convinced me," Kate said. "Let's go."

Harry revved the engine, but left the car in park. "The
system must've set Nicholas back at least twenty thousand
dollars, and what makes it work are suckers that are lucky
if they see that kind of dough in two years. I gotta be
smarter than *them.*"

"I don't see how that gets us inside."

"You're gonna. You wearin' a watch?"

Kate pushed up her sleeve over a Movado Esquire with
a gold-toned case.

"Quality merchandise," Harry said, taking her wrist.
"It's a good thing I didn't see it before." He let her arm
down slowly. "How long I been in the car, been thirty
seconds? Add another forty-five for the time it took to walk
back from the house and start counting."

They kept their eyes on the rearview mirror. A tan
Chevrolet with WALKER SAFETECH in metallic lettering
on the doors pulled up beside the stone fence and two men
in brown-and-gold uniforms hurried out with their hands
heeled to the grips of holstered guns.

"How much time is that, total?" Harry asked.

"Just about four minutes."

"They're supposed to be here in two," he said, watching
the guards sprint toward the gate. "Somebody ought to
write Walker."

"What are they doing?" Kate asked. "I can't see them
any more."

"Lookin' for burglars. But they're not even warm."

Kate dragged the back of her hand across her eyebrows
and brought it away clammy. "Why do you want them
here?" she breathed. "I've never been so scared."

"Checkin' their response time. It's pitiful, is what it is."

Soon the guards emerged from the property. One of them, a powerfully built blond, was shaking his head as they went to the car. They drove to the corner, U-turned and sped away.

"Is this your idea of fun?" Kate asked angrily. "You could have gotten us arrested, or worse."

Harry didn't hear. He had opened his door and was standing on the sidewalk.

"Now where are you going?"

"I need to stretch my legs some more." He adjusted the walkie-talkie on his belt. "Keep me posted, anything interesting comes up."

She watched him all the way to the house, till she lost sight of him at the wall. Though he hadn't told her to she began looking at her watch, and when he came back to the Cutlass flashing his sly, crooked grin, she said, "One minute, forty-nine seconds."

"Call it two minutes, then." He joined her on the seat.

At the end of a long silence Kate said, "I can see the Walker car again. It just turned onto the street."

"What's that make altogether, make about seven minutes?"

"Eight."

"Eight whole fuckin' minutes." He sounded outraged. "Nicholas should get double his money back. These guys are worse than useless."

Again they saw the uniformed men get out of the car and go up to the gate. Some of the urgency was gone from their step. The guard who had exited the passenger door, a squat mulatto, lagged behind as if he didn't want to be bothered.

Harry said, "When they come back, we better get down on the seat. They should be fairly pissed by now, and they might try cruisin' the neighborhood, see who's pullin' their leg."

"What are you doing at the house, anyway?" Kate asked.

"Kickin' the door. I've always been curious whether Walker SafeTech is as good as its advertising."

They saw the blond guard walking back to the sidewalk. His partner passed him and was waiting in the car when the blond opened the driver's door and slammed it shut again. The car bolted from the curb and raced to the corner, where it slowed for a yield sign.

"Down," Harry said, and threw himself on Kate.

As they huddled out of sight of the window Kate whispered, "Your hand. If you don't move it away this second, I swear I'll scream 'Walker.'"

"Don't take it personal," he said, and shifted his weight off her.

They heard the tan car roar down the street, then turn and speed away. Kate pushed at Harry and both of them sat up. She pulled a hairbrush from her bag, but Harry confiscated it and dropped it on the dash. "You look beautiful," he said. "Keep me posted again."

Kate said, "I don't know how much more I can take."

But she was talking to herself by then. She caught herself—and looked at her watch again.

"A minute and fifty-three seconds," she said when he came back to the Cutlass. "How many more times do you intend to do this?"

"Depends on the troops from Walker. These are not the brightest guys around, and as a rule they don't have much of an attention span. What they do have are short tempers, and by now they got to be fed up with runnin' back and forth all the time for nothin' when they could be at the office playin' hearts. What I'm bettin' they do in a situation like this, they turn off the alarm at their end and write up an order for maintenance to check out the system. Which means we've seen the last of 'em, though you never know."

"What do we do now?"

"For starters, we wait. It's Walker's move." He swept his hand along the dash and gave her back her brush. As she stroked her hair, he turned on the radio.

"Pachelbel," he said as music filled the front seat, and Kate stared at him in amazement. "Jeez, I hate that shit. You been foolin' with the radio." He spun the dial deliberately and didn't look relaxed again until he found a station at the far end of the band that played fifties oldies.

After a while he lowered the volume and asked, "How much time?"

Kate tilted her watch toward the radio's greenish glow. "Ten and a half minutes."

"Let's wait fifteen even. Then it's time to go."

"Go home?" Kate asked hopefully. "Thank God."

"Go in."

Kate grabbed Harry's good arm, digging her fingers into the bicep.

"Hey," he said. "Be careful. I only got one of these that works."

"You didn't say anything about doing it today. I'm not ready for this."

"I can't see a better time," he told her. "We've got Walker on the run."

"I mean, I don't think there ever will be a good time for me. This kind of thing, it's too nerve-racking. It's why I asked you."

Harry shook his arm free. "What you're tryin' to say, if I understand, is this is a scary, nasty business and if something goes wrong you could end up hurt. This is a job for someone like me, who it doesn't matter if he gets lost up shit creek without a paddle. Right?"

Kate opened her mouth, but no words came.

"And I'm sayin', if you're not willin' to shoulder some of the risk, I don't see why I should put myself on the line for you."

"Not for me," Kate said. "For the cocaine, for the money."

"I hope you're not proud," he said, "'cause as far as I'm concerned this is like volunteer work, my turn to give at the office. The possibilities here are not all that exciting."

"If you feel that way, let's forget it."

"Okay with me," Harry said. He switched off his walkie-talkie.

Kate hesitated and then put her hand softly on his. "Please . . . I really do appreciate what you're doing for me."

"Do you?"

"I'm starting to," she said. "I never met anyone like you before. I didn't know what you were like."

"You've been around someone just like me your whole life."

Kate looked at him skeptically. "Where would I—?"

"Try the mirror," Harry said. Then: "Now that's straight between us, I'm goin' in and you got to help. Everything I told you about before still goes. Only this time you have to be especially alert. You see anything out of the ordinary—"

"I push down on this button," she said, holding her walkie-talkie, "and let you know."

"You got it." He opened the door.

"One more thing." Kate leaned close and Harry thought she was going to wish him luck with a kiss. Instead she tapped her fingernail against his walkie-talkie. "Turn your radio on."

She fine-tuned the rearview mirror as she monitored his progress along the fence. Then she slipped off her watch and put it on the dash. Every thirty seconds or so she stared at the mirror again, feeling more tense each time she saw only the empty street. Suddenly it was unbearably close inside the car and she rolled down the windows. Her face was drenched with sweat, the black dress clinging to her body. He had been gone less than five minutes.

Ninety seconds more went by before she opened the door and swung her legs outside. She felt more comfortable like that until she realized that the dome light was attracting biting insects and, no doubt, the attention of some of the neighbors. She dropped the scanner and the walkie-talkie in her bag and went out, drawn toward the big house.

As she squinted into the darkness her heart caught in her mouth and she had to go to the bathroom more urgently than she could ever remember. Squeezing between a garbage truck and the curb a block away was a tan car with gold trim. She grabbed for the walkie-talkie, but it was dead. She swatted the plastic case against her hand and brought the mouthpiece to her lips again. "They're back," she said, and waited for his reply.

And waited . . . What was his damn name? "Harry?"

"What?" Above a brittle crackling that reminded her of a boardwalk fire she could barely make out his voice. "*Who's* back?"

"The guards. I see their car."

"Shit," he said so loud they would have done as well using tin cans connected by a string.

"They'll be here any second."

"Take the car around the block and pick me up behind the house." He was talking so fast she wasn't sure she heard him right. "You can drive, can't you?"

"A . . . a little."

"Fuck, why didn't you say something before? Never mind. Drive around the house a little. I'll be waiting in back."

"Did you get the . . . ?"

If he answered, she didn't catch it. She was racing back to the Cutlass, looking over her shoulder as the tan car threaded the needle and then came to a skidding stop for a black tomcat chasing a calico across the street. Something stung her ankle and she heard the clatter of coins on the sidewalk like tinny rain. Without looking down she pinched her bag shut under her elbow.

She dropped onto the driver's seat and threw the Cutlass into gear, stepping hard on the gas. The engine coughed and the idiot lights fluttered and she lifted her foot, waiting two agonizing seconds before putting it down again. As she steered into the street the side mirror framed the tan Chevrolet gliding to a halt and the guards tumbling out behind drawn guns.

Ignoring two red lights, she turned onto a street where blue spruce trees were all the rage. Beside a Tudor mansion that was the mirror image of Nicholas's place she saw a three-story Japanese villa with a green tile roof. Her eyes swept the empty yard between the houses, and then she was digging in her bag for the walkie-talkie when she spotted Harry doubled over a suitcase that must have weighed a ton. She reached across the seat and opened the passenger door and helped him swing the leather bag into the back.

"Let me drive," he barked.

They jumped outside, crossing in front of the car in a naked reverse, and then the Cutlass leapt into the street before she could pull both feet in. Harry killed the lights and they ran as dark and silent as a submarine toward a flashing red signal.

"How do we get out of here?" he asked.

Kate looked around blankly. "I don't know. I've never been on this street before."

"Great."

They raced four blocks to a desolate boulevard which seemed to slice diagonally through the circular grid. Harry flicked on his lights and followed the beam past a sign that proclaimed LEAVING FOREST HILLS GARDENS, veering right for a police car riding the center stripe in the direction from which they had come. He slowed outside a neighborhood tavern and warmed himself in the neon glow.

"*Woooeee,*" Harry yelled, grabbing Kate by the shoulder and pulling her close. She held herself rigidly and his kiss landed beside her mouth. When he let go, she bobbed upright like a child's punching bag. "You can charge that against my end," he said.

"Very funny."

"Where's the scanner?" he asked, feeling for it on the seat. "We better find out what the cops are up to."

"It's in my bag. I . . . I had to step out for a moment."

Harry turned to look at her with eyes that were crevasses beneath beetling brows.

"Watch the road," she said. She opened her purse and put the scanner on the dashboard. "Did you get the electric parts?"

"Shhhh."

The woman with the machine-gun delivery was ordering additional police units to Forest Gardens. ". . . report of burglary in progress."

Harry slapped his hand against the wheel and laughed. "Getaway in progress is more like it."

"The electric parts . . . ? Do you have them?"

Too much tension went into Harry's smile and then it fell apart. "No," he said. "I didn't see anything looked like that. No coke either. What I did find was a shitload of cash money and a pretty nice U.S. coin collection and some miniature portrait paintings I don't know the first thing about except they got to be worth a bundle 'cause the women in 'em are all ugly as sin and I got to live with 'em one year minimum 'cause they're too hot to move now."

Kate turned to stare out the window, but not before Harry saw tears in her eyes.

"We split this up," he said, "you can buy all the electric parts you want, open your own store."

"You didn't even look."

"Hell, you don't know for sure they're there. Be happy we made out as good as we did."

"But you said you'd get them."

"This is not a racket where there are guarantees." His tone was edgy, but with no anger in it. "I didn't know the layout and I couldn't chance turnin' on any lights. There's a Gardall SC1130 safe in the bedroom. It's a big mother, a fire safe, with plated interlocking bolts that extend into heavy-gauge prime steel walls and a key lock with a re-locking device. The damn thing weighs more than half a ton and he's not afraid to keep it out in plain sight. I didn't go near it. The electric parts could be inside, they're as valuable as you think, but you need an A-bomb to get in."

"Don't say that word."

They rode in silence to the West Side and Harry stopped for a light and said, "I don't see what you're givin' me the hairy eyeball for. Maybe you didn't get everything you wanted, but you did all right. What am I apologizing for? You did great. I was any of your other fine friends, the crappy end of the stick'd be slippin' through your fingers already. With me, at least you get your half."

"Keep it," Kate said. "Without the rest, the money doesn't do me much good."

"Don't tempt me."

"No, I mean it."

"You mean it 'cause it's the end of a rough day. In the morning you wake up with nothin' again, you look in the mirror you're gonna have to ask, 'Did I really fuck up so bad?' No," he said. "A deal is a deal. Half's yours."

He parked near the brownstone and pulled the bag out of the back, lugged it up the stoop while Kate waited with the door open, her eyes moving all over the quiet street. He went in ahead of her and carried it over the broken stairs, then dropped it on the bed and threw himself beside it pressing his cheek against the cool leather.

"It's a nice piece of merchandise," he said when she

came into the room. "You don't mind, it's part of my half."

Kate pulled one leg under her and sat on the edge of the Barcalounger as Harry snapped open the bag. He removed six small paintings that could have been of the same pinch-faced woman in a yellow sunbonnet, but weren't.

"I don't have much of a track record movin' artwork," he said, "but it's a cinch you have less, so I'll take these. You don't know a fence that owes you a favor, you end up with maybe ten percent of what they should go for."

He spread the paintings over the bed, and then dug inside the suitcase for a book the size of a looseleaf binder bound in blue leather and three more like it. "This is the coin collection . . ."

He looked up. Kate was leaning back, not paying attention to him. "It's hard to say where half of this begins," he said. "You wouldn't know what to do with 'em anyway, so I'm gonna hang onto the coins *and* the pictures. You get to keep most of the cash, though." He slipped a brown envelope held together with a string tie out of his shirt and dumped four stacks of bank notes on the mattress.

"He was usin' this for pin money," Harry said as he counted hundred-dollar bills. "It was sittin' in the top drawer of his desk. It comes to . . . thirteen K. As you were sayin', a fair night's work. I take four K off the top and the balance is yours. Now what do you say?"

Kate straightened her leg and crossed it over the other one. Then she uncrossed it. As if it was an effort, she said, "Thank—"

"Don't mention it." Harry shaped the money into two neat piles and pushed the taller one toward her. When she didn't reach for it, he asked, "You're not gonna count it?"

"I trust you."

"It's part of your problem. You better check my math."

Kate fanned the bills, then fanned them again. "I get only eight thousand."

"What did I tell you?" he asked, looking pleased with himself. He cut ten bills from his pile and dropped them on hers. "You didn't say how much coke you need, but you can buy weight with nine K. You want to be smart, you'll do some yourself. It's not what I would advise most people, but you don't let it get out of hand, it's just medicine. You won't feel so down."

"I can't get excited about this," she said, gesturing at the money as though it were contagious, "not without the electric parts."

"Maybe you can buy them, too."

"They're very rare. Those were the only ones that are available, I'm sure."

"Still, the nine K makes a nice consolation prize." Like talking to the wall, for all the response it produced. Then: "We should see each other again sometime."

She shook her head.

"Another job I'm talkin' about. You hear of anything, you let me know first."

Kate forced a smile.

"Sure I can't interest you in supper? What's it, it's close to midnight. You got to be starved."

Kate stopped forcing and the smile went away.

"You say so." He opened the suitcase again and fit the coin albums in the corners, stacked the paintings carefully in the center. He returned his share of the cash to the brown envelope and put it inside too. He shut the lid halfway and then looked around the room. "Something I'm forgettin'," he said.

"The police scanner. It's still in the car."

"And this." He unhooked his walkie-talkie from his belt. "Where's yours?"

"In my purse."

"Let's have it. Last thing we need is for you to put it out with the garbage."

Kate reached for her bag and looked inside.

"The wrong people get their hands on it, electric parts are the least of your troubles," he said. "You don't have *any* troubles."

"Why?"

"What's the diff? Let me have it."

"I don't see it," she said. "It must be in the car. But I could swear I put it in my purse."

"Don't swear. Just get it."

"I'll be back in a second," Kate told him, and ran downstairs. But nearly ten minutes went by before she came back to the bedroom looking pale and tentative.

"I thought you'd skipped to Rio without me," Harry said.

Kate didn't laugh. "I was sure it was there." She brought her purse to the bed and turned it upside down. "I . . . I don't know where it is," she said as she sorted feverishly through her things. "I must have dropped it somewhere."

Harry watched her until his color matched hers. Then he opened the suitcase and removed five bills from the brown envelope. He peeled off five more from her share and pushed the thousand to the middle of the bed.

"What's that for?"

"Headstones," he said.

13

NICHOLAS said, "You can never find a cop when you need one."

Bucyk laughed uneasily. "I was out in Pennsylvania, for the special bear season. My whole life I always wanted to shoot a bear. My lousy brother buys a share in a cabin in the Poconos, just like that God strikes him dumb. Margie, that's his second ex, wants to know why the support payment's late again, or do I think it'd be better if she has to ask a judge. So I do a little digging and track him down around Shohola, and the big sport invites me out a couple days if I promise I never found him."

Leaving Bucyk in the living room, Nicholas climbed the stone steps. He smoothed his glossy hair against the flat of his hand. "On my time you don't shoot anything unless I tell you to."

"I didn't." Bucyk lowered his eyes, but kept them on Nicholas. "What did you need to see me about?"

"Someone broke in two nights ago and took some things of mine. I want them back."

"How'd they do that? It'd be easier crashing out of Attica, all the equipment you have."

Nicholas opened the top drawer of a Lombard marquetry commode and balanced a flat gray rock in his palm. "It seems that this is the key to the Walker SafeTech system," he said. "They used it to break a window in the back of the house and then climbed in. I don't know why the alarm didn't sound. I can't get an honest answer from the people at Walker."

"You can't go to the police either." Bucyk felt another laugh coming on and he brought his hand to his mouth and coughed inside it. "What'd they get?"

"Thirteen thousand in cash, a coin collection I've had since I was a boy and half a dozen portraits of early A-merican whaling captains' wives that I just picked up at auction."

"Congratulations," Bucyk said. "What do you have it insured for, three times what it's worth, four?"

Nicholas glared at him as though his patience was over-matched. "If word gets around—and it will—that charac-ters can come in here like it's a supermarket and take what they want, I'll have to get out of business. If I live long enough. I don't intend to let that happen if the insurance company pays *ten* times the value of what I lost."

"What do you want me to do? If it's gone, it's gone."

"The time I was upstate," Nicholas said, "I celled with a small-time fence from Staten Island by the name of Whitey Louie. The man was a classic sociopath, without a spark of humanity, serving twenty-five years to life for murder two. The only time he opened his mouth was to shovel food in or to cry about his dog, a Staffordshire ter-rier he called Mikey. Mikey was another sociopath, you could say, and Whitey Louie loved him the way he would a woman—by which I mean he fed him every other day and kept him chained in the garage that he used as a warehouse. One night a pro who was looking to steal back some goods that he'd sold to Whitey Louie broke into the garage. He hadn't taken two steps when Mikey ripped open his thigh, and the pro was lucky that he was still holding his pry bar and got in a few licks before Mikey swallowed any vital organs. When Whitey Louie found the dog dead, he told me, his first instinct was to call a priest and bury Mikey in the family plot on Long Island. I believe he would have done it if he hadn't had his priorities in order. Instead, he put Mikey in the deep freeze while he made a few discreet inquiries, and the next time the pro came around to do business Whitey Louie hauled out the carcass, which was like a boulder by then, and crushed the pro's head with it. Then he drove to the Silver Lake golf course and laid out both stiffs on the eighteenth green in full view of the clubhouse."

"And this Whitey Louie, this genius, he got sent up on account of a dog?"

"You're missing the moral of the story."

"Maybe not," Bucyk said. "What've we got in the freezer?"

Nicholas opened the commode and then held up an object that was half hidden in his hand. "Do you know what this is?" he asked.

Bucyk climbed the steps and stood beside him. "A walkie-talkie," he said. "Like beat officers wear on the street."

"*Exactly* like those?"

"This one's not so big." Bucyk examined the brand name and then turned it over in his hand. "Look here," he said as if he couldn't get the words out fast enough. "The serial number's been filed off the back. Where'd you get this?"

"I found it in the shrubbery the morning after the break-in," Nicholas said. "I thought you might be able to tell me something about it."

"Me?"

"You were a detective, weren't you?"

"You want Sherlock Holmes."

"Yes, but I'm paying you."

Bucyk looked closely at the walkie-talkie again. "Okay," he said, "one burglar working alone doesn't need something like this, so you know you're up against a gang. The question is how many of them there are and who." Using his thumbnail and then a dime as screwdrivers, he went to work on the back plate. "Maybe we find out in here.

"If the serial number was still in place," he told Nicholas, "you wouldn't have a problem going to the distributor and finding out which store sold this particular walkie-talkie. What we have, it's like trying to trace a car that's missing the license plate and the engine number and the vehicle identification number." He removed two small screws and cupped them in his hand. "My guess is that whoever bought this had their own crystals. It wouldn't be real bright to use the standard frequencies, because half of Queens would be listening in. If these guys didn't, if they put in crystals, we could get a break."

"How?"

"Even in New York there aren't so many places that can do that kind of work. And each one has their own number they're supposed to stamp right on the crystal." The plate came off and he dropped it on the commode.

"Be careful," Nicholas told him. "You'll scratch that."

Bucyk said, "Can we have some light in here? The atmosphere is murder on my eyes."

Nicholas went out of the room. When he came back he placed a felt pad on the commode and a tensor lamp on top of that. Bucyk lowered the bulb over the walkie-talkie. "See, there's four crystals in there. If I can just get my . . ." He worked one loose and brought it out between his thumb and forefinger. "You see this number, 776, that's the store code. What I have to do next is find out whose it is and go down and talk to the people there." He raised the light and turned to Nicholas with a self-satisfied smile.

"Well?" Nicholas asked.

"Well what?"

"What are you waiting for?"

Bucyk's smile, and the satisfaction that had prompted it, evaporated. "Where's a phone?" he asked.

"Use the one in the kitchen."

Bucyk had found something else to smile about by the time he returned to the living room. "One of my old cop buddies is at least still talking to me," he announced.

"What did you learn?"

"Seven seventy-six," he said, holding a slip of paper nearly at arm's length, "is Randy's Radio Repair on Dyckman Street."

"Where's that?"

"Way uptown. In Inwood."

"Are you familiar with it?"

"If you're asking does the shop have a shady reputation, the answer is no. A lot of these radio nuts, they just want their privacy, so they can talk dirty to each other I think. A good store would see plenty of orders for work like this."

"You'll go there right away?" Nicholas asked.

Bucyk waved off the idea. "If I bring this in now they'll say, 'Yeah, that's our number, but we could've done the work for a million different people.' No," he said, "it's too soon for Randy's."

"What are you going to do?"

"There's this radio technician downtown on Varick Street," Bucyk said. "From time to time he works for the department, and there's times he does some work for the competition. To him it's all the same. The important thing, he knows the inside of a walkie-talkie like he lives there. I'll have him run a bench test on the crystals to calibrate the frequencies. Once I have them, I can go through Randy's work sheets for the order that matches up. I think that's the way to proceed on this."

"You know," Nicholas said, "there are occasions when you amaze me."

"Same here," Bucyk said.

"It's been more than a week. Where are you?"

"These things take time," Bucyk said.

"Evidently—"

"But sometimes it's worth the wait. I was right about the crystals. They were special orders. The frequencies were 151.633, 151.647, 151.682 and 151.723."

"That means nothing to me," Nicholas said.

"Me neither, not at first anyway, not until I went up to Inwood, to Randy's Radio. It's a big place, bigger than you'd expect in a neighborhood like this. I had to sort through four hundred goddamn work orders before I found the one that was the same as the four crystals. And when I did, it turned out the customer who wanted them calls himself Joe Smith."

"Great. That's just—"

"Hold your horses," Bucyk said.

Nicholas asked, "Did you get an address—?"

"You going to let me finish, or not?"

"Go ahead."

"No," Bucyk said. "There was no address, and of course he'd paid cash so there was no check or credit-card receipt either. What there was, though, was a new order for four more crystals, also special calibrations, and for a . . . let me try and get this right . . . for a Maxon CPO520 walkie-talkie, from the same Joe Smith. At least I say it's the same Joe Smith. Randy, he's not so sure."

"Why wouldn't he be?"

"This is where it gets interesting. After I jogged his memory, Randy said he sort of remembered Joe Smith after all. It seems when he came in the store the first time he had a dog with him, a big one, like this Mikey you were telling me about. Except that it was white, a Russian wolf-hound, Randy said."

Nicholas said, "That *is* interesting."

"When he came back again Joe Smith didn't have the dog. Maybe because it's too much trouble to hang on to a leash when your arm's in a wrist-to-elbow cast, like you've just had the first of a number of bad accidents."

"Then you shouldn't have any trouble recognizing him when you see him," Nicholas said.

"I don't expect to."

"One more thing. Before you make your point with him, there's some information I'd like you to get out of Joe Smith."

"Yes?"

"Ask him what a krytron is. Those things are taking up too much room in my safe."

Bucyk said, "I have to go now. There's an old lady standing outside who wants to use the phone."

The midnight-blue van crawled along Dyckman Street oblivious to the press of traffic. On the driver's side a large mirror was tilted away from the body like a chromed elephant's ear. At the intersection with Broadway the van stopped at a green light and remained there through two more. It didn't start up again until a man wearing a scruffy beard appeared in the glass holding a small package in his one good hand.

Bucyk leaned on the gas until the van was nearly a block ahead of Harry. He was partial to advance tails. Too often, following from the rear, he lagged so far behind that he lost sight of a subject and was shaken. This way was harder, but more reliable.

Harry turned uptown on Seaman Avenue, and Bucyk circled the block and then led the way along the edge of Inwood Hill Park. Where the street ended at Baker Field, he watched Harry go into an apartment house opposite the grandstand. Bucyk parked in front and ran into the lobby as Harry was entering the elevator. Bucyk caught the closing door and stepped in after him. "Just made it," he said.

Harry pressed four without looking at him.

"Nice day." Bucyk smiled. "If it doesn't rain."

Harry grunted. The gate slid open and he twisted around and put his back to the door and pushed out.

Bucyk followed him. "Know where the Mortons live?" he asked in the hall.

Harry shrugged. Walking away, he wedged the package against a hip with the heavy cast. With his other hand he pulled keys from his pants. He turned the doorknob, and as he dragged his feet over the sill his head snapped back as Bucyk rammed a shoulder into his lower back and drove him inside.

Harry broke his fall with his good hand, gasping for air as his midsection came down on the package. He rolled over in time to see Bucyk jam the metal bar between the Fox lock on the door and the floor plate. Harry was gathering his legs under him when Bucyk went across the room in no particular hurry and kneed him in the side.

Bucyk raised his right foot, perching on the left like a wading bird too full to strike at prey. Harry hid behind his good hand, and then Bucyk juked and buried a blunt leather toe between the exposed ribs under Harry's arm. A bleating sound escaped Harry's nose. His ear struck a corner of a low table and then the floor. "Who are you?" he wheezed.

"I'm the guy, you borrowed some stuff from a friend of his." Bucyk's gaze drifted into the kitchen where an empty dog bowl stood against a wall. "From two friends."

"They offering a reward, it gets returned?"

Bucyk poised his foot again, but put it down as a smile played a limited engagement across his lips. He unbuttoned his jacket and pulled out the .357 Magnum. "You think I'm fooling," he said, waving the gun impatiently. "We're wasting time. Where is it?"

"The coins . . . you want the coins?"

The revolver stopped moving.

"Look in the cabinet over the refrigerator," Harry said.

Bucyk stuffed the gun in his waistband and went into the kitchen. Above the refrigerator were glass doors thick with yellowing paint. Standing on his toes, he pulled all of them open. "I don't see anything," he called into the other room. "For your sake, you'd better not be bullshitting me."

Harry struggled to his knees. Eight feet away was an ancient Dumont television and underneath it, inside the drawer of an end table, was his starter's pistol. Sensing eyes on his back, he turned away. "I took 'em out of the albums," he said. "They're in three cloth bags, behind the empties."

Bucyk used both arms to sweep the cabinets clean of an assortment of beer bottles that rolled across the top of the refrigerator before splintering against the floor. Then he reached in as far as he could, but came up only with two earthenware rosé wine jugs. He slid a three-legged chair close to the refrigerator and climbed up carefully. "Yeah," he said, "I see them now, in back."

Harry edged toward the end table. He was still three feet away when he saw Bucyk balanced awkwardly on the chair with the bags in one hand.

"Now where are the pictures?" Bucyk asked.

"In the storage area under the sink."

Bucyk jumped down and dropped the bags on the counter. Below the sink metal doors on bent hinges framed a horizontal opening. As he knelt in front of the black space, he heard Harry say, "I'd be careful, I was you."

"What?"

"Isaac's sleepin' in there, watchin' over the artwork. He doesn't know you, don't be in such a hurry to stick your hand in."

Bucyk muttered something that reverberated in the darkness. The other wise guy, that Nathan, had almost fooled him like that before. Twice he didn't fall for anything. He yanked one of the doors off its hinges and stuck his head inside defiantly.

Harry screamed, "Kill, Isaac, kill, kill!"

Fucking jerk, Bucyk said to himself, and listened to the echo of his own laughter. He leaned in further and ducked under the pipes to poke around the grimy corners.

Either the guy was deaf, or else he didn't have a nerve in his body, Harry decided. Anybody normal would have panicked, or at least been startled long enough for him to whip out the starter's pistol. But the guy hadn't even flinched, just gone in deeper. It took Harry a second to realize that no reaction was as good as too much. He tore open the drawer and clamped the gun in his fist and went into the kitchen as Bucyk was backing out from under the sink.

"I told you I wasn't fooling," Bucyk said, and started to turn around. His hand was at his waist when Harry showed him a dark muzzle that was smooth where a gunsight should have been.

"Squat down," Harry said.

Bucyk's hand inched closer to his belt before it moved away again. As he went down on his haunches, Harry told him, "Now step on your hands."

"Huh?"

"Understand English?"

Bucyk lifted his right heel and slipped his fingers underneath, slid his left palm under his toes. Harry pocketed the starter's pistol and snatched the Magnum from Bucyk's pants. He pointed the heavy gun at the crouching man, hefted it experimentally and then slammed the cylinder against Bucyk's temple and watched him crumple.

"Ouch," Harry said. "That must hurt."

Bucyk fell onto his side and rolled away, suppressing a moan welling deep in his guts.

"Where you goin'?" Harry asked. "Get up."

Bucyk raised himself off the floor, holding his head, and Harry motioned him into the corner where the dog bowl lay beside the stove. "Turn around," Harry said, drawing a circle in the air with the gun, "so I don't have to see your kisser. You look like shit."

Harry pressed the Magnum against Bucyk's shoulders and traced the bulging cords in his neck up to his ear. He drew back his finger on the trigger slowly, so that Bucyk could hear the tension increasing in the spring.

"Nothin' I'd like better," Harry said, "but the apart-

ment's rented under my own name." He let his finger
relax. "Don't even think about moving."

Harry stepped back and put the gun down on the
counter. Unbuttoning his shirt, he dropped a bag of coins
inside, gritting his teeth as it nestled against his ribs. He
fit in another carefully. There was no room for the third,
and he turned it upside down and scattered the coins on
the linoleum with his foot.

"I'm takin' off now," Harry said. "You're still interested
in the pictures, check the closet. You want the coins . . ."
He dug his heel into the mound on the floor, making a cold
metallic chinking. "Be my guest. But you leave here before I'm gone five minutes, you'll wish you were never
born, got that?"

Bucyk snorted.

"So make yourself at home."

Bucyk heard footsteps retreating from the kitchen and
then a silence marred by the opening and closing of the
door. Groping in the small of his back for the tiny holster
in which he kept his second gun, a 9-mm Beretta, he told
himself: The fucking jerk must've learned that routine
from every B picture that ever got made. He waded
through the coins and hurried into the other room and
pulled open the door. As he put a foot outside, he heard
his front teeth break and then there was a moment of
unendurable pain before darkness swallowed him up.

"I told you to wait," Harry said from beside the door as
he brought the Magnum into Bucyk's face a second time
and watched him pitch onto the floor. Then he relieved
him of the automatic and rolled him inside the apartment.

"Five minutes," Harry said. "No, better make it ten."

He slipped in through the service entrance to observe
waiters divvying up tips with busboys in soiled linen jackets. A weary-eyed man tenderly piecing together a clarinet directed him to the office. He stood at the door

watching Kate hunched over a checkbook, and then coughed softly into his fist.

As if it were a great effort, she looked his way. "Oh no," she said.

"So this is hell."

She ran to the door and shut it behind him. "What are you doing here? You said you wouldn't bother me."

"Something came up. I—"

"A deal is a deal. Those are your own words."

He sat in one of the gray Barcaloungers, played with it rocking back and forth.

"Not so hard," she said sternly.

He stopped with his body parallel to the floor and raised himself with difficulty, then fell back.

"Are you okay?" she asked.

"Some of my ribs, they feel like they're busted."

"Then you should go to a hospital, not come—"

"I figured you'd want to know."

"I'm sorry you had an accident, but—"

"It was no accident." He came forward painfully until he was nearly upright. "I had new equipment on order at the radio shop," he said, "and I went down to pick it up. I never should of took the chance. Some gorilla followed me home and jumped all over me. He would of shot me, I think, except I got lucky and took his guns away."

"Did you . . . did you use them on him?"

"The idea crossed my mind," Harry said. "But what's the use? There's always more where guys like that come from."

"Was it Stan Bucyk?"

"I didn't get the name. He was my height, about forty pounds heavier, with a gut."

"That's him, that's Bucyk." Kate glanced at the door and then went to the Barcalounger. She tilted Harry all the way back, tugged the shirt out of his pants and pulled up his T-shirt. "My God," she said, and looked away. "Your ribs are practically coming through the skin. What are you going to do?"

"What *you're* goin' to do is wrap 'em for me. You got any surgical tape around here?"

"I don't know."

"Take a look in your first-aid kid, you keep one," he said. "You don't see any, send someone to a drugstore for a couple rolls."

Kate vetoed the idea with a toss of her head and blew the hair out of her eyes. "You should go to a doctor. I don't know the first thing about this."

"It's like breakin' inside houses. What you don't know, I'll teach you. . . . You got to," he said. "I can't stand the pain much longer."

She went through the closet and desk, finding a metal case with a red cross on a khaki field in the bottom drawer. She looted it of iodine and Mercurochrome and aspirin, Band-Aids and gauze before Harry said, "There, that's one."

Kate balanced a roll of tape on the Barcalounger's armrest. "I don't see another," she said.

"One'll have to do."

She pulled off his shirt and then went to the door and locked it. Harry sat on the edge of the Barcalounger and looked down at a greenish swelling below his armpit. "Wrap it tight as you can. Try and squeeze the ribs back in place."

Kate unrolled eight inches, then stopped with the tape between her hands.

"What are you waitin' for?"

"I'm looking for a good place to start," she said. "You have a hairy chest . . . very nice. It's going to hurt a lot when this has to come off."

"I'll worry about it later," he said, and slapped the tape against his pectorals himself.

Then he bent forward and Kate pulled the tape around him. "Is it tight enough?" she asked.

Harry didn't answer. Kate looked up and saw tears in his eyes. "Keep goin'," he gasped.

Kate wove the white strip around his chest five times before the roll was used up and she stepped back to examine her work. "How do you feel?" she asked.

"I can hardly breathe."

She helped him on with his shirt. "Go home and take some Tylenol and stay in bed for a few days. You'll feel—"

He cut her off. "I left you-know-who there. Home's the last place I want to be."

"Then where will you—?"

"I was hopin' you might have a place," he said, and quickly put a finger across her lips. "You might want the company. I should mention they know I'm the guy that broke into your house, and they gotta be thinkin' it's one for *Believe It or Not,* the next place I turn up is theirs."

"You're just trying to frighten me," Kate said, worry starting to show in a fluttering around her mouth. "They'd never harm me."

"Tell it to your boyfriend."

She looked at him for a long time, so still that he thought she was holding her breath. Then she said, "What do I do now?"

"Maybe you don't do anything. Maybe they get arrested for something else and your troubles are over. Or they catch up with you and your troubles are over anyway."

"I'm sorry I tried to send you away."

"Maybe they get hit by a truck."

Under her breath Kate said, "I wish."

"Maybe I'm drivin' it."

"I . . . I'm starting to see things your way," she said. "In the meantime, until we get a truck . . . ?"

"You hide," Harry said. "With me."

Kate started to say something, then caught herself. "At the brownstone? That's the first place they'd look."

"No," Harry said. *"This* is. So it wouldn't be a bad

idea, we came up with someplace fast. You still have the nine K? We could get pretty far on that."

"Most of it," she said. "I had to use some to fix up the house. But I'm not touching a penny of the rest. If, by some miracle, I come out of this alive, I'm going to need that money. Without it, I might as well go looking for them."

"I've still got some of my end, but not enough to travel on. You'd be surprised how quick money goes."

"No, I wouldn't." She returned the first-aid kit to the desk. Mostly to herself she said, "There's always Nathan's."

"I'm tryin' to avoid where Nathan is."

"Before he came to live with me, Nathan took an apartment on Seabreeze Avenue. He gave me the key. It might be all right, for a short time anyway. Nathan said it had two bedrooms."

Harry extricated himself from the Barcalounger. "They kill us there," he said, "people'll know we died pure. It's a relief."

14

THE NEW Brighton House was a five-story walk-up with terra-cotta minarets over blunted cornices, a water tank hidden inside a decaying onion dome, ALHAMBRA ARMS chipped and flaking above the pilastered entrance. A professional apartment on the first floor was given over to the office of S. Ivanov, acupuncturist and naturopath. A kosher deli shared a storefront with headquarters of the Coney Island Spartacist League.

"Here's home," Kate said.

Harry guided the Cutlass to the curb, reluctant to cut the engine.

"I know it doesn't look like much from the outside," she said, anticipating his reaction, "but Nathan said the apartment was nice."

"This is great. Just great."

Kate prepared a frown. But when she looked at Harry she saw a smile that appeared sincere.

"What we're lookin' for," he gloated. "Nobody'll notice us here."

He parked in front of a candy store and Kate slid out with a bag of coins in each fist. "Apartment 4B," she said. "The key is in my pocket. Will you . . . can I trust you to put your hand in there?"

The lobby was smoked marble, a massive oak table under a frayed tapestry a monument to forgotten elegance. The air was acrid with the onion and garlic of immigrant cooking. Beside a bank of mailboxes that had been kicked in by pilferers they found stairs and began climbing. With an eye on Kate's, Harry brought up the rear.

"We stay long enough, I ought to be back in shape," he said, approaching the third floor. "The legs."

They trudged up another flight and paused on the landing, breathing hard. They heard the thud of an object striking a wall and then a man shouting over a woman's tremulous wail and children crying. A door left ajar muffled the sizzle of frying food while letting out its odor. They walked along a scrubbed corridor to an alcove and Harry poked the key at Apartment 4B and pushed inside a living room furnished with a lumpy sofa, some easy chairs and little else.

"He had great taste, Nathan," Harry said. "Who was his decorator, the Salvation Army?"

Kate dropped the bag of coins on the sofa. "These are my things," she said. "I let him have them."

Harry went quickly to a window, snapped venetian blinds into shape and hoisted them up. Beyond a lot in the pastel of crumbled brick the sky was watery blue above the harder, unforgiving blue of the Atlantic, and all around, taking strength from the gathering dusk, Coney Island's lunatic glow. "Better'n TV," he said.

He let go of the cord and the blinds clattered to the sill, raising a puff of black dust and paint chips. "Hey," he said, "what's the matter with you?"

Kate was curled up on the couch with her knees under her chin, tears streaming down her cheeks. "I don't know," she sobbed.

"You gotta have some idea."

She dabbed at her eyes with a sleeve. "Nathan . . . he wanted to live here with me so badly." She got up and began hunting for a tissue. "I'm sorry."

"Don't be."

He followed her inside a bedroom built around a double mattress on a plywood board that was propped up like an altar with a cinderblock at each corner. A lamp with a torn shade balanced on a stack of college texts, an annotated *Moby Dick* and surveys of American literature, against a wall. Along another was an old Webcor hi-fi and an orange crate stuffed with LPs in worn jackets.

"These are my books," Kate said. "My phonograph, too. So this must be where I sleep." She brushed past him toward a room so narrow that Harry was sure he could touch both walls. On the floor a dead strip of foam under a sleeping bag curled against the molding. "And this is yours."

"I had a feelin' you were gonna say that."

They backed out to explore a kitchen that was a carbon copy of the one Harry had in Inwood except for a toaster oven and a radio on the counter. Then they returned to the living room and Kate settled into her place on the sofa.

"It's not late," Harry said. "Let's check out the neighborhood. It might be hard to believe, but I've never seen Coney Island."

Kate shook her head. "Let's stay here."

"I've had worse offers." He dropped beside her on the sofa, expecting her to cringe. When she didn't budge, he said, "You're that scared, huh?"

"Ever since we went to Queens I knew something would—"

"It makes you feel better, I'm scared, too."

Kate looked at him with eyes that were edged in black. "Please don't say that."

"So," Harry said, "what do you want to talk about? We got a lot of time to kill together."

"Don't say that either."

Harry drummed his fingers against his cast. "You're so uptight, you ought to eat. Get some food in you, you'll feel more like yourself."

"Damn it," Kate said, "I'm sick and tired of hearing that from everybody."

"Did I ever—?"

"I am hungry," she said. "But I don't want to leave the apartment. There's a Chinese take-out place on Neptune Avenue." She got up from the sofa, looked behind it, bent down and picked up a phone. "What do you want?"

"You decide," Harry said. "You're buyin', unless the delivery boy carries change for a hundred, or takes gold coins."

Harry squeezed a finger under the cardboard flap and a green blob squirted up to his wrist. Licking it, he said, "I can't do this with one hand. You mind?"

Kate brought the chow mein to her side of the floor and peeled back the flap. "You'd starve without me."

"Probably get shot *with* you," he said. "But you don't hear me bellyachin'."

"That's the nicest thing you've ever had to say about me." She spooned half the pint onto a paper plate and passed it to him, reached for another container to inhale the warm pungent smell of pineapple chicken.

"I'd beat it out of town," Harry was saying, "I could move without my insides snaggin' on my ribs." He speared a piece of chicken, brought it to his lips, blew on it and pulled it away without tasting it. "But I can't. And you're probably like every other New Yorker, think you'll die from fresh-air poisoning, you have to cross the river. So as long as we're stuck here, let's don't just wait for your friends to find us."

"What can we do to *them?*" Kate asked. "They're criminals."

"So'm I," Harry said. "They're killers, which is something else altogether. I'm not sure I'm ready to compete on that level. Up to now, bein' a burglar's been good enough for me."

"Why?" Kate asked.

"Why don't I shoot 'em?"

"No, why are you a burglar?"

"My mother made me one," he said, tearing open a cellophane packet of soy sauce with his teeth.

"You come from a broken home?"

"What . . . ? No," he said. "That's supposed to be a joke, though usually you save it for shrinks and probation officers. My folks have a dry-cleaning store in Pawtucket, Rhode Island, a cleansers they call it up there. Couldn't be tighter. My mother . . . it wasn't for her, I probably would be shootin' people, or gettin' shot at by them, or be dead several times over. The reason I'm a burglar is I like it, I like the hours and makin' okay dough for a minimum of work that I find stimulating and is always a challenge. Plus, it also gives me the chance to meet people and make new friends."

Kate said, "We're running for our lives. Can't you be serious about this, at least?"

"I am. I'd like some white rice, it's not too much trouble."

Kate opened a small container and pushed it at him. As he dug a spoon inside, she said, "You expect me to believe that you break into people's houses because you enjoy doing it?"

"For the most part, it's not a bad life, though sometimes it gets kind of lonely. Dangerous, too, but so's ridin' on the subways. I hardly do that, take the train, so in the long run everything balances out."

"Have you ever been in jail?"

"Uh-huh," Harry said, prying a ball of rice out of the cardboard and watching it break apart on the edge of his plate. "Where do you think I learned to be a burglar?"

"I didn't realize it was something you had to be taught."

Harry put down his spoon. He scraped some rice off the floor and dropped it in an empty container. "It's not . . . you shouldn't try and pick it up on your own. There's rules you have to follow."

"What were you locked up for?" Kate asked. "The first time, I mean."

"Dope. I have . . . I had a problem with that since I was a kid."

"Were you a heroin addict?"

"Later I was," Harry said. "You could say I had a sweet tooth for cocaine, too, for anything you could snort, shoot, pop or smoke. I lost a few years like that."

"You don't seem like a drug addict. You have a very hearty appetite."

"I don't do dope any more," he said, "except for grass every now and then. And coke'll always be a temptation, though I have it under control now. You do coke?"

Kate shook her head.

Harry raised his eyebrows, eyeing her as though he were staring over the top of reading glasses. Then he said, "It's evil shit. I started foolin' with it my senior year in high school, thought I was goin' to be a heavy-duty dealer. I had a wrestling scholarship to URI, and while I was waitin' for wrestling camp to begin me and a buddy scraped together four thousand bucks, don't ask how, and flew down to Peru to score kilos. Couple of real jerks we were. Eighteen years old and never been out of New England, didn't know two words of Spanish, or who the CENTAC agents were down there."

"What's that?" Kate asked.

"It stands for Central Tactical Unit, and what it was, it doesn't exist any more, was American narcs stationed overseas. Anyway, we were gone two, three days, and when we got off the plane in New York, customs took one look at our passports, saw the only travelin' we'd ever done was an overnighter to Lima fuckin' Peru, their eyes lit up like they hit the pick-six at Aqueduct. The coke was hid in a false-bottom suitcase we'd had made up by some ten-time loser in Providence. It took 'em all of ninety seconds to find it. Turned out the coke was fresh from a CENTAC evidence locker, we'd gone all the way to Peru to buy dope from a narc. Well, forget about the wrestling scholarship. Probably saved my life, I was losin' so much weight from doin' dope. Forget about URI, too. I ended up in the federal penetentiary in Danbury, Connecticut, which is not a terrible place to be I found out later. It had a nice element, couple mayors from Newark, New Jersey, a U.S. senator, shitloads of dealers. There were a couple of college professors, forgers, who ran the hobby shop and wanted to teach me engraving. But as it turned out, I don't have any aptitude for that. I had pulled a zip-six, got out in three years, and eighteen months later I was in the ACI, the Adult Correctional Institution in Cranston, medium security. That's where I learned how to do B&Es, so I could get in trouble without havin' to go all the way to South America."

"God, you were dumb," Kate said. "No wonder you landed in jail."

"Naive," Harry said. "I was eighteen years old and didn't know better than to think you could become a major importer just like that. Like I said, I'd never been out of Rhode Island, which is excuse enough for plenty of things, I was lookin' for one. The second time I got locked up, another time after that, I was strung out. That's no excuse either. Now I don't mess with drugs any more, and everything's cool."

Kate shook her head again. "Nathan was always stoned, too. You're just like him. And you're going to end up the same way."

"I don't see where dope had anything to do with what happened to Nathan," Harry said. "What got him killed, it sounds like he was tryin' to do somebody a favor, tryin' to get somebody, somebody who didn't, to give a shit about him, which is impossible and is not a good habit to get into. But, hey, I don't have to tell you that." He broke open a fortune cookie, pulled out the slip of paper with his teeth and looked at both sides.

"What does it say?"

"Nothing. It's a blank." He crumpled it into a tiny ball and dropped it on his plate. He burped. "Excuse me," he said. "That was good. Know what'd hit the spot now?"

Kate shrugged. "Something to drink? A beer? I'll see if there's one in the fridge—"

"No."

"Do you smoke?"

"Uh-uh."

"What?" she asked, impatient.

"You," Harry said.

Kate stiffened and pushed away as Harry got to his feet.

"I thought I should mention it," he said.

Kate looked up at him, saying nothing.

"Well, then, good night," he said. "See you in the morning."

Harry heard Kate shut her door and the sound of a chair dragging across the floor.

"Aren't you forgettin' something?" he called out.

"What?" she asked tensely. "What's that?"

"What I do for a livin'," he said. "Go to sleep. You're knockin' yourself out for nothing."

He was sprawled on his back with his good arm for a pillow when she came into the room. She coughed once and then again, louder, but could scarcely hear herself above the spastic gasp of his snoring. She pushed back a corner of the foam pad with her instep and Harry opened his eyes. "What's up?"

"I couldn't sleep. I need . . ."

Harry smiled. He edged over to the right side of the pad and raised the sleeping bag with his left hand.

"No," she said. "I want to talk. I'm afraid."

Harry dropped the sleeping bag and lay back. "You don't have any reason to be. They don't know where we are. They shouldn't figure it out for a while, they ever do."

"It's not that so much, as everything else . . ." She paused. "You know, having to close the restaurant and put my life on hold. What do I tell Howard? Christ, how do I even face him?"

He had no answer for that. He let her go on.

"And what do I do when . . . when all this is over. I mean, if I don't have the Knights, where do I go from here?" The words came hesitantly, as though she was working it out. "I can't go back to Times Square. I won't. But what else can I—?"

A grating sound interrupted her. She looked down at Harry and then stepped on the pad. He stopped snoring, opened both eyes wide.

"Wha . . . ?" He lifted the sleeping bag. "Last chance."

She kicked the pad close to his ribs and went back to her room.

A garbage truck woke her. She twisted her watch around her wrist, saw that it was after ten and hurried into her clothes, went as far as the bathroom before she slipped out of them and stepped into the tub. Fifteen minutes later, when she walked back through the kitchen, she found Harry with one hip cocked against the counter, scraping cold chow mein out of a cardboard container.

"Here," he said. "Have a little breakfast."

She tried on a disgusted look, found it fit. "You must have a cast-iron stomach."

"Well, no, it's just you get used to havin' different kinds of things for breakfast. Few years back, I mostly ate salami sandwiches in the morning."

"Was that in prison?"

Harry stopped chewing, surprised. "No," he said, but didn't elaborate. "You sure?" He tilted the container toward her.

Kate took the cardboard and the plastic spoon and

deposited them in the garbage bag under the sink. "Comb your hair," she said. "I know a good place to eat. A place where we can get a *real* breakfast."

"Why, what's the matter with—?"

They came out under a high blue sky and the sun nowhere in sight, damp and salty gusts hurtling down the cheerless streets, the first cold day of the season. Kate took Harry's arm and walked half a step behind him, keeping him between herself and the brunt of the wind. "I'm turning blue," she said. "I wish I had something warmer than this dress."

"Maybe in a couple of days you can go back to Seventy-sixth Street and pick up your stuff."

"A couple of days?" She shivered. "I could freeze by then."

"Better'n bein' shot," Harry said. "It gives you more time to think. Where we goin'?"

She put pressure on his elbow and turned him under the el. East of Ocean Parkway the streets were clogged with late-morning shoppers. Harry stared at thick women in cheap cloth coats deliberating over their purchases at the Korean fruit stands as gravely as if they were in an auto showroom.

"What is this place?"

"It's called Little Odessa," she said. "Most of these people are Russian, Russian Jews, born over there."

"How do you . . . ? You too?"

Kate nodded.

"You don't look like them one bit."

"I'm only twenty-two." She slapped her hips. "Give me a few years."

He was staring at her, trying to decide if she was putting him on, when she guided him inside a windowless restaurant and to a booth opposite a busy lunch counter. A waitress came with menus and Kate pushed them away and whispered something in a language he didn't recognize. When the woman retreated, Harry asked, "What was that you ordered?"

"You'll see."

"So you're Russian," he said. "What's it like over there, bad as they say?"

"I was nine when I left. There's not much I remember, except the ice cream was better than it is here."

"Your family live in the neighborhood?"

"My mother and my sister. My father's dead. Every month his brother would send him a letter from Odessa, from over there, about how the government was treating the ones who stayed, and he'd just fall apart. My mother says those letters are what killed him. He was a strong man. A laborer. Only fifty-four."

"You close with your mom?"

"I was," Kate said. "Then I started dancing on Times Square and she stopped talking to me. If I wanted to communicate with her, I had to do it through my sister. When I still wouldn't quit, she sat shiva for me."

"What's that?"

"When a Jew dies, the family spends a week mourning at their house, sitting on wooden boxes. It's like she considers me dead."

"Your mom did that?"

Kate nodded. "Uh-huh."

"She must love you a lot."

Kate was wondering how to take that when the waitress returned. Harry grabbed his fork and looked at his plate.

"This is just bacon and eggs," he said. "I thought you ordered some Russian specialty for me. I can get this anywhere."

"Anybody who'd eat cold chow mein for breakfast, anything more exotic than bacon and eggs would be wasted on him."

. . .

They walked to the boardwalk along Coney Island Avenue, past the drained swimming pools and moth-eaten miniature fairways of the Brighton Beach Bath and Racquet Club, Brighton Private.

"You never say anything about—"

Kate looked bored. "About Russia?"

"No. Times Square."

"It wasn't what you would call the happiest time of my life."

Harry slipped out of his jacket and tossed it around her shoulders.

"Ow," Kate said. "What do you have in your pockets, rocks?"

"Rocks ain't enough. You mind carryin' guns?"

"I certainly do," Kate said, and held her hands away from her body. "What guns? Why do you need guns?"

Harry took back his jacket and worked the cast through the right sleeve. "Do I have to tell you?"

"No," she said unhappily. "Not really."

They mounted charred stairs, saw the sun, and Harry shaded his eyes to stare at the green mesh of the Wonder Wheel rising above the boardwalk like the ultimate Tinkertoy. "You're tellin' me it wasn't fun growin' up in Coney Island? It's got to be every little kid's dream."

"Every kid in Pawtucket, Rhode Island, maybe, every kid who knows Coney Island from old movies and back issues of *Life* magazine. It's been a ruin forever. Just wait . . ."

Beyond the deserted handball courts of a beach park the Wonder Wheel grew larger and more distinct. "Looks good to me," Harry said.

"You can't spend your life on a ferris wheel, not unless you like going around in circles. That sounds trite, I know. But it's true. I always felt like a stranger here."

"You missed Russia?"

"Forget that," she said. "No one else wanted to see the circles. Not even my parents. And it's not like they were idealists, who'd come to America for freedom and were satisfied. They weren't religious, didn't really know what a Jew was till they got here and then they found out that being one wasn't for them. They came here to be rich. Not to work at it, they'd lost that a long time ago, with the religion. Just to *be* rich. And after ten years, they still didn't have a pot to pee in . . . And the thing is, they thought they were well off. I knew better. I went into the city all the time, wore out the sidewalks window-shopping. Christ, I hated being poor."

"What did you ever do about it?"

"I was in too much of a hurry, none of that delayed gratification the sociologists don't stop talking about for me. I was living with Nathan when I was sixteen and holding down part-time jobs all through school. I loved being independent and having a few dollars . . ." The wind eddied up off the beach and Kate covered her eyes and turned her back. "So there was no way I could go to college and be destitute for four years. I took a job in an office, but I felt trapped. I loved to dance, though, always looked good without clo— . . . well, I have a tight body, you know? So I didn't have trouble finding work on Times Square. The money wasn't great, but it was better than anything I'd seen before."

"Times Square," Harry said. "It's another place sounds like heaven when you're stuck in Pawtucket."

"It's Nightmare Alley." The wind changed direction and they started walking again. "I was the only girl I knew who didn't have needle tracks like the Seventh Avenue Express ran down her arm." She stopped, self-conscious. "Sorry about that."

"They're not my type either."

"There were girls there who'd do anything for money. Live sex shows. Sixteen a day, not faking it. With animals, even. And *liking* it, for Christ's sake, if they were stoned enough." She shivered again. "All I did was dance."

"How'd you come to the restaurant?"

"I started belly dancing uptown in addition to the bottomless work, trying to maintain contact with the human race, and I got booked into the Knights. Howard was decent toward me from the start, and—"

"I see," Harry said.

"No, you don't. He had enough faith in me to leave me in charge of the restaurant. Business picked up—just luck, I'm sure—and he offered me an interest. It was the one chance I had to put my life together, to make something of myself. And I blew it."

She looked at him expectantly, waiting to be contradicted. But all Harry said was, "How come he's never around?"

"He's in Israel. He's been gone two months."

"It's a lot of faith."

"He has no choice," Kate said solemnly. And then the words came like a dam burst. "He's in jail there. That's why I wanted you to steal back those electric devices. They're . . . I have to have them if he's going to get out."

"This is a guy who promised you a piece of a restaurant?"

Kate pushed him ahead of her. "Well, if it isn't the pot calling the kettle—"

"One thing I know is guys in jail," Harry said. "About their generous nature."

"Speak for yourself. Howard isn't like that, he's no criminal."

"He likes bein' locked up? He's there restin'?"

"He was . . . never mind," she said, "it's too complicated to get into. But you're wrong about him. He'd never do anything to hurt me."

"I didn't say he would. I'm sayin' he wouldn't do anything to hurt himself. He wouldn't give away a chunk of his business unless he expected something of equal value in return, that's all. You got anything like that? Besides that tight body you were tellin' me about?"

It wasn't worth getting angry about. He was only trying to get her goat. "You don't know him," she said.

"I know you. How you're fuckin' up again, trusting guys. Don't you wonder sometimes how come every man you know is always lookin' out for your best interests and every time you end up further back of the eight ball?"

"Howard's not like the others. You'll see."

"Yes," Harry said. "I got a hunch I will."

Who are you to tell anyone how to run her life, Kate thought, with your prison record and your drug habit and your arm and your ribs—no, that was her fault—and your broken-down car and your ugly beard that won't ever come in right? Get lost, she wanted to say. And would have, too, if she hadn't seen him looking at her in that touchy, wounded way of his, letting her know that if she suggested the idea he would have to follow up on it, because now his pride was on the line along with hers. And she needed him, or at least wanted him near, though for the life of her she couldn't see why.

She backed down. "You'll see," she said again.

They had nothing more to say to each other. They trudged past the aquarium, and Harry peered inside a wooden stockade at sea-lion pups basking in the chill glare as a company of emperor penguins paddled around a rooftop pool. Kate swung her legs through the backrest of a bench, sat watching him until he came back and announced, "I'm hungry again."

"You just ate."

"Must be the salt air," he said, patting his belt buckle.

"Think you can last another half hour? I want to take you someplace and I don't know you that well, I don't know if you can handle it on a full stomach."

"Where's that?"

She marched him to a street where a boarded-up freak

show still promised the five-year-old mother of twins, Jo-Jo the Lobster Boy, Bigfoot. They stood beneath the Typhoon watching six empty cars rattle around the giant roller coaster's track. Harry stared at the rickety scaffolding, wondering what was holding it up, deciding that a single passenger shifting his weight would send it crashing down like a matchstick bridge. Kate nudged him through the turnstile and ran for the first seat in the front car. He got in beside her, gripping the safety bar with his good hand. Kate pried his fingers loose. "Only sissies hold on," she said.

A man in sharkskin pants cut off at the knees released the cars into a tunnel which angled upward so sharply that all the light seemed to have poured out of it. They came into the brightness again at the top of an almost perpendicular drop. Harry stared out over the Lower Bay to the gray shore of Sandy Hook, and then they were falling, plummeting weightlessly as the beach rushed up to meet them. Kate threw her hands over her head and kept them there as Harry let out a mocking *"Woooeee."* He reached outside the car and suddenly the safety bar snapped forward and he straightened his knees and began raising himself. Kate screamed, "Don't," and wrapped both arms around his shoulders and wrestled him down, held him tightly.

Harry relaxed, watching Coney Island whirl around him. They raced up a second incline, dipped and turned dizzily, and as they rose again he saw another car bearing down on them and yanked back the bar before he realized that it was a D train pulling out of the elevated subway station across Surf Avenue. He turned to Kate with a sheepish grin, but she took little satisfaction from it. Then the hills evened out and the cars slowed, and with the black tunnel looming above them she caught her breath and said, "Don't ever touch that bar again."

"I was always curious how those things worked," he whispered in the darkness. "Turns out, it's like pickin' any

other lock, only easier." Then the bottom dropped out of
their stomachs a second time and the roaring in her ears
drowned him out.

"I see what you mean about runnin' around in circles,
about goin' up just to come down," he was saying when the
man in the sharkskin shorts let them out of the car. "It's
fun, but it doesn't get you anywhere. I think it's time we
went back to the apartment, figured something out."

They walked toward Seabreeze Avenue through
bombed-out blocks. Junkies had burned out the residents
on both sides of the street, stripping the buildings of pipes
and fixtures to be sold for scrap metal while the darkened
shells were left standing as crack houses and shooting gal-
leries. Harry detoured around an apartment building re-
duced to a mound of bricks, as though it had imploded,
and, having seen enough, picked up the pace to a steel-
gated avenue.

Kate asked, "Are you thinking of homesteading?"

"I was hopin' maybe I'd see a drugstore. That roller
coaster sloshed my insides around pretty good. I need to
have my ribs taped again."

"You won't find one here." She took his hand and they
backtracked to the boardwalk. "You won't find anything
here."

She sat him on a corner of the bed and took off his shirt
and his T-shirt, probed his ribs with her fingers. "How do
you feel?"

"I'm makin' up my mind," he said. "Do it some more."

"You're impossible."

"Only when you don't know me. You do, I'm real easy."

"Oh? Why would anyone bother?"

"Maybe I'm the best they can do."

"Think so?" Without his answer she reached beside the
bed and put a brown paper bag in his lap. "Play with this,"
she said. "I'll be back."

"Where you goin'?"

"Bathroom. There ought to be a scissors in the medicine chest."

Harry poured eight rolls of tape onto the mattress along with a disposable razor and some shaving cream that he hadn't wanted, a toothbrush that he had. More than ten minutes went by before she came back with a pair of blunt-nosed scissors. "The bathroom next door?"

She shushed him. She sat facing him and plucked a corner of the tape over his heart, then tugged sharply. "Does that hurt?"

Harry winced.

"I warned you it would," she said, as she peeled back several inches more. "Get ready now. This is going to smart."

She tore the tape down to bare skin. As Harry squeezed his eyes shut, she put her hands against his shoulders and pushed him onto his back, slithered on top of him. "Hey," he gasped, "you're crushin' me."

She pressed her face to his neck, his cheek. "What are you going to do about it?" she whispered.

Harry inhaled deeply through the taffy hair and felt the blood surge to his skin. *Woooeee,* he wanted to shout. He said, "You wouldn't believe the punishment I can take."

"We'll see." Kate kissed him, and pushed off carefully, and then bent down and took off her shoes.

"That the way they do it on Times Square?"

She stood up quickly. Harry saw color in her face and thought that he had just shot himself in the foot. He was trying to think of something to say when she reached behind her back and he heard a zipper slide in its track. "No," she said as the dress fell away. "More like this."

"That is tight," Harry said, and kicked off his own shoes.

Jesus, Harry said, that *is* tight.

15

HARRY stirred, opened his eyes. Kate was sitting against the headboard with her legs under her, watching him. She put her fingers on his eyelids and pressed them shut, kissed them. She said, "You know, just because something happens once doesn't mean it's going to happen again."

"I thought it happened three, four times already," he said. "I wasn't countin'."

"You know what I'm trying to say."

Harry yawned. "Yeah, but why say it now?"

"I don't want there to be any misunderstanding later."

"There's gonna be," he said, "you don't let me go back to sleep."

"Just so long as you—"

"I'm not lookin' you should make an honest man out of me, that's what's worryin' you. Usually, I'm the one who says it's time we had a little talk, though I try and wait at least till everybody's dressed."

Kate flushed.

"On the other hand, I'm startin' to get used to bein' around you. It's a comfortable feelin' and beats sleepin' with strangers, which is unhealthy and is something I generally avoid, although it'll do in a pinch."

"Don't think I feel any differently," she said. "About you, I mean." She reached for the blinds, bent one of the slats and gray light pushed aside the gloom.

"What're you doin'?" He moved her hand away.

"People are coming home from work already. We should try to salvage part of the day."

"What've we got to do that beats this?" He didn't let her respond. "I didn't expect a roll in the hay. I can't say I wasn't thinkin' about it, 'cause I was thinkin' about it all the time. Now you're tellin' me I got lucky, and let's leave it at that. You made your point. But your timing is way off."

Kate shifted uncomfortably. "If I didn't get it off my chest right away, I was afraid I'd do something I'd regret."

"What's that?"

She hesitated. "I'd attach myself to you."

Harry stroked her thigh, and she covered his hand with hers. "It'd sound better, you didn't look like you were swallowin' arsenic."

"That's just what it would be for me if I stayed with you," she said. "My life's such a mess the way it is. And yours . . ." She lifted her hands, then brought them down and cinched them around her knees. "I need someone, something to hang my hat on. Can you imagine what we'd be like together in a few years?"

"As I understand it, that line of thinkin' went out a while ago," Harry said. "A woman in her twenties, she should be lookin' for some excitement, find the right guy for that. She gets in her thirties, she can ditch him for Steady Eddie, to have kids with. In her forties, she keeps herself in shape, she can trade up to an older guy who'll be glad to give her things, a fancy house, furs, like that. She gets bored, there's always plenty of young guys don't do anything in the afternoon. She reaches her fifties, her sixties, well, I don't know too much about that. And after, about all you're interested in is someone to change your bedpan. I never said we should stay together the rest of our lives. But it'd be nice we played a few encores and see where we go from there."

Kate said, "I'm not worried about what happens when I'm seventy. I'm worried about whether I'm going to see tomorrow."

Harry pushed himself up to a sitting position and leaned back beside her. "You get around to tapin' my ribs, I can travel," he said. "I can ride a roller coaster without it killin' me, I don't see any reason I couldn't survive a few hours on a plane. Let's see how far we can get on the money we have—mine, you don't wanna touch yours—and worry about everything else later."

She pulled away. "What good does it do when we have to come back?"

"For starters, it keeps us alive. Which is a step in the right direction every time."

"What about clothes?" She looked pained. "I still haven't gone back to the brownstone."

"You'll buy new ones."

"And, aren't we forgetting somebody?" More pained, yet relieved to have an argument he couldn't dismiss so easily.

"Who? Ormont? You got your own problems. There's nothing you can do for him anyhow."

"Isaac," Kate said.

"Jesus."

"We can't just let him starve. When I left, he had enough food and water in his bowl for only one day."

"The mutt's got some camel in him," Harry said. "He can hold out till you send someone the key."

"He'll be dead."

"I happen to know for a fact he can go lots longer than . . ." He saw her waiting to ask how he knew, and stopped. ". . . Now, you wanna get out of town, or you wanna stick around till they find us? Like I gotta ask you, like it's a tough choice."

"Oh, keep quiet," Kate said. "It's almost time for supper, and I haven't even had lunch, and you expect me to make my mind up about something like this."

"What's the big deal? We get on the plane and go."

"That's easy for you to say. You have nothing to come back to."

"What've *you* got?"

"I need to think about it," Kate said. "Why don't I make supper and we'll see just how badly you want to stay with me. You can take a shower while I run down to the store for a few things. Does that sound fair to you?"

Harry swung his legs over the side of the bed and padded out of the room. "Medium rare," he said.

She hadn't returned by the time he stepped out of the tub. He went into the bedroom and got into his clothes, then pulled the blinds. Seabreeze Avenue was alive with pedestrians moving head-down from the subway through an October thundersquall. He wandered into the kitchen. Under the toaster was a note in a determined feminine hand.

> *I may be late so make*
> *yourself at home. We're*
> *having supper with Isaac.*
> *I've gone to pick him up.*

Kate sprinted the last block to the brownstone, looking over her shoulder. The key was in her fingers. She ran up the stoop and slammed the door behind her, threw the bolt and chained it, put her back against it as if the big bad wolf were threatening to blow it down. In the anteroom she stood catching her breath as she shook the rain from her hair. "Isaac," she called into the darkness. "Isaac, are you okay?"

She switched on a light and climbed toward the landing. A damp breeze fluttered against her cheek, and she made a mental note to close all the windows before she left. She heard a stair creak above her and halted with a foot in midstride. "Isaac?" she said again.

Her answer was the scuff of leather against the runner. She backed down two steps, pivoting as she grabbed the banister and began running.

"Kate?"

She pumped her legs harder, taking the steps two and three at a time.

"Kate, where are you going?"

Her knees felt rubbery. She lunged for the door, opening it before she dared turn around. A light came on over the landing illuminating brown loafers without socks, baggy cotton trousers, then a white shirt open at the neck. Her body tensed and she backed onto the stoop. *"You?"* she called inside, unsure of herself. "Is that really you . . . ? *Howard?"*

He came onto the landing tousling gray ringlets over his forehead. "You look like a dybbuk is chasing you," he said. "Who did you think it was?"

Kate didn't answer. She came back in and went up the stairs, meeting him below the landing. He looked tanned and fit, with an amused smile that announced he'd never seen such a fool. But she was beyond embarrassment. She threw her arms around his neck and let him hug her, her tears wilting the collar of the fresh white shirt. "I thought—"

Clinging to him, she began to sob. He put a firm hand on her shoulder and prodded her upstairs, sat her at the kitchen table and drew a glass of water from the sink. "Yes?" he said, trying to hide the smile that refused to go away.

"I still can't believe . . . How could you do this to me? What are you doing here?"

"What questions," he said. "This is still my home, isn't it?"

Isaac Grynzpun crawled out from under the table and rubbed his back against Kate's legs. She started, then dropped to her knees to pet the big dog all over. Then she began crying again. "I . . . I thought you were locked up in jail."

"I was," Howard said.

"But when did you come back? How did you get out?" Forcing herself to look him in the eye.

He let her see his smile. "No thanks to you."

Kate stood over him and kissed him again.

"Where *were* you?" he asked. "I was waiting, and waiting, and—"

"Oh, Howard," she said through her tears. "I'm sorry, so very, very sorry."

"Not half so sorry as I."

"I know," she said contritely.

"And what about my restaurant? When I left, I still had one. Now it's closed."

"God," Kate said. "I have so much to tell you."

"I should say the same thing. But mine is such a complicated story. I think it would be better if I heard yours first."

"Tell me all of it," she demanded. "Tell me right now. Don't leave anything out."

Howard bent an elbow behind his back, turning to show her the twisted arm. "Since I have no choice . . . But I must warn you in advance there are details I am not prepared to divulge, even to you."

"I understand," she sighed, as if the fact in itself was a trust too heavy to bear.

"Good, then," he said, sipping from her glass. "As I told you over the phone, new bureaucrats have installed themselves at the highest echelons of the IDF, the Israel Defense Forces, men with whom I have no relationship. As eager as they are to get their hands on my electronic gear, that is how severely they view the other goods I bring to Israel." He shrugged. "And who can blame them? These men had me kidnapped, brought to them so they could order me to give up all the krytrons that I had or they would prosecute me as a drug smuggler. They wanted also to teach me a lesson, show me who is boss. In the future, they said, my special privileges would cease. When I refused to cooperate, they threw me in prison, and a waiting game ensued. I would be there yet, if the prime minister's office did not intervene. The IDF men were instructed that the krytrons were needed immediately and so I would be allowed to pass unmolested through customs one last time. And that is how I am here today."

The corners of Kate's mouth, sagging under the weight of apprehension, collapsed. "Now I see everything."

"I don't," Howard said. "I see only a closed restaurant, and your strange behavior, and my house in ruins. When I went to the vault, I found poorly repaired stairs covered by a runner which does not quite match the old one. And inside—nothing. Can you explain these things to me?"

"I . . . I can't even explain them to myself."

"That's no answer."

"It's all I have," she said. "If I tell you what I do know, maybe you can make some sense of it for *me.*"

". . . And I was worried you would be bored," he said, smiling faintly. They were in the bedroom, Howard on the edge of the Barcalounger while Kate sat up in bed with her heels against the footrest. "That, I thought, would be your biggest problem when I was out of the country."

"It was the only one I didn't have."

He smiled again, apologetically, it seemed to Kate. "I suppose it is my fault. If I hadn't been so eager to see you take on a little responsibility, none of this would have happened to you."

"How were you to know? It was just one of those things." She reached beside the bed for her glass. "Or ten, or twenty of them."

"But still not so many as cannot be resolved. I am acquainted with Nicholas a long time, and he is not unreasonable. If I talk to him . . ."

"This is a *reasonable* person!" She was up off the bed, screaming. "Your house was burglarized, Nathan's dead, and I was almost charged with murder. And you say he's just folks?"

"The way he was when he brought you to his place, the

man who charmed you, that's Mike Nicholas. Much in the same way that the real Detective Stanley Bucyk shot Nathan. *He* is a thorn in my side ever since he was a bagman for the police and I was not his most cooperative . . . er, client. I ask Nicholas how he can employ such a thug, and he tells me I answered my own question."

"There must be a good reason why he wants someone like that working for him," Kate said.

"That is not our concern. I will reason things out with Nicholas. That is to say, I'll buy him off. After all, your new friend—and what you are doing with such a character is the greatest mystery of all—did take some things from his place. But, as Nicholas still seems to be holding on to my most valuable possessions, I am sure that a deal can be worked out to everyone's satisfaction."

"I refuse to believe it's that easy."

"Why not?" Howard asked. "Nicholas is a cocaine importer by profession, not some gonif, some hoodlum who looks for trouble he doesn't need. I think he would be more offended to hear you speaking of him as one than by your breaking inside his house."

"You're sure of that?"

Howard nodded vigorously. "The man who tried to ransack my home, he doesn't sound as smart, or as brave as he would like for you to believe. I would bet that Nicholas's was the first place he ever broke inside, the first place like that, and he gave himself a bad fright when he realized the kind of person it belonged to."

"I wouldn't count on it. It seemed to me that he knew what he was doing."

"In any event, not even he has anything more to fear. I will call Nicholas, and explain everything, and a deal will be worked out, rest assured. Nicholas will tighten the controls on Bucyk and you will be able to come out of hiding and show your face around our restaurant."

"I hope so."

"And where *have* you been?" he laughed. "In case I

have to reach you, can you give me a phone number at least?"

Kate opened her mouth, and closed it just as quickly.

"Surely, you trust me with this piece of information."

"Of course I do, Howard. It's just that . . . I know this is going to sound silly, but Harry, that's my . . . that's your burglar . . . Harry says I can't keep a secret. And I'd hate for him to pick up the phone and hear your voice and know that he was right."

"This prize catch, he's a jealous man, no less?"

"Oh, you're making me feel ridiculous, both of you. I . . . I'm living in Brooklyn, back in Brighton Beach," she blurted. "Is that good enough for you?"

"It is, if you promise to phone me, say this evening, so I can tell you how my negotiations with Nicholas went. How does that sound?"

Kate's eyes were glistening again as she went over to the Barcalounger and kissed the top of his head.

"Go now," he said. "And leave everything to me."

"Nick, how are you?"

"Ormont. What brings you back? I heard you went home and got the royal treatment."

"And give my regards to your parole officer," Howard said.

Nicholas laughed. "He works for me now." Thinking about it, he laughed some more. "Something I can do?"

"I believe you already did. I believe it was your man who came in here shooting like a cowboy and took some things that don't belong to him. What is all this about?"

"It's about Stan Bucyk," Nicholas said. "You remember Stan. As I recall, you were the one who introduced me to him."

"So I know he doesn't let out a breath without your telling him it is okay to take in the next one."

"Stan's a big boy now. I've put him on a longer leash. From time to time he gets all tangled up, and it's more like a noose around his throat. I can't help that."

Silence.

"Ormont . . . Ormont, are you still there?"

"Thinking." After a longer silence Howard said, "It changes nothing. If I were run down by your car, I would sue you, no matter who was behind the wheel. I will expect to see Bucyk shortly with my things."

"Krytrons?" Nicholas asked. "Is that what we're talking about? I've been having the dickens of a time trying to figure out what they are."

"They wouldn't be worth any more to you if you knew."

"What are you offering for such a rare commodity?"

"A certain young man."

"Couldn't you make it a young woman instead? They're more to my liking."

"His name is Harry, Harry something or other, the fool who looted your home in much the same manner as Bucyk ransacked my brownstone. If you give your word not to harm a mutual friend, I will tell you where he can be found."

"I get him for how many of the krytrons?"

"For all."

Nicholas made a *tsk*ing sound with his tongue and his teeth. "I don't see much profit in that. How about sweetening the pot? Can I interest you in more blow? I just received a quantity of pharmaceutically pure—"

"Not at this time. But there is something else *I* want from you."

"I'm giving up too much as it is."

"Hear me out first," Howard said, letting his voice rise for effect, then dropping down to little more than a whisper. "I want Bucyk. What he did inside my house is unforgivable. What he tried to do to me through this friend, that is worse."

"Why? I heard nothing happened," Nicholas said, amused.

"But why did anyone have to try?" Not whispering any more.

"You won't be sore if I suggest that Stan is not your biggest fan? He didn't enjoy calling on you when he was carrying the tin, and he doesn't resent you any less now that he works for me." He paused, letting everything sink in. "I promised Stan I would let him show me what he could do on his own one time, and that I would help out if I could. What he wanted to do, he wanted to do to you. He's a manipulator, Ormont . . . and I'm a man of my word. What choice did I have but to go along with him?"

"I'm sure you were greatly inconvenienced."

"No harm was done to anyone, except to that Russian kid, and Stan says that was unavoidable. If you don't believe me, ask the girl."

"To me, Nick, damn it. The harm was done to me. Letting Bucyk get at me through—"

"I don't see how," Nicholas said. "I treated her like a lady."

"You don't have to see. I want . . . I needed her—"

"And a good time was had by all. The girl has an appetite for luxury, Ormont. You should indulge it once in a while. It might bring results. I understand that so far they have been short in coming."

"It wouldn't be that for your own reasons you resent me as greatly as Bucyk does?" Howard said. "That you would like to see me embarrassed, too, that you thought Kate was a pushover."

"Ormont, how can you even think such things? Without my money where would you be?"

"Where you would be without my laundering so much of it for you. No good, Nick. I want Bucyk. I want to see him dead. You can deliver him in that condition, or I will have it taken care of myself. We both know I'm doing you a favor."

"You're right about Stan. He is more trouble than he's worth. But I can't let you have him right away. He has an important job to do for me. In fact, he's working on it at this very minute."

"What kind of job?" Howard asked anxiously. "Where a job?"

"You were going to tell me where yourself, weren't you?"

"I . . ."

"Quick, Ormont. I've got to run. My other phone is ringing."

"In Brooklyn," Howard said. "All the way out at the end of the subway line. In a place called Little Odessa . . ."

The single-prong plug fit neatly in the lighter socket. Bucyk dropped the small coil inside a can of Campbell's tomato soup and balanced it on the console between the seats, watched it simmer. He looked up to stare through the rain at the brownstone half a block away, flicking on his wipers, running through all four speeds before deciding on the slowest one. The aroma of the soup distracted him, and he searched the glove compartment for a plastic straw and inserted one end carefully between his cracked lips.

He switched on the radio. There was only hard rock and news on the AM band, more of the same plus some elevator music on FM. He sent the antenna higher and scoured the dial again, settling for a hockey game. It was the one sport he wasn't interested in, hockey and horseshoes, maybe. But the partisan roar of the crowd heartened him as though the cheers were meant for him. Any port in a storm, he thought, as he glanced at his watch again. He had been parked on Seventy-sixth Street for most of the day, and was feeling damp all over. He wondered if the girl was ever coming out.

He warmed his palms on the can as he sucked the soup

over temporary crowns. Checking the brownstone again, he saw the door open, and put the wipers on high. Ormont came out with an umbrella and leash in one hand and Kate on his elbow. The wolfhound went straight for the ginkgo tree at the curb. Ormont yanked him away and then gave him his lead. His second choice was a plane tree two doors down. Bucyk decided that if he were still carrying a summons book, he'd have cited Ormont for not cleaning up afterward.

He watched them dart back toward the house. Kate whispered something that made Ormont laugh, and then she kissed him—on the cheek, Bucyk noticed with some satisfaction—and when she stepped away, she had the umbrella. Then Ormont ran up the stoop and followed the dog inside. Bucyk twisted the key and backed the van around the corner, keeping an eye on Kate as she hurried toward Broadway.

Nicholas's phone was busy. The damn thing was *always* busy. He waited a minute before dialing again, and was answered by the same angry signal. Trying to remember the other number, the one he had been warned was only for emergencies, he pushed the quarter back into the slot.

"What took you so long?"

"She must've been in there a goddamn hour," Bucyk said. "I thought she was gonna spend the night. Then I remembered how hot she was for Ormont's body and I figured maybe *he* was leaving. She just went out, heading for the subway. What do you want me to do?"

"Do you think you can beat her train to Brighton Beach?"

"That where she's been hiding? Shit, I should've figured it out myself."

"You should have," Nicholas said. "But it doesn't matter now. Get there as fast as you can and wait for her outside the subway."

"Which station? There's lots of them in that part of Brooklyn."

"The Little Odessa stop."

"That's . . . yeah, that's Coney Island Avenue. On the D."

"Follow her wherever she goes, and then call me here and I'll meet you."

"It'll take you an hour, minimum, from where you are," Bucyk said. "What if they go out while I'm waiting?"

"In this rain? The weather bureau says a major storm is coming."

"You never know."

"You've got a point," Nicholas said. "I'll plug in the damn answering machine. Leave a message so I know where to find you. I'm already gone."

Bucyk pulled the receiver away, careful not to let the hard plastic brush against his jaw. He reached deep inside his jacket and adjusted the stiff new shoulder harness and the holster it held tight against his ribs, let his fingers flick against the rasped grips of a Taurus PT 99 Protector. "You're not the only one," he said out loud.

He was parked in the shadows when she came down from the elevated station, walking briskly through the rain as if outdistancing all her fears. Keeping half a block behind he stalked her along Brighton Beach Avenue, through dark streets blackened by the worsening storm. At Ocean Parkway an old woman in a red and yellow babushka smiled and said something to her, and they ducked under an awning to gesture exaggeratedly with flailing hands. Traffic forced him past them in the curb lane and he saw her look right at the van without a hint of recognition.

From a side street he watched as she kissed the old woman good-bye and then crossed the parkway. Close to the beach there were fewer cars on the road, and he let her get a block ahead before he followed her onto Seabreeze. When she went inside an apartment house, he drove into the shade of an ailanthus thicket and cut the engine. A Con Ed crew in blue waders was scurrying around a manhole like fishermen in an underground stream, and the light bubbling up from their excavation illuminated the building entrance. He wrote the address in a spiral notebook with an NYPD shield on the cover. Then he slipped outside to search for a pay phone that worked.

He came back in a downpour and turned on the heater, directing a warm blast of air at his damp clothes. He was monitoring the sparse traffic for Nicholas's car when a station wagon pulled up and a man in a dark raincoat backed out covering his head with a newspaper. Bucyk flipped on the radio, played it so loud that at first he didn't hear the tapping on the window. Then he swept the fog from the glass and saw Nicholas with the rain running down his cheeks.

"That building there," Bucyk nodded, reaching over quickly to let him inside. ". . . I was looking for the Porsche."

Nicholas shut off the heater and opened the vents, tossed the raincoat lightly around his shoulders. "I used a car service from Mermaid Avenue. The robbers charged ten dollars for an eight-block ride. I couldn't take the Porsche into a neighborhood like this. It would stand out like socks on a rooster."

"Where'd you stash it?"

"In a lot on the other side of Neptune Avenue. I hope it's safe."

"Part of it is," Bucyk said, showing a lopsided grin that didn't seem worth the pain. "The fog lights, the radio, they're safe with whoever's got them by now."

"Something like your teeth."

Bucyk looked back toward the apartment house. "The dentist says no one'll know. He says the caps'll look better than the real ones even."

"They should," Nicholas said. "They're costing me

a bundle. I'm giving you better benefits than the department."

Bucyk started a feeble laugh. Nicholas finished it for him.

"You mind changing the subject?" Bucyk asked.

"What would you rather talk about?"

Unbuttoning his jacket, Bucyk came out with the Taurus. "Hunting," he said.

Nicholas held out his palm and Bucyk slapped the gun into uncallused flesh. Nicholas removed the clip expertly. He switched off the safety and dry-fired it. "Where'd you get this?"

"You could say I always had it."

"Do you think you can hang onto it without some punk taking it away from you?"

Bucyk replaced the shells and stuffed the Taurus back inside the holster. "We'll find out soon," he smiled. "Won't we?"

Nicholas didn't return the smile. "I don't want to find out. I want to know it in advance. If you screw up like last time, I'm telling you now, I'll cut you loose. Until we get back the Mag, the damn thing is a loose cannon rolling around our decks."

"Why? Anyone takes it off the punk, it's no skin off our nose. It's not like it's registered in my name."

"Do I have to tell you that if he's picked up with it your former employers will run it through ballistics as a matter of routine, and that they'll see it was used to kill the Russian?"

"You know what happens then?" Bucyk said. "The punk gets nailed for murder two, that's what. Going after him like this, putting him out of his misery, we're doing him a favor. Shit, if it wasn't I had a personal grudge against the bastard, I'd say let's dime him and save ourselves the bother."

"That's all we'd need. He'd be screaming your name to

anyone who'd listen. Yours *and* mine. . . . No," Nicholas said. "We came here to do a job."

Bucyk wound down the window and put his hand out. "You think the rain'll let up, think he'll be coming out?"

"There's one thing more. When you're through with the punk, I've got something else for you."

Bucyk turned quickly toward him, shaking his head. "The girl? I don't see why it's necessary she—"

"She has to be silenced," Nicholas said firmly. "But, you're right, taking her out is not the way to go about it. We can get at her as effectively through other people."

Bucyk appeared to relax. "I told you, the punk's dead."

Nicholas didn't seem to hear. "Who can she go to when she finds herself alone? Back to the police? Considering all they've done for her so far, I doubt that. It's more likely she'll come to us, come crawling. If she does, and if she asks nicely, I might throw her a little something. Make her a partner in my restaurant." He laughed. "Of course, if she doesn't ask nicely . . ."

"You already have a partner in the Knights," Bucyk said. "Remember?"

"Not for much longer. Not after you take care of him."

"*Ormont?* That's who . . . ? I thought he was your buddy, your cash cow."

"He was," Nicholas said. "But then he asked me to do a contemptible thing, something that shows just how little he values my integrity."

"Yeah? What's that? What'd he want, a pussy like that?"

"He wants you dead, Stan."

Bucyk sat up sharply. He rolled up his window and squeezed out of his seat and went to the back of the van. "You mind keeping' an eye on the building while I catch a few winks?" he asked. "I see where it's gonna be a long night."

16

KATE knocked twice, then twice more. She opened her umbrella and set it beside the door, listening for footfalls that never came. She searched her pockets for the frayed knot of string that held the keys and came inside with her shoes in her hand.

She hurried through the empty rooms calling his name. A few twisted strips of tape on the bedroom floor were the only evidence that he had been there. In the kitchen she found a ball of paper in the sink, and she spread it against the drainboard to read the note she had left him. That he was gone didn't surprise her. The surprising thing was that he had stayed as long as he had—and the moisture she felt on her face. Angry with herself, she blotted her eyes with a paper towel and examined the dark smears. What was the matter with her, anyway? This was what she had wanted, wasn't it—not having to face him, to tell him herself?

She walked back to the bedroom and slipped out of the wet dress. As she went to the closet, she noticed that the window was wide open and that a small puddle had collected on the sill. She lay the dress on the bed and was hurrying to the window, when she felt her limbs go weak.

Someone was on the fire escape, plodding toward the apartment along the metal rungs. Her instinct was to run into the hall hollering for help, trapping him there. But as she moved away she glimpsed herself in the mirror wearing only her bra and panties, and suddenly modest, picking the worst of all times for *that*, she froze.

His back was to her, the upper half of his body hidden behind the blinds. She was attempting a few steps toward the door when he bent inside and she saw the cast on his arm and allowed herself the luxury of a breath, then so many of them, quick and shallow, that she nearly toppled onto the bed. He spotted her over his shoulder as he slid off the sill carrying a heavy object on his hip.

"What were you doing out there?" she asked.

He looked at her as though she didn't exist. He brought his load to a small table and placed it carefully against the wall. She saw that it was a portable television with a silver handle and bent rabbit ears on top.

"You said supper was gonna be late. You didn't say five hours late. I didn't have the key, and I didn't wanna get locked out, so I hung around lookin' at the walls and when I got done I went over to the neighbor's, and borrowed this."

"I don't believe you did that," she said angrily.

"Nobody saw."

"I mean, how could you just go into someone's apartment and take their TV? That's a terrible thing to do."

"They have another one," he told her. ". . . Color. They also have plenty of nice stuff they shouldn't keep lyin' around, stuff I didn't take. It makes you feel better, I'll bring this back when we don't need it any more." He pushed the dress out of the way and sat down. "Where's the mutt?"

"What?" She went to the bed, but when he reached out to her she snatched up the dress and pulled it over her head. "Oh, I left him at the brownstone."

"He wasn't hungry?"

Kate shrugged.

"Then where the hell were you all day? You know what I was thinkin' must've happened to you?"

"No one told you to," she said in a voice that reminded her vaguely of herself.

"Since when'd you get so independent? The other night you were too uptight to sleep without me tuckin' you in bed. Now you're telling' me to mind my own business?"

"That's right," she shouted. "And lower your voice. We don't need everyone in the building knowing our problems."

"There's somebody in this building who'd like to know what the goddamn problem is."

Kate threw up her hands in an awkward stage gesture. "What's the use? This could never work out, not you and me. Who are we trying to fool?"

"Fooled me," Harry said. "You fooled me good. I thought we were gonna beat it out of town, see what it'd be like by ourselves without all kinds of crap to worry about."

"It would be just like this."

"You'd rather be dead?" Not sarcastic, not trying to score points. "What're you gonna do instead?"

"I . . . Stop worrying about me," she said. "You're in lots deeper trouble than I am. You can have my money, my end of what we took, if you'll use it to get as far away as you can. Worry about yourself."

"I'm tired of that. I thought it'd be nice worryin' about somebody else for a change."

"Not me. I'm sorry."

"Come here." He patted the mattress and made room for her by putting his knees together.

Kate stayed where she was. "Please . . . leave now. Or I will."

Harry got off the bed. He slid his hand in his shirt and rubbed his sore ribs. "Okay, that's what you want." He grabbed the TV by the handle and carried it to the window.

"Where are you going with that?"

"I told you," he said, "I was gonna bring it back when we didn't need it any more."

In spite of herself she smiled, brushing away tears. "God damn you, why are you making this so hard for me?" She took the TV from him and brought it back to the table. Then she circled her arms around his neck and pressed herself against him. "Don't go. Not just yet, I mean. There are things I should explain."

He walked her to the bed, pushed her down gently. "No," she said. "That's not going to make it easier."

"What do you want to do?"

"I don't know. Have you eaten yet?"

He shook his head.

"I haven't either," she said. "Let's go out. I know a special place . . . a place you're going to love."

The storm had gathered in intensity, gray sheets of rain riding a salt wind out of the east. As they hurried toward the beach Harry tilted the umbrella over his shoulder and a looping gust turned it inside out, wrenched the fabric from the ribs. He dropped it in a garbage can and the gale sucked it out again and sent it rolling into traffic. Kate clung to his bad arm, burying her head against his body. "Where'd you say this place was?" he asked her.

"On Stillwell Avenue, around the corner from the Typhoon."

"Pretty far, on a day like this. What's so special about it?"

"It's in the subway arcade," she said. "After we talk, you can go upstairs and you'll never have to see me again."

"My favorite kind of cookin'," he muttered.

"Don't be mad at me."

"No promises," he said, and let her hold him a little tighter.

They hurried down Surf Avenue behind the boardwalk. In the shelter of high weeds sprouting from a sidewalk sand dune, they stopped to let Kate dry her face with a handkerchief. Harry saw the fresh mascara running down her cheeks. "Something you wanted to tell me," he said as they began moving again.

"Howard's back."

His heel dragged in the sand, but he didn't break stride. "You saw him this afternoon?"

She nodded.

"You knew he'd be there?"

"No," she said, shouting it into the wind. "I lost ten years' growth when he said hello."

"I thought you said he was in prison. In Israel."

"He was."

"Then what's he doin' out?"

"It's not important. I mean that part of it doesn't concern us. What matters is that he's in New York and that he made me another offer, an even better one, to run the Knights for him."

"To move in with him, too?"

"Please don't hate me," she said. She felt his foot catch again, more noticeably than before. "I need something new, something better than this. Howard can change my whole life for me."

They crossed a street that ran into the aquarium parking lot. The rooftop pool was empty. A fine day for ducks, Harry was thinking, not for penguins. He started to say something, but then changed his mind. "You think those other two are gonna pack up and quit lookin' for us 'cause Ormont's in town?"

Something told him that she was going to say yes.

"Howard's known both of them for a long time. He can straighten things out easily. Everything was just one big mistake."

"What happened to Nathan, he can fix that, too?"

"Do we have to talk about it?"

"Uh-huh."

They followed the avenue away from the boardwalk. At a street dead-ending at the beach they stepped into the gutter, standing unprotected in the rain as a garbage truck turned in front of them. Harry glanced up to see the Typhoon's dark skeleton disappearing in low clouds a block away.

Kate was saying, "Howard says he can smooth things out so they'll forget they ever wanted to hurt us. That's good enough for me."

The garbage truck completed its turn and crept toward the beach. Harry and Kate were almost on the sidewalk when a blue van cut across three lanes of Surf Avenue and bore down on them from the side. Kate screamed, "Look out," and pushed him onto the curb, felt the breeze from the speeding vehicle tickle the hairs on the back of her neck.

"Fuckin' lunatic," Harry yelled, and shot the driver the finger.

Kate pressed a hand to her chest, steadying herself. Squinting over his shoulder, she saw the van continue halfway down the street, then wheel into a U-turn and tear back toward them. "Oh my God, it's Bucyk. Howard mustn't have talked to them yet. Come on," she screamed, grabbing at Harry's sleeve. "He's trying to run us down."

They charged along the deserted avenue past disco bumper cars and a Fascination parlor that was shuttered for the season. Caged by latticed shadows, Harry hesitated under the Typhoon, his legs churning as though he was treading water. Then he slipped into gear again, clamping Kate's wrist in his good hand and dragging her around the corner.

"Where are we going?"

"Beach," Harry said. "He can't drive that damn truck in the sand."

Tripping over his heels, Kate struggled to keep pace. Her arm was still locked in his as she spurted two steps ahead of him. They were less than fifty yards from the boardwalk when the sidewalk erupted in pebbly shrapnel, and she saw Nicholas at the railing, pointing a shiny gun that looked like precious metal against the dark raincoat around his shoulders. Without slowing, Harry swung her into a taut semicircle, and then they were racing back toward Surf Avenue. Behind them Kate heard a second bullet carom off a hydrant.

Harry was in the lead now, pulling her with him as her legs began to give out. Her lungs were burning, and she cursed all the nights she had spent in smoky rooms.

"Run," he yelled. "We make it to the subway, maybe a cop'll scare 'em off."

Kate pushed herself forward, breathing through her mouth. She was about to come even with him when he stopped suddenly and she bruised her chin against his back. The squeal of tires forced her eyes to the middle of the street, where the blue van was angling at the sidewalk. She panicked then and would have backed against the Typhoon's chain-link fence if Harry hadn't yanked her into motion again, shoving her toward a gingerbread booth where a fat woman in a sharkskin suit jacket was shooing away two tattered black children. Harry threw five dollars at the woman, didn't wait for change. He ran around the kids, prodding Kate into the narrow loading area where the roller coaster's six cars should have been.

"What are we doing *here?*" she asked.

Looking down the empty track, he went inside his jacket for the Beretta. "Think you can shoot this?"

She put both hands on it, pushed it away. "Not at a person."

"They're tryin' to kill us, you know."

"I can't," she screamed. "I can't."

Then the cars glided along the platform and three couples drenched to the skin came toward them laughing uncontrollably. "Maybe you won't have to. Let's follow these nice people out. Your friends wouldn't try anything in a crowd."

Kate took a long, soothing breath, but gulped it back as she saw his eyes narrow. "What's wrong?"

"*Shit!*"

She followed his gaze to the ticket booth, where Nicholas and Bucyk were pushing money at the fat lady. "What do we do now?" she asked him.

Harry didn't answer.

"Think of something," she pleaded.

"I'm tryin', damn it. Nothing's comin'."

She looked toward the booth again. Nicholas and Bucyk were muscling the laughing couples aside as they hurried to the loading area. Harry dropped her hand and ran for the front car. When she took off after him, he shoved her back roughly.

"Get away from me," he hollered. "I gotta get as far from you as I can."

She stood there, defeated, watching him run. She saw him pull out the Magnum, then wave it uselessly as the black kids got in the way, racing him to the front. He tripped up one little boy, pushed him into his friend and jumped in the first seat. Nicholas and Bucyk brushed past her with guns partially concealed by the raincoats draped over their arms. She felt tears in her eyes once again as Harry surrendered the Magnum and Bucyk relieved him of the Beretta.

His lone act of resistance consisted of refusing to leave the roller coaster. She saw him looking small and injured beside them, shaking his head like he was going to snap it off his shoulders. Poor bastard, she thought—forgetting just how frightened she was herself—poor, runty tough guy, too terrified to move, or even to think. Howard had been right about him, like he was right about everything. She laughed, realizing that it was too late now for even Howard's good sense to do her any good.

Bucyk was stuffing Harry's guns in his jacket as he came back for her. He pushed her into the last car and sat with his body angled against hers. Up ahead she could see Nicholas with his weapon buried in Harry's ribs, the bad ribs, sliding into the front seat.

"So what's new?" Bucyk laughed through puffed lips.

Kate twisted away, avoiding his smile. "What's going to happen to us?"

"Whaddaya think's gonna?" He leaned forward, adjusting the guns in an inside pocket so that he could sit comfortably. "We're going for a ride. Then, if you want, I'll buy you some cotton candy and a frank. We're all gonna have a swell time today." He folded the raincoat over his lap. In his hand she saw a gun that was even nastier-looking than the ones Harry had showed her. "Well, maybe not everyone."

An attendant came by and pulled the bar over their knees, then went to the first car and locked Harry in with Nicholas. Nicholas dug his gun deeper into Harry's ribs, savoring the wince it produced. "I had no idea a roller coaster could be so much fun."

"Let Kate go, at least," Harry said. "She didn't know what she was getting herself into."

Nicholas tried the muzzle against another rib. "She had a good idea the night you two broke into my house."

"What's the big deal? You got just about everything back. What are you out, you're hardly out anything."

"You underestimate me," Nicholas said. "I'm a very sensitive fellow. When I found out that my home had been entered, it was as though I had been personally violated by you two."

"By me," Harry said. "Kate only went along for the ride."

"That's not what I heard."

"I don't know where you get your information from, but it was all my idea, my score. There's no reason for that ape to hurt her."

"Stan?" Nicholas said, his head tilting back as the cars lurched away from the platform. "Stan would never harm the girl. As you must have noticed, he's quite taken with her."

Some of the pain went out of Harry's face.

"So I'll deal with her myself. As I'll deal with you."

In the tunnel Nicholas played the muzzle hard against Harry's side. "I wouldn't try anything in here. I wouldn't even think of it."

"You say so," Harry croaked.

"Just stay nice and calm, and answer a few questions for me, and who can say, you might live an extra two or three minutes."

The darkness diluted and Harry felt the rain on his face. He looked over the boardwalk, but saw only the derelict tower of the parachute jump piercing the blackness.

"That night at my place, you were looking for something . . . krytrons. Tell me what they're for." Waiting for an answer, Nicholas surveyed the emptiness. "Tell me, or I'll blow you away this second."

Harry cringed, inching away from the gun until his back was against the side of the car. "Oh," he said like Kate would. He put his hand outside and felt for the lock on the safety bar. "Oh, *that!*"

They crept to the edge of the incline, and Harry watched Nicholas take a deep breath and hold it. As they spilled over the top Nicholas reached automatically for the bar, falling forward as Harry sprang the lock and the steel rod shot away from their laps. Nicholas put his free hand out to push back against the gathering speed, and with the other raised the gun at Harry. Harry swiped at the weapon and it went off beside his ear, the pain as intense as if he had caught the bullet. The ringing that filled his head told him that he was still alive and that he would never hear much else with that ear again.

They were dropping, careening into the hairpin curve that would bring them to the second hill. Harry wrestled the gun out of Nicholas's hand, saw it clatter through the scaffolding to the street. Nicholas threw a short punch to the side of the jaw and the momentum carried him into

Harry, pinning the good hand against his chest. Before Nicholas could land again, Harry brought the cast up sharply into the other man's chin. Nicholas recoiled, punching blindly with both hands, but Harry was too out of control to notice. He grabbed a fistful of the glossy hair and slammed Nicholas's face into the cast, smashed it again and again, crying out as the knitting bones shattered in his arm. Then he pulled back on the hair and saw the fine nose spread over Nicholas's face, drove it one more time against the plaster.

They dove and looped and soared over another hill, and Harry lost his balance and clung desperately to the seat. Behind him he made out the top of Bucyk's head coming over the rise. He twisted around just as Nicholas's limp form was toppling over the side of the car. Harry let go of the seat and grabbed Nicholas's raincoat, watching as though from a distance as it came off in his hand and the other man fell away from him. Too late he reached out again as Nicholas pitched headlong into the scaffolding, snagging on a beam long enough to make eye contact before hurtling to the roof of the gingerbread booth.

The car whipped over a smaller rise, and when Harry glanced back again Kate and Bucyk were hidden on the other side. Below he glimpsed Nicholas's body sprawled face up with a leg curled grotesquely underneath, the arms spread open in supplication, inviting him to jump. Harry pulled his eyes away, and grim curiosity brought them back. Nicholas's face was a pulpy mask, but the glossy hair appeared hardly mussed. At the corner of Stillwell the black kids he had seen before were pointing to the top of the booth.

His arm was on fire. Two large cracks in the plaster seemed to be letting the pain leak over his entire right side. Shivering, he picked up Nicholas's raincoat and threw it over his shoulders. He felt something bulky in one of the pockets, and pulled out a billfold and then a ring of keys. He was examining them when the car slid through the loading area and the tunnel and came out into the rain. The roller coaster slowed for the big hill, inched over the top, and then stopped moving, and he looked down at the street, toward the wailing of sirens muzzled by the storm. He shuddered again as he buttoned the raincoat and swung his feet onto the track, hunting for the easiest way down . . .

Bucyk made a tent of his raincoat and raised an elbow for Kate to join him inside. "The hell's going on? I'm getting drowned."

Kate knotted a kerchief over her head, moved farther away.

"You know who you look like, like that? Like one of those old Russkies—"

"I don't want to hear it."

"Hey," he shouted, rattling the safety bar. "Let's get this show on the road." He cupped his hands around his mouth. "Hey, Nick, how you two doing? Having fun?"

His answer was the sound of the wind and the keening of a siren above it.

Shielding her eyes from the rain, Kate took her bearings. They were stuck below the crest of the big hill with the front cars already out of sight. A flash of red light drew her attention to the avenue and she raised herself cautiously. The ticket booth came into her field of vision and she saw the broken body on the roof, knew at once that it was Harry. She wanted to sob, but had run out of tears. She forced herself to take a second look through clear eyes.

Bucyk put a hand on her shoulder and forced her down. "What's the matter?" he asked. "Scared?"

"This thing is always getting stuck."

"A roller coaster? How?" He peered down over her side of the car, but the ticket booth was out of view. He saw an emergency vehicle on the street and another arriving. "Looks like trouble," he said. "Like somebody's hurt."

"No," she told him. "They send for an ambulance whenever anything goes wrong with the Typhoon. They don't take chances."

"Good idea."

They sat there for fifteen minutes before the cars jolted over the hill with a metallic groan and Kate saw that the front seat was empty. Bucyk did, too, and strained for a better look. Kate pulled him down and threw her arms around him, feeling for the guns against his body, pressing against them as he hugged her to his side. She didn't let go until they crept into the loading area, where two policemen and an ambulance attendant met them.

One of the officers, a lanky blond who couldn't have been older than Kate, helped her onto the platform. "Did you see what happened, miss?" he asked.

"Ask him," she said, stepping quickly behind the uniformed men. "But ask nicely. This man is carrying three guns."

17

HOWARD dropped onto the dark brown Barcalounger that was his favorite and leaned all the way back. His entire body hurt. He pulled out his shirttails and rubbed the proud flesh beside his spine. After forty years the scar scarcely had faded, the angry reminder of a blunder he had devoted his life to trying not to repeat. As though he needed a reminder on a day like this, when the pain filled his chest again like molten iron. He tucked in the shirt and reached for a bottle on his desk. As he did, he saw one of his waiters passing outside the office.

"Malik," he called out, "why don't you join me in a drink?"

The sad-eyed man came in dutifully, reluctant to risk intimacy with his boss, or not to. "It's early," he said. "I haven't eaten."

"Neither have I." Howard patted his chest as though it was his belly. "What do you say to some dinner first?"

"If there's time . . ."

"If I say there is," Howard told him, "there's plenty."

"Let me go to the kitchen. I'll see what's good."

Howard stopped him with a stare. "Let's have real food." He scoured his desk for a Chinese take-out menu and began circling his selections with a felt-tip pen.

The waiter rolled the menu into his breast pocket and went away. Minutes later he was back in the office, as uncomfortable as if there was a gun to his head.

"That was quick," Howard said. He was cradling a tumbler in his hands.

"There's a man outside. He says he wants to see you. He says he has something you'll be interested in."

"I'm sure he has." Howard raised the glass to his lips. "But tell him we'll get along somehow without. These salesman, I should charge admission . . ."

"He's not a salesman."

"No? Who is he, then?"

"I don't know," the waiter said, unhappy in his role of intermediary. He held out a worn hand wrapped around something Howard couldn't quite see. "He told me to show you this. He said you'd be interested."

Howard flipped through the sleeves of a soft pigskin wallet, and came forward in the Barcalounger so quickly that his feet slapped against the floor. He took a twenty from his own wallet and tossed it at the waiter. "Treat yourself to the dinner for three at Lum Fong's. I'm not hungry any more. And Malik, before you go, show the gentleman inside."

Harry came into the office raking his hair with his fingers. To Howard he looked exhausted, a sleepless man in slept-in clothes. Howard stood up to greet him. But when he offered his hand, Harry raised the heavy cast that immobilized his right arm. The plaster was a pristine white, the only thing about him that seemed fresh and clean.

"Where are you keeping yourself?" Howard asked, studying the tired features. "We've been worried about you."

Harry circled warily and then sat in the dark brown Barcalounger. "Why? You don't know me. You don't know the first thing about—"

"I know everything about you. Everything that Kate does. And Isaac." When that produced only a pained smile, he added, "We were afraid you'd been hurt."

"I was hidin'," Harry explained.

Howard retreated to the desk and raised his hips onto it. As if it were expected of him he asked, "Where?"

"In various places. After your pal had his accident on the roller coaster, it didn't seem like such a hot idea for me to be out in the street."

"He wasn't my friend," Howard said.

"It wasn't any accident either. At least no one would've believed it was. I thought I could be facin' a murder rap. Only now I see in the papers where Bucyk's takin' the fall for that one, too."

"You have Kate to thank," Howard said. "She told the police Nick and Bucyk were trying to kill her because of what she knew about Nathan's murder. Under the law, that makes what happened to Nick Bucyk's fault. The detectives like neat packages, and Bucyk and his guns no doubt make up the neatest they have seen in some time. They were only too happy to believe that Kate was alone."

"She covered for *me?*"

"For all concerned," Howard said. It occurred to him that his chest had stopped hurting; he poured another drink anyway. "But that's not what brings you to see me."

Harry pushed back in the Barcalounger and put up his feet. Howard tried not to look dispossessed. He motioned toward the wallet. "It was this?"

"And these," Harry said, tossing a ring of keys at the desk.

Howard got a hand on the key ring, but dropped it. "Americans are all baseball players," he said as he bent down with an embarrassed grin. "You know how to catch since you are little children."

"Got any ideas what they open?"

"Here are car keys. But these others, I don't—"

"That one there," Harry told him, "is for a safe-deposit box at the CitiCorp bank on Utopia Parkway. It'd be too bad there was anything excitin' inside, 'cause there's no way we get a peek at it that I can figure. The other one is for a Gardall SC1130 safe like the one Nicholas was keepin' in his bedroom. I got a hunch you're interested in what he had in there."

"Am I?"

"You tell me."

Howard sloshed a few drops of water from a copper pitcher into his glass. A long drink brought a softness to his mouth. "Of course I am," he said. "Why pretend otherwise? If you believe Nick was holding goods belonging to me in that safe, well, so do I. I don't mind admitting that I would love to have these back. The question is, what do *you* want."

"I was thinkin' in the neighborhood of twenty-five thousand dollars cold turkey might be fair."

The hardness—and then some—returned to Howard's face. "I think it's highway robbery for keys."

"Those damn krytrons, whatever the hell they are, have got to be in that safe." Harry became aware that his good hand had balled itself into a fist. "You sayin' now you don't want 'em after all, that two men are dead on account of 'em and you were just playin'?"

"That key is worth nothing to me . . . nothing." Howard put down his drink. "Not when I have no way of getting past Nick's security system." He glanced toward the door and barely perceptibly showed his palm.

Someone darted by in a tan raincoat, a slender figure topped with taffy hair. Harry opened his own hand and raised it. "Hey," he called out, "you don't say hello any more?"

Kate stopped reluctantly. Tiny brass bells dangled from her ears and she was heavily made up. Harry counted eight rings on her left hand, more on the right. Below the raincoat golden slippers whisked against the flattened shag.

"Hello," she said emptily.

Howard nodded and she came into the office, pinching the raincoat around her veils and halter top. She snatched

Howard's drink off the desk and carried it into a corner. "This man has made me an outrageous proposition," Howard said. "I would like your opinion if I should consider bargaining him down."

"I don't know anything about your deals."

"You know him. You can tell me whether to take this seriously, whether I can trust him."

Kate shrugged. "Why would he trust us?"

"Evidently, he doesn't. He's trying to hold me up. He wants twenty-five thousand dollars for the key to Nick's safe, if that's what he has."

Harry said, "That's the key. And twenty-five K is the price. How you get in is your business. You interested, or not?"

Howard twirled the key ring around his finger. He shook his head.

Harry pushed up out of the Barcalounger, plucked the keys from Howard's hand.

Kate watched him walk away. "Thirty-five," she called after him.

"Who gave you permission to—"

"Offer him thirty-five thousand, if he'll empty the safe himself."

Harry kept walking. When he reached the door, he dug a finger in his bad ear and turned the other one toward them. "You want my professional services, they don't come cheap. I'll go inside for you, but it'll cost another twenty-five K."

"You can do this?" Howard asked. "The police are not watching Nick's place all the time?"

"Yeah," Harry said.

"Yeah? Yeah, which?"

"I was out for a look this morning, and an unmarked car comes by every hour or so. But that don't mean the job can't be done. For fifty K, nothing's impossible."

Howard made a face like he'd found a scorpion in his

shoe. "You'll want half in advance. I'm giving ten percent."

"We'll discuss terms later." Harry raised his cast with his
good hand. "I can't do it alone. You interested in comin'
along, maybe learnin' a new trade?"

"You're joking, yes?"

Kate said, "I'll go."

"I wasn't askin' you. I'll find somebody."

"Howard," she said, "tell him everything is off if I can't
go with him. I wouldn't trust him with five thousand dollars. I've been out there before. I know the kind of help
he needs."

"Take her." Howard unscrewed the cap from the bottle
again. "I want her watching out for my investment."

"Your investment," Harry said, "is ten K up front, and
I don't move a muscle till I see you bringin' along the
whole fifty. There's nothing in the safe, I can't help that."

Howard stiffened his elbows, raising himself off the desk,
then sank down. "What you are demanding is entirely
unreasonable."

"Yeah," Harry said, and made the keys disappear in his
hand.

"The three of us will go," Howard said without hesitat-
ing. A pull from the bottle amplified the resignation in his
voice. "When is the best time?"

"You tell me."

"I should? What do I know about—?"

Harry said, "You know how long it takes to raise that
kind of cash."

In a sweatshirt and jeans and her old shearling coat Kate
dashed out the service entrance. Around the corner on
Seventy-third Street the green Cutlass was parked behind
a leased BMW 735i that was Howard's latest plaything.
She saw Harry duck out of the German car stuffing two

thick envelopes in his pants. A gaslamp in a brownstone's short yard threw spasmodic light on Howard motioning her to the driver's door.

"For his own good I should have bargained him down," Howard said. "He's a wild man, you know. He'll kill himself with fifty thousand dollars, throw it all after whores and bad drugs."

Kate bent inside the window. "I wouldn't count on that." She smiled, then thought better of it. "What makes you say—?"

"He told me."

Kate backed away. "Are we taking your car, or his?"

"Both of 'em." The words came from behind her. "I'll just hand over your stuff and be on my merry way."

"He has his ten thousand?"

As though he couldn't bring himself to say it, Howard whispered, ". . . All."

"I'd better ride out with him."

"Who invited you?" Harry said.

Howard touched the gas and the BMW began to purr. "I must insist that you let her."

Kate got into the Cutlass as Harry was fitting a key into the steering column. "Why, it starts from inside now." Also purring. "Aren't we getting lazy?"

The BMW pulled into the street. Gunning his engine, Harry swerved around and nosed ahead at the crosswalk. "Let's just don't talk, huh?" The light changed and they sped down Broadway, turned again and headed toward the park.

"Fine with me," Kate said. "That's perfectly fine." She slouched against the door, then sat erect and pressed down the lock with her elbow, then leaned back again. "I . . . you know, I have my own room at the brownstone."

Harry adjusted the mirror. A cab had maneuvered between the Cutlass and Howard's car, and he slowed to let the intruder by. He tugged at his ear. "I don't hear so good."

When they came off the bridge, Kate said, "I don't imagine you remembered to bring fresh batteries?"

Harry pointed to his ear.

"I must be out of my mind going back there with you," she shouted at him.

"Yeah," he said.

The German car caught up again on Queens Boulevard and Harry kept it close the rest of the way to Forest Gardens. It was three-thirty by the police scanner in Kate's lap when they passed under the arch and cruised the wooded streets toward Nicholas's place.

Kate said, "This will never work. The guards can't possibly be stupid enough to fall for the same trick twice."

Harry started to touch his ear. Kate swatted his hand away. "Damn you," she hissed.

They drove down Nicholas's block and turned. A cream-colored Mercedes-Benz limousine took up the spot where they had parked the last time and Harry continued almost to the corner. He waved the BMW ahead. Howard found room on the other side of the intersection, then walked back to the Cutlass.

Howard's chest was hurting again. "What do you want me to do?" he asked.

"It's up to you," Harry said. "You can hang around and keep an eye out, or go in with me. We're playin' on your nickle."

"You're sure you can get inside without alerting—"

"Howard will stay here," Kate interrupted. "With my eyesight, he's the best lookout we have. Also, I've been in the house before. Moving around in the dark, I'll have some idea of where I am. You don't mind, Howard, do you?"

Howard stood taller. He said, "Tell me how I do this."

It was Kate who reached into the backseat for the walkie-talkies. "It's simple," she said as she got out of the car and hooked one of the radios to her belt. "You listen for police calls to the neighborhood and at the same time you watch for private security guards. If you see them, you press—"

"How do I know who I'm looking for?"

"In a few minutes you'll be closer to them than you could ever want." She glanced into the front seat for Harry's approval, but the Cutlass was empty. She saw him heading up the walk, and chased after him along the flagstones. "I didn't finish telling Howard—"

Harry pointed to his ear.

"Damn," she said, and ran around to his left side. "Howard doesn't know what he's supposed to do."

"He'll figure it out."

When they came to the door, Kate stepped in front of him. "My turn," she said, and drew her leg back.

Harry shoved her out of the way. He punched a four-digit number in the SafeTech unit on the panel as Kate retreated onto the lawn. When the alarm didn't go off, she inched back and said, "You figured out the code? How?"

"Remember how smart you told me Nicholas was?"

"Brilliant. Are you saying you're smarter?"

"The guy was such a brain," Harry said, "he couldn't get in his own house unless he had the combination written down."

"You knew all along that you could just walk in. You should have said something."

"Nobody asked."

"So you charged Howard another twenty-five thousand dollars for turning a key?"

Harry dug a stubby planchet out of his pants and fit it in the door. "Two keys."

Kate entered ahead of him, moving cautiously through the blackened foyer. "Be careful," she said. "There are steps here somewhere."

Harry went the other way and switched on the wall lamp.

"Is that wise?" she scolded.

"I'm not a bat. I don't work in the dark."

Kate brushed back curtains from a living-room window. Howard was in the Cutlass with the scanner pressed to his ear. "What happens if someone does come?"

"We're not gonna be here long enough to find out."

He prodded her into the bedroom and turned on another small lamp. Where the safe had stood there was only a bold spot in the carpeting edged in dust.

"The police have it," Kate said. "You've been taking this too lightly, I could tell."

In an untroubled voice Harry said, "It's a monster, a safe-chest combination. It's gotta be around. Look in the closet."

Kate slid open the door and they saw the safe camouflaged in a pile of men's shirts. "Check out this beauty," Harry said. "Interlocking tongue-and-groove closures on all sides, heat-resistant up to seventeen hundred degrees. No way the cops got in. You can see pry marks on the chest unit where they tried."

Kate said, ". . . I'm sorry."

"I told you I know this racket."

"I mean I'm sorry about everything."

Harry covered his good ear. "Stop yellin'. You want I should be deaf on both sides?"

"You were right about the safe like you were right about Nicholas. Like you were right about Howard. He gave me an interest in the place all right, and he expects me to dance three shows every night to earn it. What he really wants from me, I don't know."

Harry swept the shirts onto the floor. He unfolded a cloth sack from his jacket and spread it on top of the safe. "You know."

"No, that's one thing you were wrong about. He gave me a room on the top floor of the brownstone, and most days I don't even see him till I get to the club. Sometimes I think that all he's interested in is having me deliver those

krytrons to Israel for him. Getting them back, he's ob-
sessed with it."

Harry crouched beside the safe's lower unit. "Bring the
light over, so I can see what I'm doin'."

"I'm sorry," Kate said again. "I'm sorry I didn't go away
with you." She went back for the lamp and carried it as
close as the cord allowed.

"That's good."

"You're not even listening to me," she said.

"What?"

"What?" Kate shouted. "What? Is that all you ever say?"
She was sniffling. "I'm sorry. That's what."

"Late for that," Harry mumbled.

"At least I admit I made a mistake. You could be man
enough to accept my apology."

Harry had the key ring in his hand. "I accept," he said.
"Get out of the way."

He pushed the key into the door, jiggled it delicately,
then forced it, cursed, pulled it out. "You believe those
clowns used a pick on a lock like this. It's a miracle, they
didn't ruin it. Get me a pencil, huh?"

Kate found a mechanical pencil in a teak writing stand.
"Will this do?"

Harry extracted the graphite and crushed it against the
key. When he tried the lock again, the mechanism
twanged softly. He tugged at the door and it eased open
on silent hinges.

The safe was piled with bundles wrapped in thin paper.
On top was a small gray box that Harry pulled out first,
buttoning it inside his shirt when the lid refused to yield.
"That's my tip," he said.

Kate guessed that there were forty bundles in the safe.
As Harry brought out the first one, it nearly slipped from
his hand. "Heavy," he said. "What're they made of, gold?"

"Who cares?"

"Not me." He brought out two more and stacked them
beside the first. "Still, a look wouldn't hurt."

Kate returned the pencil to the writing stand. "Hurry up," she said. "You can look in the car."

"What's your rush? I thought you liked it where the other half lives."

He tried peeling the paper from one of the bundles, but found that it had been glued on. He tore the wrapper with his teeth, revealing a smoked glass bowl tapering into an inverted bulb. In the weak light he couldn't decide what to make of it. He held it toward the lamp. "All the grief these caused," he said. "They don't look like much, whatever they're for."

Kate went back to the closet and began placing bundles inside the cloth bag. "If you really have to know," she said as though she was being imposed upon, "they're parts for an A-bomb, for the trigger."

Harry said, "Wow," and moved closer to the light. "Ormont must be gettin' zillions for 'em from the right party." He brought the krytron to his mouth and kissed it. "I love everything about this."

Kate began to sob. "You do," she said. "I'll bet that's all you could ever love. These fucking things . . ." She scooped up a bundle with two hands. "I hate them."

Kate heaved the glass into the darkness. As it smashed against the wall, Harry winced. "Ormont asks how come we're runnin' short, you'll tell him."

Kate reached inside the safe again. Harry yanked her away. "I think maybe you better cool off."

He sat her on the bed and then stepped over the broken glass. "Well," she heard him say, "will you look at this?"

Kate squinted into the gloom, but could make out only his humped shadow against the wall. She got up off the mattress and aimed the lamp at him. Harry was down on his knees, pinching glass slivers out of some white powder that he had shaped into a neat mound.

"What *is* that?" Kate asked.

Harry was grinning ecstatically, too engrossed in what he was doing to answer.

"I asked you, what's that?"

"Coke," Harry said. "About half a pound."

"Don't be absurd. It's part of the krytron."

"Yeah?" He rolled a crisp dollar bill into a tight cylinder. "Do some."

Kate came closer. She kicked away pieces of glass and bent down beside him.

"Now you know why Ormont would've moved heaven and earth to have these back. . . . Nuclear triggers." He laughed. "It's just a scam for movin' all this nice blow out of the country, and you were goin' to be his mule."

"You're fantasizing. You wish this was drugs."

"Yeah," Harry said, and lowered his face over the white mound.

"What are you doing?"

"What's it look like I'm—?"

She was all over him, then, digging her nails into the back of his neck. "You're crazy," she screamed, "you'll ruin your life."

"Get offa me." With one arm he was no match for her. Until she ran out of gas she had to be as strong as the woman he read about in the *Star*, the one who picked up a truck that ran over her baby.

Kate knotted her fingers in his hair and pulled his head away. "I love you," she shouted into his good ear. "I mean I could, I think."

"Bullshit," Harry said.

"I do," Kate screamed. "I love you. I do." She yanked his arm behind his back and slipped her hand under the elbow, pushing down hard on his wrist. "I'll break this, too," she said. "I saw how in a movie. If you don't get away from that stuff, I swear I will."

Harry fixed on the cocaine. "Who do you think you're trying to fool, Kate?"

"Remember, you asked for this."

Harry felt the ligaments tear around his elbow, heard something snap. "I give," he cried out. "I give, I give."

"Did I break your elbow?"

Harry looked at his good arm, wondered if he still could call it that. It was hanging at a strange angle, turned inside out, like an old screwball pitcher's. "God, this is killin' me," he said. "Lettin' all that coke go to waste."

Kate nudged him toward the safe. "It doesn't have to." She peeled the paper from one of the krytrons and then twisted the bulb out of the glass bowl and let the cocaine pour through her fingers.

"Please don't do that," Harry said. "It's like throwin' away food while babies are starvin' in Ethiopia."

"You can deal it. We'll go partners."

"This kind of weight? Where am I gonna find a buyer?"

"Do I have to tell you everything?" she said. "We'll sell it back to Howard. He's been taking so much money out of the Knights, and from everything else he has going for him, that he had to rebuild the vault to hide it all. You thought you were holding him up, but the fifty thousand came from petty cash." She unscrewed the bulb from another of the glass bowls and spilled the cocaine into the sack. "First we have to bring him his krytrons, though. Like you say, a deal's a deal."

When Kate carried the sack outside, she found Howard in the BMW with the engine running, his hair plastered against his forehead with perspiration. "Where are they?" he asked.

"Inside," she said. "All wrapped up in a clean white sheet and ready to go. But Harry hurt his other arm. He needs you to help bring them out."

"That bag," he said. "What's in it?"

Kate winked conspiratorially. "Souvenirs."

Kate brought the sack onto the passenger's seat as Howard marched up the walk like he had a date with a firing squad. She turned on the heater and made herself comfortable in the soft leather. The thing was, she saw clearly now, Howard really did care for her; but the fifty-eight-year-old Israeli with the bullet hole in his back had to be at least ten times as dangerous as any burglar from Pawtucket, Rhode Island, ever could hope to be. The police scanner barking out the report of a burglary in progress in Forest Gardens forced open her eyes. She reached for Howard's walkie-talkie, and felt the wind go out of her as she remembered the one still on her belt. She was chewing on her lip as she slid over the gearbox and fit her feet awkwardly on the pedals.

Grinding into first, she steered away from the curb. But when she stepped on the clutch again, the car bucked and then stalled, and she pushed helplessly at the stick. She leaned on the horn, looking through the gate at two dim figures wrestling a white ghost along the flagstones.

"You hear that?" Harry said. He had stopped moving and was peering at the street over his end of the sheet.

Howard's face was red turning to purple. "Just a little more." He blinked away the sweat that was running into his eyes. "We're almost there."

"We ain't even close. We gotta get goin'."

"You promised to help me, I gave you money . . ."

"I'll give it back," Harry said. "Most of it. Come on, these krytrons ain't worth shit to you now anyway."

"What do you know—?"

"I ain't got time to argue." Harry let go and the cloth fell out of Howard's hand with the clatter of breaking glass.

Harry ran across the lawn, looking back to see Howard on his hands and knees, tying the corners of the sheet around the paper bundles. "You comin'?" Harry called to him.

Howard looked up, then began dragging the sheet over the grass.

When Harry got to the sidewalk, the BMW was stopped with its nose pointing into the driveway. He jumped in the passenger's seat and put his left hand on the stick. "Step on the clutch," he said. "Now the gas. I'll work the transmission for you."

Kate backed away with one eye on the house. "What about Howard?"

"He's happy doin' what he's doin'."

"We can't leave him. The police will be here any second."

"It's his choice," Harry said. ". . . Now gun it."

Harry wound through the gears as Kate steered along the black streets. When he could see city lights framed by a railroad trestle, he took the wheel from her and guided the car out of Forest Gardens. On Continental Avenue he pulled up to a hydrant and set the emergency brake. "The coke," he grinned. "I gotta have another peek."

He swung the bag onto his lap, but turned toward Kate without looking inside. His face was the same color Howard's had been. "The hell's goin' on?"

"I dumped the cocaine in the sewer," she said. "I was afraid the police would find me with it."

"You did *what?*"

"I had to."

"Who're you tryin' to fool, Kate? You don't scare so easy."

"I was scared," she insisted, "scared that if we kept it, you'd mess yourself up again."

"I wasn't gonna do twenty pounds. I would've found a buyer."

"Either way," she said, "*you* end up in the sewer."

Harry looked at her for a very long time. He drummed his fingers against the dash, then poked one through Nicholas's key ring and twirled it, let it fly into the darkness. "Easy come, easy go," he said with a sickly smile.

He was toying with the stick when Kate put another key in his hand. "You mean what goes around, comes around," she said.

"What's this?"

"The key to Howard's. The money he was going to give us for the cocaine is just sitting inside his vault now. And with all the trouble he's gotten himself into, who can say he'll ever get the chance to enjoy it . . . ?"

But Harry was already out of the car, running around to her side and tearing open the door, squeezing in on top of her. "Lemme drive," he said.